Dudley Road

M. Jandreau

To my wife, Megan, for a lifetime of support, love, and being my voice of reason.
And to my daughter, Samantha, who, when just three years old was asked if daddy could write a scary story, said "uhm, no thank you."

Inspired By True Events

Prologue

It was May of '97, the first time I'd heard the story — the legend, the tale, whatever we want to call it — of Dudley Road. It was my senior year of high school and I was just a seventeen-year-old kid. A dumb kid. Who thought he was invincible and fearless. Once I started hearing the specifics of the story, I realized it seemed like almost everyone I had ever met — and everyone they knew — had heard some variation of the stories. Almost everyone but my very small group of friends and I, that is.

I grew up in a small town in rural Massachusetts, one town over from where it happened. I'd only heard of it through some friends from high school who had grown up in Billerica, the town where it'd happened. Once I heard the initial telling of the story, it was almost like I'd been initiated into some unspoken of club, as if everyone else who knew about it suddenly was approved to talk to me about it.

The first version of the story was the one that stuck with me the most. I've heard varying tales since, with slightly different details and minute variances. But the way I'd first heard it is how I will always remember it. I'll preface what I'm telling you now with the insight that I've never — up to and including today — verified any of the facts or researched the story. But this is how I heard the story all those years ago.

The first time I was told the story was like any other day, unremarkable and ordinary. At school lunch with some of my friends, Bernadette, asked if we'd ever heard the story of Dudley Road. Some friends nodded, some shook our heads. Bernadette then repeated a story I'm sure she'd told many times before that Tuesday afternoon.

At some point in time, an inmate at a local insane asylum escaped and fled through the woods, eventually stumbling on a nunnery on Dudley Road. The inmate broke in and spent the night savagely raping and beating the nuns. One of the nuns ended up getting pregnant from being raped. She became torn between her servitude to God and her belief in all life being good. She ended up taking her life by hanging herself on a tree directly across the street. Ever since, the area surrounding the nunnery has been haunted. People say, if you listen closely enough, you can hear the nuns scream from the woods, as if their torture is still happening.

My first thought when I heard the story was that I didn't know of any insane asylum anywhere in Billerica. As an adult and now knowing where Dudley Road is, I couldn't imagine someone escaping from the only local prison I knew of (Billerica House of Corrections) and running from there to where Dudley Road is. It's too far. Even for a crazed escaped inmate who's fleeing authorities. It didn't seem plausible to me.

But, at the same time, I didn't know everything about Billerica. Perhaps there was some insane asylum I was unfamiliar with or that had closed down since the escape. It was tough to know exactly what could be true and what wasn't. And while the internet existed back then, it was a very different thing. It wasn't full of endless information, memes, Facebook, etc. So the thought never crossed my teenage mind to go look it up. I just took what I'd heard as gospel and brought it back to my group of friends.

All these years later, I did some research into Dudley Road, as well as the nunnery. Primarily to make sure I remembered the story correctly. It was a long time ago, and the story is the least important part of what happened to me, to us. The story was just a legend, but what happened to my friends and I over that summer was anything but.

In my research, I found were even more variations of the legend, tangents from what I'd heard, slightly different but slightly the same. And some tellings that had no similarities to what I'd heard.

Part One

One

It was early June — like it is now, as I write this — and my three best friends and I had just finished our jam session, or as we liked to call it, "band practice".

"Man," Dan said. "That was great."

Dan was my best friend. We'd met in '92 through my very first girlfriend, Melissa. He and I hit it off pretty quickly and had a lot of similar interests; we liked the same movies, the same bands, and we had an enormous love of Queen. The band, not the monarch. We became best friends shortly thereafter, and I spent most of my teenage years at his house, sleeping on the floor in his room, playing in his basement, and just being a kid with him.

He was referring to the jam session we'd just had. Our band — the word band being used here in the loosest of forms — "Downfall" had just finished practicing in the basement of my mom's house, like usual.

"You know I love a good Metallica solo," Kevin said.

"You really nailed Ride the Lightning, Kev," Brian added, giving Kevin a thumbs up.

The three of them smiled.

I was mostly keeping quiet, debating whether to tell them about the story I'd heard or not. I knew Dan and Kevin were big into the supernatural, but I didn't know how Brian would react. We'd always given him a hard time about fearing everything, but I think it was due to him being close to his mother, and not an actual fear of everything on the planet.

Kevin walked past Brian, towards the stairs, and patted him on the belly. "Hungry?" he asked.

"Don't touch my stomach!" Brian yelped. He was always conscious about his weight. He wasn't fat, he was just bigger than the other three of us, who were admittedly thinner than we should have been. Dan and Kevin were both tall and lanky — Dan more so than Kevin. I was shorter than the two of them, but still thin.

The four of us, with our dark hair and dark eyes, could have been in a commercial for an Italian restaurant. I'm not sure of the other guys' heritages, but we all sure looked like we could be Italian.

Kevin loved to sit on the stairs after we'd finished jamming. I think, subconsciously, it was his way of saying he was ready to leave. Most times, I was okay with getting out of the house once we were done, but I had no motivation to get moving.

"You okay?" Dan asked.

"Huh? Oh, I'm fine," I replied with a shrug.

But I knew I wasn't okay. I was dying to tell them what I'd heard and ready to beg them to go there with me and see what we could find.

We hung around for another couple of hours that day, mostly talking about what movies we'd seen recently.

Dan told us how much he loved Scream 2. We had a good laugh remembering how much Jen, Dan's girlfriend, and Wendy, Jen's best friend, and my crush, were terrified of the original. "The second one is just as good," he told us.

Brian had just seen Lost Highway and had nothing but good things to say about it.

"Jen's been begging me to see Titanic," Dan said. "I'd rather die."

I cracked a smile, trying to engage in the conversation.

"You gonna take her?" Kevin asked.

"I'll go see it," Brian said, half smiling.

"Of course you would, you fuck," Kevin poked.

"Hey, a good movie is a good movie! And I hear it's excellent," Brian said, standing to stretch his legs.

"I probably have no choice," Dan said. "What Jen wants, Jen gets."

We all chuckled. We knew Dan was not in control of their relationship.

"I'll go, too," I said.

"You mean if Wendy goes?" Dan asked, making a kissy face. It was no secret I had a crush on Wendy. I think everyone knew, except her.

I shook my head, trying to half-deny it. But he was right.

The faint sound of a horn came from outside.

"That's my mom," Kevin said. "Anyone want a ride home?"

"I should go," Brian said.

"Can you take me home later?" Dan asked me.

"Yeah, you can hang out."

It wasn't uncommon for Dan and me to hang out after the other guys left, just the two of us.

"Ok, see ya," Kevin said, grabbing Brian by the arm to pull him upstairs.

It was a perfect opportunity to tell Dan about Dudley Road, but I decided not to. I'm not sure why, but I thought it might make more sense to keep it to myself for a little longer. Perhaps see if I could learn anything new before sharing the stories with my friends.

Two

Graduation was just around the corner. I looked forward to being done with high school, and Dan looked forward to his last summer before senior year.

Like a million other times before it, I gently knocked on the door to his house and walked right in, not even waiting for someone to answer. I waved to his mom, Kathy — who was like a second mother to me for most of my teenage years — and his little sister, Rachel, as I passed through the kitchen into the hallway, and then knocked on Dan's door.

I always knocked on his door, because who knows what a 15-year-old is doing in their room with the door closed. I closed my door because I liked my privacy, and Dan was no different.

"Come in," he said.

I opened the door and walked into his room, no different from any other day.

"Hey," I said. He was playing F-Zero on Super Nintendo. I always thought he was the coolest because he had a stereo and Super Nintendo in his room. No other friend of mine until then had either of those in their own room. Our video game consoles were always in the living room. I'd guess to keep my older sister, Jen, from fighting over who got to play and when.

"Hey," he said, not taking his eyes off the screen.

"You ever heard of this place called Dudley Road?" I asked. I had never considered myself a subtle person. I often blurted out what was on my mind and worried about the consequences of it later.

"No, why?"

"Someone I go to school with told me about it the other day and it's been stuck in my mind since."

"Just some road?"

"Yeah, but it's more than that," I said. "It's supposedly haunted."

Dan's eyes widened as he put down the Super Nintendo controller. "Haunted? You know I love a good story. Tell me more."

Dan and I spent many nights looking for ghosts and telling haunted stories during our sleepovers in his basement. Sometimes we'd camp out in either of our backyards and listen for spooky sounds in the middle of the night. We were by no means ghost hunters of any sort, though. We were just interested in seeing what we could find out.

"That's the myth, anyway."

"How? Haunted how? And where is it?"

I had his attention.

"It's in Billerica, but I don't know where exactly."

"How is it haunted?" he asked, leaning in closer, his cheeks getting flush with excitement. I could tell he wanted me to get to the point.

"Supposedly there was an asylum nearby and someone broke out and found a nunnery on Dudley Road. He broke in and raped a bunch of nuns all night long. He got caught a couple of days later, but one nun got pregnant. She hung herself across the street because she felt so terrible about the whole thing."

"Shit," he said. "That's fucked up."

"I know. I doubt it's true," I said.

He took a second, staring at me, before responding.

"Are you fucking with me?" he asked, not breaking eye contact.

"That's the story how I heard it," I told him. "I know nothing more or less than what I just told you."

"We have to go," he said, jumping off his bed. "We have to find this place."

I grinned from ear to ear. "I was hoping you'd say that! Let's go."

We spent the rest of the day driving around Billerica trying to find Dudley Road. Hoping we'd just stumble onto it by dumb luck. We eased into Billerica from the part of town we knew where it connected to our town, Tewksbury. While we had been in Billerica plenty of times in our lives, we didn't know it as well as we knew our own town, so there was some bit of learning curve to finding our way.

We drove by the Billerica Mall, a shell of what it was when we were kids, now just housing K-Mart and the discount movie theater.

As we made the right at the light, we saw the Taco Bell we'd been to so many times before.

The center of town was as foreign to us as any other place we'd never been. A small gazebo. The library. A church. Some shops. The Walgreens. It felt like any other small town American town.

It had got dark that night before we stopped and asked for directions.

I pulled into the parking lot of the Lil' Peach convenient store, hit pause on the Creed CD we'd been listening to on repeat, shut the car off, and we grabbed some drinks. Then, asked if the person working knew where the road was.

As I paid, I casually slipped it in.

"Do you know where Dudley Road is?"

The man behind the counter seemed to be ten feet tall and looked down at me over his glasses. "Are you boys planning to do anything stupid there?"

"Stupid? What do you mean?" I asked. He knew what we were up to. He'd probably heard about kids going there all the time.

"You know it's haunted, right?"

"That's why we want to go there," Dan spoke up.

He continued to look down at us from over his glasses while counting back our change from the register. "I didn't tell you how to get there, if anyone asks."

I couldn't imagine anyone caring who pointed us in the right direction. "Of course."

"Good," he said, handing me the receipt. "Go out of here, make a right on Concord Road, keep going for about ten minutes. Dudley Road will be on your right. The first half is between Concord Road and Nashua Road. Cross over Nashua Road and you'll be on the part of Dudley Road you want to be on. That's the part that is haunted."

The way he'd said "haunted" wasn't sarcastic. It wasn't condescending or rude. It was matter of fact. He said it like he knew, possibly from firsthand experience, that Dudley Road was haunted.

"Thanks," I said, scooping up our Cokes and my bag of chips.

We left Lil' Peach and did our best to remember the directions he'd given us as we cruised off, blasting "My Own Prison" for the fiftieth time.

It turned out his directions were right on the money. It was almost a straight shot from the store to Dudley Road. Streets stemming from both sides of the main road we were on, jutting off into neighborhoods, presumably full of people who had no idea what we were up to.

"I wonder if he's been here before," I said as I made the right on Dudley Road from Concord Road.

"Probably. He seemed to know exactly why we wanted to come here," Dan said.

The first section of Dudley Road was unremarkable. The stretch between Concord and Nashua Roads was full of regular houses and normal yards. Everything seemed perfectly normal until we got to the very end of the road, about to cross over Nashua Road to the next section of Dudley Road.

"Look," I said, pointing to my left. "That stone wall looks like someone smashed into it."

The property on the corner of Dudley Road and Nashua Road had a stone wall wrapping its property line around the corner. It was about three feet high and looked like it was, at one time, constructed to mark the property lines. Right at the curve, next to the street sign marking Dudley Road, the stone wall had collapsed.

My brain raced. What happened to that wall? Did someone crash into it fleeing Dudley Road? Had something chased them across the street, and in a hurried panic, they crashed?

"I wonder if someone crashed into it trying to speed away from something scary that happened?" Dan asked, tapping me on the shoulder and pointing to the wall I'd just pointed out.

"Oh shit, you think?" I replied.

"It's perfect that we're here right as the sun's going down. It makes it extra spooky," Dan said.

He and I sat in silence for a few minutes, trying to grasp what we were about to do. The trees across the street seemed to stretch as far as I could see, just slightly opening up to allow Dudley Road to continue from where we were, to where we were going.

We sat at that intersection for another minute before I pulled across the street to the other side of Dudley Road. A covered bus stop was on the opposite corner, by the street sign. A small bench, big enough for two or three people, sat under a covered roof. The whole wooden structure looked like it had been there for decades. I thought of all the kids that lived nearby huddling in it during a rainstorm while waiting for their school bus. I wondered if all those kids knew what hauntings lurked right up the road from where they lived.

As we eased down the road, we passed a couple of normal looking houses on either side — nothing out of the normal with anything we'd seen so far.

That didn't last long, as we pretty quickly found the nunnery. I turned off the stereo to not draw any attention to us.

On the right side of the road stood an enormous building. It had two-story tall arches leading to the inside and looked to be made of stone or had some sort of stucco exterior. It was beige and seemed to blend into the surrounding woods.

On our immediate right, preceding the nunnery, was a 10' gate with barbed wire at the top. It ran the perimeter of the building, connecting at the near corner. The far corner of the fence followed the driveway along the right side of the building, running off into the dark woods. I couldn't see far enough back to see how long the driveway was.

As we slowly rolled down the street, I recall noticing more details about the building. A large bronze sign read "Daughters of Saint Paul" off to the left, near the brick walkway leading up to the building. To the sign's left, a statue of Mary stood, with its hands extended out, palms up. It seemed warm and welcoming.

"Daughters of Saint Paul," Dan read aloud as he noticed the sign. "It says something else underneath it, but I can't read it."

"Me either, but this has to be the place, right?"

"What's the difference between a nunnery and a convent?" Dan asked.

I didn't know. I waited for him to look to his left and shook my head.

We kept driving down the road, finding nothing else remarkable once we'd passed the building that we were convinced was the right place.

A white farmhouse stood at what seemed like the end of the road. I could see a number of Christmas trees growing in the yard.

"Weird place to grow Christmas trees," I said.

"Yeah, how bizarre," Dan agreed.

"Looks like this is the end of the road," I said, pulling up to the front of the house. In hindsight, the people who lived there probably saw thousands of cars pulling up out front of their place and turning around.

As I eased the car to an almost stop, Dan shouted, "Wait! Look!" and pointed to his right.

The road continued to our right. There was a very sharp turn, probably greater than 90° to our right. But he was right, the road kept going.

I turned the wheel, pointed us in that direction, and hit the gas.

That part of Dudley Road was, in my memory, much creepier than the nunnery we'd just discovered. It's also where we'd come to spend a lot of our time and nights in the coming months — but I'll get more to that soon.

As the road turned to our right, the pavement disappeared, turning to a completely gravel road. The trees that lined the paved portion of the road seemed to come together over the car's roof, forming a tunnel and blocking out the night sky. The road narrowed almost immediately, where it was barely wide enough for my car, let alone someone driving in the other direction.

Branches scraped the doors as we drove through the now pitch-black night. No streetlights overhead, no houses lined the road anymore, not a sign of any type of life, even wild life, anywhere near us.

I truly felt the absolute silence around us.

As Dan and I crept along this darkened portion of Dudley Road, ever so slowly, in my white 1989 Mitsubishi Galant, I felt a sense of eeriness about me. Was I feeling that way because of some supernatural forces or was I feeling that way because I had heard the legend and wanted to believe it was true? I'd always been into exploring dark and supposedly haunted places, ever since I was a child walking around in our basement in the pitch-black. But this felt like something different.

"It's fucking creepy out here," Dan said, peering off into the dark woods out the passenger side.

I didn't say anything back to him, but in my mind. I agreed with him. It was so creepy and just purely void of any ounce of light at that point.

We bounced over the potholes and uneven surfaces at a snail's pace. The branches continuing to scratch the car's doors had somehow lowered overhead. They were closing in on us from all directions. I remember wondering how we'd back out of the road, should we not be able to get out, if we continued on.

As we kept driving, it felt like the opening kept getting smaller and smaller, and I wondered if it'd eventually come to a dead end of pure brush that we couldn't pass.

I have a vivid memory of Dan and I both putting our windows up simultaneously. It was about that time where the branches along the road would have poked their way into the car. We didn't coordinate. Instead, it felt like something had told us to put the windows up. Something compelled us to do it.

We drove for maybe ten minutes when we came to a clearing on our right. It looked like a small parking lot, though not paved. The dirt space looked like a natural clearing in the woods, directly connected to the road. I guessed it could fit five or six cars.

"Should I turn around?" I asked Dan, genuinely not knowing if we should keep going or not.

"I guess," he seemed disappointed. "We should probably head back. It's almost ten and the girls will be out of work soon."

We had always referred to Wendy and Jen as "the girls". It seemed more of an "our girlfriends" descriptor, but only Dan and Jen were dating. Wendy was just my crush at that point. Jen and Wendy were best friends and had known each other since childhood. The girls and I had all worked together, which is how I'd met Wendy, and then Jen, once she started working with us. She and Dan started dating a few months later.

"You're right," I said, confirming the time on the radio. "We should head over there to pick them up."

We pulled into the clearing to turn around, pausing for a moment to stare straight into the woods. I don't know why, though. Maybe we hoped for some sign that we should (or shouldn't) be there. Maybe we hoped for something scary. Maybe we were looking for some supernatural thing to shoo us away. But we sat there for just a few minutes in silence, only illuminated by the lights from the dashboard in the car. I looked out into the woods, thoughtless.

Waiting. Hoping. Excited.

I'm not sure what had me so excited. I think, given the situation, most teenage boys might put on the same brave face as I had. But not many of them would be excited, not many of them would want — even welcome — of something to happen in that situation.

Billerica to Burlington wasn't a long drive. I knew the general direction we had to go, so it wasn't a worry of being late to pick them up that drove us from the clearing that night. But something did.

As we drove past the building on our way out, just before I'd reached to turn the radio back on, I felt a sense of panic. Just for a brief moment. Just a quick flash of panic — that type of panic you feel as an adult when you think you've lost your phone or car keys. It washed over me and then was immediately gone.

Three

THE '50S BURGER RESTAURANT that the girls and I worked at was at the tail end of the Burlington mall, down at the end of an offshoot wing. The mall itself closed at ten, but many of the restaurants — ours included — stayed open later since they had their own entrances. Some weekend nights, we were there until well past midnight. Sometimes because of customers not wanting to leave at or near closing, sometimes because there was a lot of cleanup to do after a busy night, and sometimes just because we all had nothing to do after work and we hung out goofing off. The last one depended on which manager closed that night. Some managers were out by 11:01pm. Others took their time. Others let us hang out and goof off until we felt like leaving. Debbie was the favorite manager for most of us. She was a no bullshit boss who just wanted to clean up, cash out, and get the hell out of there.

We strolled into the restaurant as we'd done so many other times, popping down at the counter — stools 1 and 2, away from the busy section — and I helped myself to a Coke behind the counter. I'd done it so many times that I didn't even bother asking someone to get it for me anymore. The soda fountain was right under the counter by those stools, so I just reached over and poured a glass.

Jen was the first to emerge from the swinging door to the back, both arms full of ketchup bottles. Both of the pockets on the front of her Johnny Rockets branded apron were stuffed to the brim with bottles, as well. The more you carried, the fewer trips you had to make to the back to restock every table before the end of the night. It took her a few minutes of putting ketchup bottles on tables that didn't have them and swapping empties for full ones to notice us.

"Hey guys," she yelled across the mostly empty restaurant, "be right over!"

She and Dan weren't overly affectionate towards each other in public, they just had this way about them that made you know they were together and were a good fit. The way he looked at her when she wasn't looking. The way she smiled when she heard his voice. The way they held each other's hands, or how he stood behind her with his arms wrapped around her. It was sweet.

Wendy must have heard Jen call out to us from the back, as she came bounding through the swinging door shortly after that. She also had arms full of ketchup.

"Burger?" one cook I enjoyed working with, Francisco — though we called him Paco, for some reason I still don't know — asked us.

"No thanks, Paco. I'm good," I said.

"Me neither," Dan chimed in.

Jen had made her way over to us with a look of dread on her face.

"Busy night?" Dan asked.

"You have no idea. It was insane all night," she said while Wendy made her way over. She stood to my right in the space between the counter and some shelvings where we kept extra plates and napkins, resting her arms on the counter. It was comical when she did this, as she was barely five feet tall. Her arms just barely made it up onto the counter.

"I made good money, though," Wendy said.

"Same," Jen agreed, "what did you guys get up to tonight?"

"I'll tell you about it in the car," I said, not wanting to talk about it in public, in case anyone around us was listening. I don't know why I felt the need to be so secretive, but something compelled me to keep it hush hush.

Jazmin — or Jaz, as she insisted we call her — came out from the back. "Almost done?" she asked.

It was her way of reminding the girls that they were still working and, although I was physically present, I was not. I was distracting them. Jaz was usually the manager who let us goof off after hours, but it seemed like she wanted to get out of there, so she was hurrying everyone along.

"Hi Mike!" she said. "Hi Mike's cute friend." She was always flirting with my friends. I never knew how old she was, but I know she was older than I was by at least a handful of years. I remember going to her apartment once for a big party, so I knew she was old enough then to have her own place.

"Hey, Jaz," we both replied half-heartedly.

We waited another ten or fifteen minutes while the girls finished cleaning up and escorted the last customer out, locking the door behind him. They finished counting up their tip money, exchanged it for larger bills from the register before Jaz collected it all, and we headed out. There was — is — something about working a long shift at a burger joint you can't shake after you leave. This thin layer of grease that cakes your body from head to toe, which is even worse when you're working the grill. There's this sense of "phew, it's over" when you walk out of that place after a long day, especially a busy one.

"Night Paco," I said as our group split from he and the rest of the back of the house crew near my car. I could see their cars towards the back of the lot.

Since it was essentially the stone age, I unlocked the car with my key and opened my door to hit the unlock button for the other doors. Dan sat in the back with Jen, which meant Wendy would sit up front, next to me.

I'd had a crush on her since the day I met her. She was tiny —
just about five feet tall — and had the most beautiful brown eyes,
which complimented her long brown hair.

"So, what did you guys do tonight?" Jen asked again.

"You want to tell her?" I asked Dan.

"Yes!" he said, more excited than I'd remembered him being for
a while. "You guys ever heard of Dudley Road?"

"Oh no, not you guys too!?" Wendy said immediately.

"What?" I asked, looking over at her, as we pulled out of the
parking lot to head to her house.

"Everyone around here has heard the stupid stories about that.
The ghost convent," she said, even using air quotes.

"You don't think it's true?" Dan asked from the back seat.

"No, it's not true, and it's stupid," Jen said.

"What's the story you've heard? I just heard it from Mike earlier
tonight," Dan said.

"I heard it from someone I go to school with. Maybe what you
heard is different," I added.

"Wen, how did you hear it?" Jen asked.

"I've been hearing it since I was a kid. It's always been folklore
around here because it's not far from here. The story I heard
was that there's a convent in Billerica on this road and some
crazy guy kidnapped a nun, took her into the woods, found some
abandoned house, and raped her. She got pregnant and hung
herself rather than telling the priest about the pregnancy. They
never found the guy and supposedly he lived in the abandoned
house for a while."

"That's kind of what I heard, except he didn't kidnap her. He
broke into the convent and spent the entire night raping and
beating the nuns there," I said.

"There's so many versions of the story, but none of them are
true. When I told my parents about it when I was twelve, my
dad took me to the library to look through old newspapers and

we couldn't find any evidence of anything ever happening that sounded even remotely like the stories," Wendy said.

"I heard it the same way as Wendy," Jen said. "I think we both heard it from one of my older brother's friends. Over the years, I think every new group of older kids that tells it to younger kids changes it slightly or adds something to it."

"Well…" Dan said, "we went there tonight. We drove down the street, by the nunnery or convent or whatever it is and down this long creepy dirt road."

"Did the boogeyman jump out and scare you?" Wendy laughed.

"No, smartass," I said. "But Dan's right, the road itself was super creepy. Something just felt funny the whole time we were there."

"It's an urban legend," Jen said as I made the left onto Wendy's road. "It's not true."

"Whether it's true, we went there, and we got creeped out. I don't know if it's haunted, but I got a weird feeling the whole time we were there," Dan said.

I pulled into Wendy's driveway behind her dad's car and put the car in park, once again turning off Creed. I turned to look at Jen and Dan in the backseat. "I want to go back," I declared.

"Are you nuts?" Wendy yelped. I could tell she was a little uneasy about the conversation.

"Not nuts, just inquisitive," I said as she opened the door.

"There's no way I'm going with you." She said as she closed the door. The light on the front porch of her house turned on at the same time. It meant her dad was waiting up for her, as he usually did.

"She's such a chickenshit," Jen said. "She's always been afraid of ghosts and haunted stories."

"You have to come with us," Dan said. "It's so cool, but weird and creepy."

"What's to be afraid of?" I asked Wendy out my window. "If it's not real, why wouldn't you come with us?"

I knew I wanted to go back and explore more, to check out the woods and see if we could find anything creepy. I knew Dan wanted to do the same. I don't think he cared if Jen came or not, but he probably wanted her to come along because they were still in their teenage lovey-dovey honeymoon phase.

"I'll think about it," she said while we pulled into her driveway.

"Good," Dan said, jumping out of the car to race around and open Jen's door for her.

"Bye Jen," I said while she got out.

"Bye, thanks for the ride."

"Can we go back right now?" Dan asked when he got back in.

"If I don't get you home soon, your mother is going to kill us both. But we'll go back. We'll definitely go back."

This was just the first of many times we talked about Dudley Road that summer. And although I'd come to know that place like the back of my hand, I still think back on that first night very fondly, very vividly, remembering every exact detail about how things looked, how I felt, how alone we felt out in that clearing for those handfuls of minutes before we turned around. I still get chills when I think of going back there today.

Four

I STAYED UP ALL night thinking about the legend and the two varying stories we'd heard so far. The girls were right. It seemed like much of the story had been changing and evolving. As each new generation heard it, they changed something slightly about it.

Was the rapist a convict? Was he a patient at a mental facility? Did he break into the convent or kidnap one nun that was outside? Where was this abandoned house he supposedly took her to and why was it out in the middle of the woods? Had anyone found any evidence of a house out in the woods?

Question after question raced through my mind all night as I lay awake, the faint sounds of WAAF playing on my clock radio.

My eyes darted around the room while I tried to not think of what had happened that day. My "Braveheart" poster sat across from a "White Men Can't Jump" poster that I'd only kept all those years because I'd used some names at the bottom of it to name the first main character in the first book I'd written, when I was twelve. It had some sentimental value to me.

My desk sat across from my bed, the hum of my computer barely audible over the sounds of the radio, the flicker of the monitor's power light bouncing off the walls and ceiling, the only source of light, other than the red LEDs of my alarm clock.

The only thing I'd know for certain was that I had to go back. I had to find some evidence that something had actually happened there. I don't know why, but I had to be the one to prove that the legend — or at least part of it — was real. I guess, in looking back at my life, I'd always had a what my therapist calls a "superhero complex". I had to be the guy who did the superhuman things. I had to be the guy who was able to do things others couldn't. And, for whatever reason, that included being the person to either prove or debunk the Dudley Road stories.

I remember watching the sun come up out the back window of my bedroom that morning. I was always a night owl as a teenager, but I was usually asleep by the time the sun came up. I didn't get a wink of sleep that night. The anxiety of the whole situation distracted me from ever feeling tired.

Perhaps it was as a sense of security. Nothing bad ever happened in the daytime, right? If the sun was up, I was safe from whatever haunted thing might have climbed in my car that night and come home with me. Isn't that what happens in horror movies? The Exorcist, Night of the Demons, Event Horizon, The Evil Dead, The Amityville Horror. They all taught us the same lesson. The thing attaches itself to the protagonist and they need to cleanse themselves of it. The sun would protect me from that, wouldn't it?

Whether it did, I finally fell asleep shortly after sunrise, and slept until noon that day.

I slept a long, dreamless sleep. I slept hard, to where I had pillow lines on my face when I finally woke up.

The only thing able to wake me from my deep sleep was the incessant ringing of the phone on my nightstand.

I knew who it was before I even picked up, and I knew what he wanted.

"Come get me. We're going back," Dan said before I could even get through saying hello.

"I'll be on my way in ten," I said. I was glad I had a friend who was as crazy as I was.

Five

DAN'S HOUSE WAS ONLY a few minutes from mine and Dudley Road was only twenty minutes from his house. A quick stop at McDonald's on the way there and we were pulling down Dudley Road just before one o'clock that afternoon.

I didn't officially have a goal for that trip or really any other trip we'd make there. But I found myself taking note of things we either missed the night before or things we just couldn't see due to how dark it was.

I rolled slowly by the nunnery from the get go. Since I now knew how far down the road it was, I could drive slowly leading up to it, not just when I'd noticed it.

The house immediately preceding the nunnery had a small patch of grass just past their driveway that was all run down, mostly a giant patch of dirt, which was probably once a lush, green lawn. I'd wondered if that's where other inquisitive people had pulled over to look at the nunnery more closely.

Again, my mind raced. Had anyone parked and gotten out of their car and tried to go inside? If so, had anything happened to those people? Did they see anything? Did they learn anything that hadn't made it into the stories we'd all heard?

"It's almost creepier in the daytime," Dan said.

I nodded and kept paying attention to everything I could see.

The trees lining the right portion of the property, separating it from the neighboring house, were thick and tall. Mostly pine trees, currently full of pine needles, creating an almost completely solid barrier between the two properties. They extended back into the property as far as I could see from the road. I couldn't make out the back of the building, but it seemed like the trees wrapped around to the left, engulfing the whole building in trees. I'd later find out that the entire area behind the nunnery is a forest, connecting all the way over to the clearing where we'd turned around the night before.

We rolled past the entrance to their driveway. It extended back a bit from the road past a house on the corner, gated with a small call box on the left. The fence and gate were easily ten feet high and were closed at the moment.

I practically let the car drive itself along that portion of the road as we both peered out the passenger window at the building.

All the details I'd seen the night before were still as vivid as I remember. The arches along the front of the building, one of which I could now see, held the door to get inside. The statue of Mary on the left. A long fence, clearly marked Private Property, ran the length of the property, about ten feet back from the road.

"Let's go knock on the door," Dan joked.

"Hi, nuns. Can we come in and talk about your friend who was raped? Is that real?" I said, laughing.

"We're such assholes," Dan agreed, chuckling.

We were. We really were.

We drove the rest of the way past the building and hung the hard right at the Christmas tree farm, which we could now see was on both sides of the street and not just in front of us. A handful of houses sat along the right-hand side of the road as we made our way to the clearing we'd turned around in the night before. Big, beautiful homes that felt incredibly out of place on the road, given their history and folklore. I counted six houses along the right-hand side of the street. On our left were open fields, though it was tough to see what was over there through the overgrown trees and shrubs lining that side of the street.

Like the night before, I pulled into the small clearing and put the car in park, leaving the engine running and the radio on. I'm sure we'd seen it the night before, but now in the daylight the sign reading "Governor Thomas Dudley Park" was more visible. It was the typical sign you'd see at a state park; no littering, open dawn till dusk, etc.

"Even this is pretty creepy in the daytime," I said to Dan, turning the radio off.

"Should we go out into the woods?" he asked.

"Not today," I said. "If we're going to go out there, I want to be prepared." I had been a Boy Scout when I was younger and still maintained some of that mentality of being prepared — water, flashlight, pocket knife. You know, the essentials for hunting imaginary ghosts in the woods.

"Pussy," he joked.

The truth is, I wasn't scared. Back then, things like this didn't scare me. Life's much different now that I'm older and have been through so much. But seventeen-year-old me? He was fearless. But he also wasn't a moron. There was no way I was going out into those woods without at least a compass to find our way back to the car.

"Let's keep going down the road and see where it goes," I suggested. "Maybe there are more entry points to the woods."

Dan agreed, and I backed out of the clearing, heading in the same direction we had been heading before turning off into the clearing.

The road seemed to get worse as we went along. It was muddy, even though it hadn't rained recently, and it got slightly more narrow as we drove along.

Another house popped up on our left. Like the others, it was much bigger than I expected a house on this road should be. I had thought the folklore would affect the overall size of the houses. As if real estate developers or property owners would only build tiny shacks on this street and they'd instantly become run down. It was an eerie juxtaposition between this incredibly old-looking, and presumably haunted nunnery and these new, modern, beautiful, enormous houses we'd seen on the road.

We drove along at a snail's pace, taking in all of our surroundings. Another big house on our right. Followed by another and another. We passed four big houses before the road opened up. It was like someone had flipped a switch and everything was back to normal.

The canopy above our heads disappeared. The road turned from gravel to pavement — albeit run down pavement in rough shape — and the trees lining both sides of the street disappeared. We were suddenly out in the open, both literally and figuratively. The weight of eeriness lifted as soon as I crossed from the gravel part of the road to the paved part.

On our right was a house that looked slightly older than the other houses on the road we'd passed already, a farmhouse sitting behind it. Some old cars and a truck were out back by the farmhouse.

Both it and the farmhouse on our right had fences around part of their yard. Not tall white fences like you see people install for privacy or chain-link fences that people use to keep animals out. But those old-fashioned type fences where it's just three horizontal wooden beams going across between the posts.

"Horses," Dan said, pointing to my left. "There are horses over there."

That was it. That was the type of fence I was trying to put my finger on since I'd seen it. There were horse pens on both sides of the street.

I didn't count the other houses along that portion of Dudley Road. It didn't feel necessary since it felt like an entirely different place to the part of the road tied to the folklore. But I remember every single one of the houses had horse pens. Some bigger and more extravagant than others. Towards the "far end", as we referred to it, of Dudley Road, the horse farms were huge. Acres of fenced in property where we'd often see horses running around, almost in the wild, but still penned in.

"This is so weird," I said.

"How is this the same road?" Dan asked.

"It's all one road, right?"

"It has to be. We didn't make any turns, and I didn't see any different street signs," Dan said.

We drove to that end of Dudley Road, which connected further down from where we'd entered Dudley Road with North Road. From there, I knew my way back to Dan's house in Tewksbury.

"Head home?" I asked, as I made the left out of Dudley.

"Yeah, let's go." Dan agreed.

Any time we'd come to Dudley Road over that summer and felt truly creeped out, we'd exit that way. We'd drive out of the creepy part of the road, into the part we felt safe in, past all the horse farms and houses we knew normal people probably lived in, and back out onto the main road that got us back up.

There were still so many answers to questions I hadn't even thought of yet. So many things that we hadn't even thought of possibly happening that were on our horizon.

Six

AFTER THAT SECOND TRIP by ourselves, Dan and I decided to see if our other friends, Kevin and Brian, would be interested in tagging along. The four of us had been close for the past four years.

Brian lived a few doors up the road from Dan, and they were best friends for a while before I came along. They met Kevin at school at some point. Since we were all into music, we all got along and for a period, we were all in a band together. Brian and Kevin played guitar, Dan played the bass, and I was the drummer. I digress.

If the four of us weren't all together, at least two of us were. Since Dan was with me on that day, I figured Kevin and Brian were together. They spent most of their time together working on music at Kevin's house. Brian's mother had re-married a couple of years before, so he had a very young sister. Little kids and loud guitars didn't work out well, so they'd often go to Kevin's house to write or rehearse. Kevin's mom was a single mother, so she worked a lot to provide a good life for Kevin.

We pulled into Kevin's driveway mid-afternoon and let ourselves in. I could hear the guitars from the street, so I knew they wouldn't hear the knock. We were all close enough that it didn't matter, so Dan and I just let ourselves in.

The guitars stopped one at a time when they saw us from the living room.

"Hey, check this out," Kevin said, ripping right into some guitar lick he'd either recreated or made up himself. He often started conversations this way, straight into guitar. He hadn't been playing as long as Brian had, so I think there was some sort of rivalry between them. As usual, the lick he'd played was incredible. He could hear a song once or twice and play it perfectly. This lick was Metallica's "Seek and Destroy", specifically the first guitar solo.

Dan walked over and turned the amplifier off mid-strum.

"Hey," Kevin said, "I was playing!"

"Listen," I said. "Something kind of crazy is going on."

Kevin put his guitar down on the floor. Brian gently placed his in its case. They both sat and looked at me.

"What do you know about Dudley Road?" Dan asked.

"The haunted convent?" Brian asked.

"Yeah, that. What do you know?" I added.

Kevin shrugged.

"I heard the story when I was a kid," Brian said. "Something about a nun getting raped by someone who escaped a mental hospital."

"That's the gist of it, but there are more parts to it I don't really know," I said. "Have you ever been there?"

"Is it real?" Kevin asked.

Almost cutting me off, Dan replied, "It's real. We just came from there."

"You guys are fucking crazy," Brian blurted out. "Why would you go there?"

"Why not? It's creepy and they say it's haunted," I added.

"Who says it's haunted?" Kevin asked.

"Everyone," Dan said. "Or at least, everyone who has been there says it's creepy."

"We found it the other night," I told them, "and just went back today during the day. We want to go check out the woods around it sometime."

I filled them in on the rest of the legend, all the variations I knew so far, all the bits and pieces we'd known up to that point. Kevin seemed interested, as I figured he would be. Brian didn't seem at all interested, but I knew he'd go along with it anyway, because that's how he was.

"So you want to come?" Dan asked, looking back and forth between the two of them.

"I'm in," Kevin said immediately.

"I don't know," Brian said, pausing. "What do we hope to get out of it?"

"Nothing, really. I doubt we'll find anything, but why not go try?" I asked.

"Ok, fine. I'll go. But can we stop by my house first, so I can drop off my guitar and tell my mom I'm out with you guys?"

We always gave Brian a hard time about being a momma's boy. We probably spent too much time busting his balls about it. In hindsight, he was just a good kid who respected his mother.

We swung by his house and dropped his guitar off right around four that afternoon. Her car wasn't there, so he must have left her a note. He'd never leave home without telling her where he was going.

"Let's go," he said, hopping in behind me.

And, like that, prepared with flashlights and a compass we'd taken from Dan's house, we were off to explore the woods surrounding the nunnery for the first time. I was excited, as were the rest of the guys. We had that buzz as if all of our moms let us have a camp out in Dan's backyard on the same night and we know we'd get to stay up all night eating junk food and telling ghost stories. Though we were amped up and excited to do it, I think we were all a little glad we decided to make our first trip into the woods during the day.

Seven

As I PULLED OUT onto the street to cross over to Dudley Road, Dan started pointing out the things we'd discovered. He said it was to remind himself, but also to catch Kevin and Brian up on what we'd seen.

"There's the spot where people seem to park and walk around," he said. "And there's the nunnery. See the tall fence around the driveway?"

Kevin and Brian said little from the backseat. Just some occasional "uh huh" and "yeahs" to confirm they were taking in what Dan had told them.

As we made the hard right by the Christmas tree farm, I could feel Brian shifting around in the seat behind me. I looked in the rear-view mirror to make eye contact with him. I knew he was the least likely of us to be doing something like this, but also wanted him to know I appreciated him being there. A silent connection between the two of us to tell him it wasn't a big deal.

Dan kept pointing things out as we drove along. The tree branches covering us from all sides, the eeriness of all the vast houses on this otherwise deserted road, how it seemed like had just stopped out here in the middle of nowhere.

I pulled into the small clearing that we'd eventually start calling the "give up point". Once things started really escalating, it was here that we'd retreat to and decide if we needed to give up and head out at the safe end of the road or not. It was our home base, of sorts.

I parked the car and was the first to open my door. No other cars were there, though it seemed like there should be. It felt more like the entryway to a hiking path at that point than any sort of ominous or creepy route into the woods.

As I closed the door to the car, the guys got out, stretching their legs in unison. We all paused to take in our surroundings.

"One legend says there's an abandoned house out here somewhere," Dan said.

"Where the nun got raped?" Brian asked.

I nodded. "Yeah, one version of the story says he took her to some house he found. The other story says he broke into the nunnery and did the raping there," I said.

The clearing was unremarkable — a small dirt patch off the road, big enough to fit a handful of cars. There were three different paths you could take into the woods from there. After a short deliberation, we took the middle path. We also decided, this time, that we'd stick together.

I consider myself fairly brave, but I can't sit here and tell you I was brave enough to be the first one to walk off into the woods. I followed Dan in. Brian was right behind me, and Kevin brought up the rear.

My memory tells me we walked for hours. The woods growing more and more dense. The sunlight getting blocked out more and more as we ventured on. In reality, I don't think it was the hours' long journey I remember it as. It was probably a much shorter trip that first time into the woods.

"Should we look for any old looking houses out here?" Brian asked. "Or, like, what are we doing?"

"We're just walking around," Kevin said. "Would you relax?"

"If we see something, we'll check it out," I added. "I just want to see if there's anything out here."

We kept walking into the woods, feeling like we were going in circles, but I knew we were walking in a straight line. Aside from all the trees getting more dense, the ground covering of brush had thinned out, so we could head anywhere we wanted to go.

Snapping twigs and the gentle sway of branches were the only sounds that we heard.

After we'd been walking a while, Dan called out from the front of the line, "What's that over there?"

I couldn't tell where he was pointing, but to the left, a few hundred yards away, was a solid wall of trees. It looked to have stood separate from the rest of the woods. Like part of a video game that didn't render properly. It stood out from the rest of the forest.

"What is that?" I heard Kevin faintly ask.

"Let's go check it out," Dan said, not waiting for a response.

Before I knew it, he'd veered off the beaten path, dodging the rows of trees on our left, heading to the wall of trees he'd seen.

I felt like he sped up some, but maybe I'd unintentionally slowed down.

I watched as he seemed to take longer and longer strides to get to where he wanted to go. Then he stopped suddenly and knelt. I couldn't tell from my viewpoint, but it looked like he was stopping to tie his shoe.

When I caught up to him, I saw he was looking at something on the ground. It was an old newspaper.

"What is it?" I asked, as Brian and Kevin caught up with us.

"The Billerica Gazette," Dan replied. "It's dated June 8th, 1951."

"Shut up," Brian said. He bent down to inspect the newspaper. "How... What the..."

I took a closer look. I couldn't figure out what I was looking at.

There, before us on the ground, was a newspaper that looked brand new, except for a bit of yellowing. It showed no tears, rips, bent corners, or water damage. It was like it came straight off the printing press, sat in the sun for a few minutes, then got deposited in this very spot. Never to be touched again. For almost fifty years.

"How has the weather not destroyed it?" Kevin asked.

He was right. If the paper had been sitting out in the woods, even for a few days, it should have been ruined. Rain falling through the trees would have made it show a sign of age. Morning dew and mist should have warped the pages some.

Dan picked it up to examine it closer. The ground beneath it was flattened and brown. The paper had been there long enough to kill the life underneath it. But the paper itself showed no signs of age at all. It was, for lack of a better description, perfect.

We took turns flipping through it, seeing if one of us could find something relevant that the others missed. There were no stories of nuns or escaped mental patients. There were no police or doctor reports of rape. There was nothing of significance at all. Even the date didn't seem important to any of us.

I was the last to hold the paper and was careful to put it back down in the same spot we picked it up from. I don't know why I felt that was important, but the feeling was there, so I did it.

"Holy shit," Dan called out. He'd wandered ahead while the rest of us took our turns looking at the paper.

I looked up and saw he had gone the rest of the way to the wall of trees. I just caught a glimpse of him as he disappeared behind the largest tree at the end.

"Wait up," Kevin shouted and hurried behind Dan, leaving Brian and I with the newspaper a few yards away.

We followed right behind Kevin and were just a few seconds behind them when we rounded the tree Dan had gone behind.

There, on the ground of the forest, we saw the outline of a house. The walls and roof were completely gone, taken back by mother nature, their wood long since rotten away. A bottom handful of rows of a brick chimney were laying on the ground across from us. I could see a small pile of hardware pieces; a few doorknobs, some window pulls, a fire poker. Save for a few pieces of wood here and there, there was nothing left of what we assumed was originally a house. The footprint was small, maybe fifteen feet by twenty feet. It seemed like it used to be all one room.

"Is this it?" Kevin asked.

"You mean the house?" I asked, making eye contact with him.

"Yeah, is this where it happened?"

I shook my head.

"I don't think so," Dan said. "This looks like a house, but I don't think it's been a house for a really long time."

"Look," Brian said, pointing to the far corner across from where Dan and I were standing.

There, were stacks of newspapers tucked neatly into the corner of the former frame, tied into little bundles with strings. Dozens of them. All pristine, more so than the one we'd found just outside. Only the top newspaper from each pile had slightly yellowed. That one sacrificial newspaper on top had sheltered the ones below it, which showed no signs of aging or yellowing. All are in perfect condition. All perfectly flat. All from the summer of 1951. They were all editions of the Billerica Gazette, and they all seemed to be meaningless.

"Grab a pile and look through them," I said, grabbing a pile for myself.

We each flipped through the piles, careful not to untie them from their bundles.

"Nothing important here," I called out first.

"Why would someone keep all this garbage?" Dan asked.

"People are nuts," Kevin said.

As I finished flipping through my stack, I put it neatly back where I'd gotten it from before grabbing another. The fifty or so newspapers in my second bundle also yielded nothing noteworthy.

"They're just someone's old garbage," Dan said.

"Why the fuck aren't they falling apart?" I asked. "It's like someone made them yesterday and put them out here."

"Why would someone do that?" Brian asked.

"I don't know," I said, "why would someone keep all these old papers if they weren't put here for a reason?"

I couldn't figure out where they came from or why they were sitting out in the woods. The newspapers seemed to distract us from the house that had fallen down in the middle of the woods, off the pathway most people would follow if they were hiking.

"Whatever this place is," Kevin said, "nature is hiding it behind a wall of trees."

"What if someone used to live here?" Dan asked. "And they wanted their privacy, so they built their house behind a wall of trees?"

"Why would anyone want to live out here? Everyone says these woods are haunted," I said.

"What if whoever it was lived here before the woods were supposedly haunted?" Brian asked.

I felt Kevin and Dan both stop what they were doing and turn their heads towards Brian. I did the same. The three of us stood in silence in what could have been someone's living room at some point. What if Brian was right? What if this structure we were standing in had pre-dated all the creepy things that happened on Dudley Road?

"I didn't think of that." I was the first to speak after a few minutes of silence.

I don't know why, but something about Brian's words triggered me into wanting to leave. Maybe it was because it was getting dark and the idea of being out in the woods at night was terrifying. Maybe it was an eerie feeling that maybe whoever lived there had died and they were still out in the woods. Maybe there was another part of the Dudley Road story that people didn't know or had forgotten. But I knew it was time to go.

"Why don't we head back?" I asked. "This is sufficiently creepy for today."

No one said anything. They didn't agree or disagree. They just silently followed me back to the main path and out of the woods.

No one spoke until we were in the car with the doors closed.

"That was fucking weird," Dan said. "I love it."

"Why were there so many newspapers?" Brian asked.

"I don't know," I said. "I'm more concerned with how they weren't destroyed by nature. Something in the woods seems to keep them safe."

The music was so loud it scared all four of us as soon as I started the car. I did then — and always have since I've been driving — turned the radio completely off when I shut the car off. I did it on purpose because I never wanted to start the car and be scared like I just was that moment. Somehow, the volume was up all the way and the station had turned to a classic rock station.

"Fuck!" Brian said. "You turned that off when we got out. I saw you!"

"Are you sure?" Kevin asked. "Maybe he didn't."

"I turned it off," I mumbled, barely audible. "I know I did."

"I know he turned it off," Brian reiterated.

We all exchanged looks of confusion. A slight hint of fear escaped in my glance across the roof of the car in Dan's direction.

As if by some weird happenstance, or some haunted happening, or something else I can't explain, "Witchy Woman" from The Eagles was playing on that classic rock station. A station I didn't normally listen to, had not previously had on in the car, and did not have saved on my radio. There was no way that someone accidentally bumped the radio and hit a preset station. There was no way I or Dan had accidentally hit something before getting out of the car to change from 107.3 to 100.7. There's no way that either of us did it. There's no way someone went into the car and changed it while we were in the woods.

But something. Something changed the station and turned the volume up so loud that my ears rang for the rest of the night.

Something did it. And that something would continue doing things like that for quite some time.

Eight

Days had gone by and all I could still think about was that creepy house or structure or whatever it was. Why was it there? How long had it been there? It was consuming everything that I did or thought or said to where I'd completely zoned out at work. I stared at the fry machine, when Wendy came up behind me and pulled the fries that I'd been cooking out of the oil.

"You okay?" she asked.

"Huh? What?" It was like I'd been in some sort of haze. "Oh, yeah, I'm fine."

"You don't seem fine," Jen said from my right.

I wasn't, but I couldn't say that. Not out loud, not to them, not at work.

"I'm okay. I promise," I assured them.

I took the plate of fries I was waiting on to the table I was serving, plopped it down in the middle, doing our traditional ketchup pour on the extra plate, and then headed through the swinging door to the back of the restaurant. I walked straight by the dishwashing area and out into the loading dock.

Wendy followed me out, just a step or two behind me. During slow times, it wasn't uncommon for us to hang out back there. It was one of the few places we could go where we could talk without customers hearing us. It was wide open outside, but still private enough that we could be away from most people.

"What's going on with you?" she asked, sitting next to me on an empty milk crate.

"We went to Dudley Road the other day. Dan, Kevin, Brian and I," I told her. "We walked out into the woods and found this creepy old house that had fallen down."

Jen came out and sat on the other side of me. She handed me a plate of french fries. Sharing a plate of fries outside was a rite of passage with me. Something I'd done more times than I can even remember.

I spilled everything that had happened the other day. I told them about the creepy house and the newspapers. I said how no one was freaked out about the ominous radio being turned on when we got back in the car except for me. I kept telling them how much everything we'd seen out there felt so out of place, but also so incredibly normal at the same time.

"Dan told me about most of it the other night," Jen said. "He didn't seem as creeped out by it as you seem now."

"I'd be scared shitless," Wendy said. "I don't like ghosts."

"Who said anything about ghosts?" I asked.

"No one," she said.

"But you know something out there is haunted," Jen said. "Ghost. Paranormal whatever. However you refer to it, it's a ghost."

"I didn't get a feeling of ghosts. Well, I was creeped out. But I didn't get any feeling of someone watching me or anything. It was just weird. I guess it was more mysterious than anything else. Do either of you know anything about that house?"

"No," Wendy said, "and I asked my dad about it and he knew nothing about it, either."

"I've never heard of it, either," Jen said. "But part of the legend says this guy took her to a house and raped her. Do you think, maybe, that's the house you found?"

"I don't know," I said. "I don't know what part of the legend is real. If any of it is."

"Were there any clues to when the house fell down or who lived there?" Wendy asked.

"No. Just the stacks of newspapers. There weren't even any other signs of life there. No old furniture. No dishes or silverware. It was just… empty. Except for those newspapers."

"And they were all from 1951?" Jen asked.

"Every one of them. I didn't look at every single one, but I think every issue from that year was there. All practically brand new."

"I want to see it," Jen said. "Take me there."

"Not me," Wendy shuddered out the words. "There's not enough money in the world to get me to go there."

"You have to go if I'm going," Jen said, looking across me at Wendy.

"Hey Mike, your table is asking for you," Raul, one of the cooks, poked his head out the door.

I handed the plate of fries to Jen and stood up. "Figure out if you're coming," I said to Wendy, "and when you want to go."

I walked back inside and let the door shut behind me, hoping they'd want to go with us the next time we decided to go. I wanted to get a closer look at the house. I hoped that a second visit could provide some more clarity.

Wendy eventually agreed to go to the woods with Jen and I. I knew that meant Dan would want to go, too. Since I was the only one driving, that meant we didn't have room for Kevin and Brian in my car, so they couldn't come. I looked through the schedule at work to find the next day that all three of us had off.

"Tuesday," I said. "We're all off Tuesday. That's when we'll go."

Nine

I PICKED DAN UP after we got out of school and headed to Burlington. He'd just gotten off the phone with Jen, so we knew Wendy was already at her house, waiting for us to pick them up.

They piled into my car, Jen behind Dan and Wendy behind me, just before three o'clock that afternoon. In typical over-prepared fashion, Wendy had a backpack with her.

"I brought snacks, flashlights, and a disposable camera," she said. "Just in case."

We all poked fun at her before leaving Jen's driveway. But in reality, I was thankful she thought ahead to bring some things with her. I had been ill prepared, even after all those years as a Boy Scout. I only joined in on making fun of her to fit in with Dan and Jen. It felt natural to do so.

As we drove over to Dudley Road, we made small talk. Unimportant conversations unrelated to what we were planning to do that day. We could have been going anywhere that afternoon, as we had dozens of times before. We were a foursome, even before Dan and Jen started dating.

The overall mood seemed to change from jovial and lighthearted almost immediately when I made the left onto Dudley Road. The sky seemed darker, though the sun was still shining. The sound of the dirt on the corner of the road seemed to signal some sort of change in the atmosphere.

As we drove past the nunnery, Dan told the girls the same story he'd previously told Brian and Kevin. He pointed out all the same things that he'd pointed out the last time we'd come here. This time, as we drove by the front of the nunnery, we saw a small group of nuns walking towards the front entrance. They were behind the black wrought-iron fence, fifty or so feet away from us. The sound of my car didn't seem to faze them. They just kept going about their day.

It was a quarter to four when we pulled into the turnaround spot.

"This is too creepy already," Wendy said, partially covering her eyes.

"Wuss," Dan said. He still seemed to be fearless about this whole thing.

Before I shut the car off, I purposefully made sure the radio was on a station I would remember — WAAF — and the volume was all the way down. I shut it off entirely, just for good measure.

I put all four windows up and closed the sunroof before killing the engine. The quietness was instantly eerie. I was the first to open my door and step out. A warm breeze swept around me, engulfing me in a gentle, safe feeling. It felt calm and reassuring, but I knew to keep my guard up. I tried to focus on how the woods felt so peaceful at that moment. I tried not to think about what creepy thing would happen to us today.

"Let's fucking do this," Dan said as he got out of the car, ruining my moment of serenity.

"I'm scared," Wendy said, racing around the car to hold Jen's hand.

"It'll be fine. We're just going for a hike," Jen said. "Nothing's going to happen."

I took a moment to look around the clearing. I'd been there a couple of times already, but I hadn't really taken any time to look at it. So far, it'd just served a purpose of allowing us to park the car, or turn around and head back home on that first night. I wish there'd been something remarkable about it. An old tree that had a face in it, or some branch that made a creepy sound when the wind hit it just right. But it wasn't anything special. It was just a small clearing on the side of a road that felt eerie — nothing out of the ordinary.

"I'll go in the front. Mike, you go behind the girls, so we can keep them between us."

"Okay," I said. I wasn't in love to be at the back of the line, but I didn't have much of a choice. Jen didn't seem very scared, but Wendy seemed terrified, so I knew I couldn't make one of them bring up the rear.

When we set off into the woods that day, I felt positive. It was the middle of the day, there was plenty of daylight left, and we had already gone to where we were going. I didn't feel like anything could surprise me.

I timed the walk out to where the wall of trees was to just over half an hour — about a mile and a half, maybe a little less.

Dan didn't run off ahead this time, instead waiting for the girls to go around the wall of trees first. He wanted to see how they reacted to seeing the house, he later told me.

To my surprise, neither of them was as freaked out as I expected. They both, much like me, were more curious about the house's origins than scared. They both spent a good amount of time looking through the newspapers.

"You were right, Mike," Jen said. "It's every edition of the Gazette from 1951. Every single one of them, in order."

"Weird. I don't know why. Do you know of anything that happened that year?"

"I don't know of anything," Jen said.

Wendy shrugged as I looked at her.

I spent a good half an hour looking around the rest of the house that wasn't newspaper related. I was hoping to find something we'd missed the last time we'd been there.

There was no spot for a bathroom, no plumbing of any kind that I could see. I figured even if the house had completely fallen apart, the plumbing would still exist underground. But there was none. I peeked my head out what would have been the back of the house, looking for an outhouse or some kind. I couldn't see any.

Dan and the girls were still flipping through the newspaper stacks, trying to make rhyme or reason out of them. Wendy took a few photos of them with the camera she'd brought.

I walked off through what looked to be the remnants of a doorway, though just a few inches off the ground now. I took about ten steps back out into the woods, away from the direction of the trail, and stopped. For a few seconds, I closed my eyes to see if I could hear something or feel something.

I could feel nature all around me. I got the feeling you get when you know you're truly alone, even though I knew my friends were just a few yards away. They were out of earshot, but I could still see them from where I was if I opened my eyes.

I felt the wind kick up around me, causing the trees to sway and creek, the leaves rustling all around me.

"Mike!" I heard Wendy call out.

I opened my eyes and turned around to face them, still standing in the house by the stack of papers.

"What's up?" I asked, as I re-entered the structure, careful not to trip on the corner of the foundation sticking up through the underbrush.

"Listen," she said. "Shh."

"What am I listening for?" I asked, before being shushed again.

I closed my eyes, standing almost smack dab in the middle of the house, and listened.

It was faint at first, but the more I listened intently, the louder it seemed to get.

First off in the distance, but then growing closer. I heard it.

I heard a woman screaming.

Not words. Not pleading for help. Not begging for mercy. Just screaming, as if she'd been hit repeatedly. Screams of pure pain.

Then, like a punch to the chest, she screamed out the word no. Loud and long, like a frustrated parent telling their kid not to stick a fork in an outlet for the millionth time. The word seemed to ring forever.

And then it stopped. The screaming was gone. The wind died down, and the sky seemed to lighten up.

I looked to my left, at Dan. His face was white, his eyes wider than my own. Wendy, directly across from me, had grabbed Jen and tried to hide behind Jen's much taller frame. I couldn't believe what had just happened.

"Holy shit," Dan said. "Holy fucking shit."

Holy shit was right. I didn't imagine it. All four of us heard it. All four of us experienced it.

"Was... was..." Wendy said, "was that real?"

Had we been in any other woods at any other moment in time, I wouldn't have even needed to think about the answer. Of course, it would have been real anywhere else. Of course, someone would have needed help if we weren't on Dudley Road. But here? Was it real? Was there someone out in the woods who needed help?

"I don't know," I said. "I don't think so."

Whatever we heard, if real, was sign enough that we needed to head back to the car.

"Take a few more pictures of the whole place," I told Wendy as we headed back to the path.

She did. She spent the rest of the roll of film before we headed back to the car.

The walk back to the car seemed to go much quicker than the walk to the house. We covered the mile and a half in about twenty minutes, with Dan first emerging into the clearing.

My car was still the only one there. I could see it from the trail, about fifty yards still into the woods.

From the front of the line, I heard Dan say, "what the fuck?"

"What's wrong?" Wendy asked.

"You locked the car, didn't you?" Dan asked.

"Yeah, I always do. Why?"

As I got closer, I could see that all four doors were open. Swung to the widest point that their hinges would allow.

"Who would do that?" Wendy asked, grabbing Jen's hand.

"And why?" Jen asked.

"And how?" Wendy added.

As I exited the path into the clearing, it hit me. "This is impossible," I said, holding the keys to my car.

"What is?" Dan asked.

"The windows are all down, too." I said, barely able to speak the words.

Had I just forgotten to lock the car, I could understand someone seeing it and playing a prank on us by opening the doors. But it was, as I had just said out loud, impossible for the windows to be down. I had the only key to the car in my possession. There was no option to put the windows down remotely in a car like nowadays. The only way to put the windows down was to have the key, put it into the ignition, turn it to RUN, and press the buttons on the driver's armrest.

"Let's get the hell out of here," Jen said.

"I'm not getting in the ghost car!" Wendy screamed.

But we had no choice. We had to get in the car to leave.

It was the first time we intentionally left through the other end of Dudley Road. Past the peaceful horse farms and beautiful houses. It was the first time that I felt like something out there was trying to mess with us. The radio being turned on before could have just been a fluke. But this, the doors and windows all being wide open, was something else. This was ominous and intentional. Something knew why we were there. That something was trying to scare us off.

Something didn't want us poking around anymore.

I felt more scared than I had until that point. My knees had a small shake to them, my hands had gone numb from the fear. I put on the best brave face that I could, but I think my friends knew me well enough to see through it. Just as I knew they were all scared, they knew I was, as well.

Ten

We didn't speak much on the ride home. We just quietly — and forcefully peacefully — listened as the multi-disc CD player randomly selected tracks from Tool's Ænima, Matchbox 20's Yourself or Someone Like You, and Radiohead's OK Computer. I periodically looked in the rearview mirror at the girls, or peered over at Dan next to me. Everyone was quietly looking out their respective window. As if any of us were afraid to talk about what had just happened. Like the words would somehow make what happened worse or more terrifying.

We drove all the way to Jen's house to drop her off first, with no words. The radio chugging along on random, but volume turned down to almost silent. All the windows were up. The air conditioning pumping through the vents was much louder than the radio. The occasional bump in the road causing an unexpected thump made the four of us more scared than a pothole should have.

No one spoke, even as Jen got out of the car. Normally she'd have said goodbye, even given Dan a kiss. But she silently, and slowly, got out of the car and closed the door quietly behind her. I normally would have just driven off, but I waited. We all watched patiently as she made her way up the walkway and opened the door. Even after she went inside and closed the door behind her, I didn't feel right leaving. I waited longer. I counted, silently, to myself, to fifteen before a light turned on in the otherwise dark house. It wasn't that late, and I never asked where they were, but it seemed so odd that no one was home when we arrived.

We continued our silence over the next ten minutes on the drive to Wendy's house. As if not speaking could protect us from anything bad happening.

The car had barely stopped in her driveway before she flung the door open.

"Bye," she said, barely audibly, and ran up the driveway. Her house was lit, both outside and in. Her dad usually left the light by the door on when he knew we'd be out until after dark. There was something about that generation and needing to leave the light on. It seemed like all of our parents did it back then, but it's not something I do now.

Like at Jen's house, we waited for Wendy to get inside. She waved quickly before closing the door behind her. I knew she was safe when the light went off.

I looked over at Dan and gave a quick shrug, as if to say "okay, it's time for us to go home now."

We were about halfway to his house before he said anything.

"Today was fucked up," he said, startling me.

"I know. How the hell did my car get unlocked, and the windows put down?"

"That was some supernatural shit," he said.

"You think so?"

"Well, what else would it have been?" he asked.

"What do you mean?"

"Think about it. The only way someone could have put the windows in the car down would be if they had a key, right?"

"Right."

"If you had lost your keys in the woods and someone else was out there and found them, I could see them doing that to mess with us. Then leave the keys in the car."

"But that didn't happen."

"Right," he said. "You had the keys the whole time."

"I don't get it. It really freaked me out, though," I said.

"Me too," Dan said. Even without looking at him, I could tell that he was shaken up. This sort of thing didn't normally bother him.

I'd driven from Burlington to Dan's house more times than I could count. From any of the various jobs I'd had at the mall, I'd gone straight to his house after. Or from his house to work. I basically lived there. I'd done it so often, I could do it with my eyes closed.

But I missed a turn.

The even odder thing is that I didn't even notice until we were just about at my house. My autopilot would have normally just brought me to Dan's, but that night it had tried bringing me home.

Was I just shaken up over the entire thing?

Dan didn't seem to notice, so I didn't mention it. I kept driving, ignoring turning into my neighborhood, and made a really long turnaround through town to head back to his house.

I could see the light on in the living room as we drove down the street. His dad, Charlie, would most likely be in there reading the newspaper, as he had virtually every other night. His mom, Kathy, would likely be in the kitchen washing the dishes from dinner, probably wondering where we were. His little sister, Rachel, would be fast asleep already.

Neither of us said anything about it, but I instinctively got out of the car and followed him inside.

As she'd greeted us so many other times, Kathy asked if we were hungry. She always kept leftovers for us, even if she didn't know when we'd be home.

I don't know if she enjoyed cleaning up after us, but I can never remember putting a dish in the sink at Dan's. We just finished eating and the plates would be gone. As if some ninja came by and swooped in to clean up our mess.

"We're going downstairs," Dan said, more to inform his parents than to ask permission.

"Be quiet, your sister is sleeping," his father called out from the living room.

"Let me know if you boys need anything," Kathy said, as Dan closed the door behind him.

Although the light was on by the time I hit the bottom of the stairs, I still felt scared. I'd been in their basement almost every day for five years at that point, but something about that night felt different. Not spooky, not terrifying, just different.

There was this old day bed down there. It had two big drawers under it where we kept board games in that we liked to play. There was also an old dining room table with a couple of chairs we could use for anything we felt like doing down there. It was small enough that I always assumed they'd used it until Rachel was born about four years before. Now that they were a family of four, they needed a slightly larger table. So we got the old one in the basement to use for whatever we felt like doing.

I climbed onto the daybed, sliding back against the wood-paneled wall. Dan pulled a chair out from the table, slid it against the wall across from me, and sat down.

We both, perhaps subconsciously, had put our backs against walls. I don't know why I did it. It wasn't something I normally would have done in the basement. I'd normally have sat on the floor or sat at the table. We'd then spend ten or fifteen minutes figuring out what we wanted to do.

"Why is it so quiet?" Dan asked after a few minutes.

He was right. There were no sounds of life that we normally would hear. The usual hum of the computer from his dad's small office was inaudible. The television from the living room directly above us was gone. Footsteps of Kathy walking around the kitchen or making her way in to sit in the living room were missing. No sound from any cars driving by, which we could normally hear. Everything was still and silent.

"That's unusual," I said. "I don't know why."

"It's freaking me out," Dan said.

"Me too," I said. "Me too."

We sat in silence for a long while. So long that we both visibly jumped when Kathy opened the door and came halfway down the stairs. Something that should have not scared us. Something she'd done hundreds of times before, but that night was the icing on top of the fear cake we'd baked today.

"We're going to bed," she whispered, to not wake Rachel up. "Are you boys staying down here tonight?"

I looked across at Dan. I could tell he wanted me to stay and I think he could tell I didn't want to drive home alone.

"Yes, thank you," Dan said.

"Okay, keep the noise down. We'll see you in the morning," and she was gone up the stairs, closing the door behind her.

I don't remember the rest of the night. I'm sure we eventually snapped out of it and found something in the basement to occupy us until we fell asleep down there. I'm sure we didn't spend the whole night scared, wondering, and afraid of every little noise that we'd been so used to. I'm sure everything was fine. But I don't remember any of it.

The last thing I remember from that night was Kathy saying she'd see us in the morning and leaving.

Eleven

I WOKE UP THE next morning, still in my clothes. I had slumped over onto the daybed and fallen asleep at some point. The clock to my right said it was just after six. Charlie was up and getting ready to go to work. His footsteps moving from their bedroom to the kitchen must have been enough to jostle me awake.

I looked around the room, adjusting my eyes to the sun shining through the small windows above ground level, to find Dan. He'd fallen asleep on the floor, on a foldout chair that turned into a single bed-length cushion. I'd slept on it in his room dozens of times. It wasn't very comfortable, but it was good enough for most situations. Especially situations where you, perhaps, didn't want to go upstairs by yourself to get something better. Or, worse, go sleep upstairs by yourself, even if it meant sleeping in your own bed.

He was still asleep, tucked under the only blanket I'm sure he could find before he passed out. An old, torn-up, barely holding itself together Thundercats blanket. It must have been from when he was a kid, but I couldn't remember ever seeing it before that morning. And, come to think of it, I never saw it again.

I sat up, trying not to make any noise, adjusting my back to compensate for a less-than-stellar night's sleep. I cracked and popped like someone well beyond my years, doing my best to be comfortable, but not make too much noise.

I spent some time looking around the room while I waited for Dan to wake up. I noticed some old books on a bookshelf I'd never noticed before. I focused on the chair holding the body-length punching bag to the drop ceiling. I noticed I could, once again, hear the hum of Charlie's computer coming from the office, even with the door mostly closed.

I'd been down there so many other times before, but never felt like I had the run of the place. I was always doing something with just Dan. I was sometimes part of a group playing a board game. I couldn't ever remember being down there while Dan was still asleep. We, for whatever reason, usually woke up at the same time.

Everything seemed so new to me. The stacks of boxes off to my right all seemed taller than I remembered. The table seemed farther away than it normally did. The door off to the laundry area was closed, though it was usually open. I could smell sawdust coming from Charlie's workbench, that while I'm sure was always present, I couldn't recall previously noticing.

It seemed like my senses were heightened when left to my own devices.

"Oh, hey," Dan said, sitting up. "You been up long?"

"No, I just woke up," I said. It was a bit of a lie. I'd been awake for twenty minutes, according to the clock.

The noise upstairs had stopped when Charlie left for work a few minutes before Dan woke up. But, suddenly, the sound of a five-year-old Rachel running around in the living room seemed to get louder.

"Dan, Mike," Kathy said, opening the door, "Rachel is up. She wants to see you. Hungry?"

Before Rachel was born, Kathy would usually let us sleep all day. We'd just be teenagers and stay up late, making as much noise as we wanted. We'd wake up at ten or sometimes later, and it was no big deal. But once Rachel was born, we'd get up early and play with her. She loved The Lion King. We watched it on VHS, almost daily, sometimes multiple times a day. It was one of the few things that could keep her tiny mind calm for an extended period.

"We'll be right up," Dan said, making his way to his feet.

I followed suit, stretching my back even further than I was able to do from the daybed.

He went up the stairs first, greeted with a screech of "Danny!" when Rachel saw him.

I looked back down at the basement from about halfway up the stairs. I don't know why. I don't know what I expected to see down there.

"Mike!" Rachel called out to me.

"Hey kiddo," I said, climbing the rest of the stairs and shutting the door.

Like so many other mornings, we sat at the table while Kathy brought us scrambled eggs and toast. Some mornings, if we were lucky, we got bacon, too. That day was a lucky morning.

As we ate, Rachel zoomed around the house. The hallway by the bedrooms connected to the living room on one end and a smaller hallway on the other, where the basement door was. It created a long rectangle that Rachel usually used as a race track. She did lap after lap while waiting for us to finish our breakfast.

"Simba!" she yelled as we were finishing. It was her way of telling us she wanted to watch The Lion King. We both expected that was how we would spend our morning. We'd watch the movie for the umpteenth time while Kathy got ready for work later.

I plopped down on one end of the couch, Dan on the other, and Rachel made her way into the middle of us. The VHS was already in the VCR, so we had to turn the TV on and press play.

My mind drifted as the movie started. I thought about everything that had happened the day before. I thought about what could happen if we went back. I wondered if Dan wanted to go back.

I looked over Rachel's head towards him, sitting on my left, and I just knew he wanted to go back. As scared as we both were, the adrenaline outweighed the fear. I didn't care how afraid I was, because I felt like we were out there trying to solve the question no one but us had asked, even if only to ourselves; is there something actually haunted out in the woods? And, if something was haunted, could we find the supposed house that existed? Would we find something else out there? Something that could explain what we'd seen so far?

I didn't know when we'd go back. But I knew we would. I knew we'd get back out there and explore more. Maybe during the morning, so we had more daylight. Even though the woods were thick overhead, the sunlight still made its way through and that, even if just a little, helped me feel better while we explored the woods.

"Hey mom?" Dan semi-shouted toward the kitchen.

"Yes?" She called back.

"Did you ever hear anything about Dudley Road, in Billerica?"

She didn't respond. Dan looked over at me, and we made eye contact.

"Mom?" Dan yelled.

She approached the entryway to the living room. "I don't know much about it. But I know it's bad news."

"Bad news?" I asked.

"Yes. You boys stay away from there."

She didn't wait for a response, she just issued her decree and scurried back off to the kitchen to clean up from breakfast.

Weird, I mouthed across the couch to Dan. He nodded, then shrugged.

If Kathy knew anything, she didn't want to share it with us. It made me wonder what she knew and if she had any first hand experience at Dudley Road.

Twelve

WE DIDN'T OFFICIALLY CALL a moratorium on going to the woods, but we sort of avoided going there. I suppose we avoided it intentionally for a while. It just felt too creepy after the last time we'd gone. Even though it was only a bit of a weirder thing that happened to my car, it seemed to have progressed from the first time the windows were open.

I didn't want to risk making things worse, so I purposefully didn't go there and didn't suggest it to anyone else.

For almost a week exactly.

Over that week, Dan had brought it up twice in casual conversation. Not going back, but just discussing what had happened, what we'd seen, how weird it all was.

Every time he brought it up, Jen quickly changed the subject. Or Wendy left the room. Sometimes both.

It seemed like they were just as freaked out about it as I was, if not more.

It was early evening on a Friday. I was at work, waiting tables. Wendy and Jen showed up together before it started getting busy for the Friday night rush. I'd guess it was around five-thirty.

"Hey Mike," Wendy said, as she emerged from the back of the restaurant. Jen was right behind her.

"Hey Wen. Hey Jen," I said.

Cisco, one of the evening cooks, said hello to both of them in Portuguese, as he'd done a hundred other times.

"I'm going to kill Dan," Jen said in my general direction.

"Why? What'd he do now?" I asked.

"He keeps trying to freak me out. Every little opportunity he gets, he tries to do something that he thinks will scare me in a cute way. I want to punch him in the face."

"He's been calling me and breathing heavy into the phone when I pick up, too," Wendy added.

"He can be such a dick sometimes," I said.

"Has he done anything to you?" Jen asked.

"No, but I haven't seen him since last week. I talked to him a few times, but haven't been to his house since the morning after we last went there."

I used "there" because I knew they'd know what I was talking about. I also didn't feel the need to say the words "Dudley Road" or "the woods" out loud. I did that more often in conversation with my friends that knew about what we'd been through. Even when telling Kevin and Brian about the last trip, I avoided actually naming it. Like it was Voldemort or Beetlejuice or Candyman. As if saying it out loud would make something terrible happen.

After telling Kevin and Brian, both of them agreed what had happened was even more strange than the time they'd gone with us and seen the house in the woods. Neither of them explicitly said they didn't want to go back, but I could tell from Brian's voice that he'd had enough and had no intentions of returning. I was sure Dan would talk him into it, eventually. Not that Dan was a bully, but he had a way of getting Brian to do things he didn't want to do.

A line started forming at the door just as we'd finished divvying up the tables amongst us. Besides Jen, Wendy and myself, Jessica and Megan — who were older than us and friends with one another outside of work — were also waiting tables that night. I let the girls take three tables, and I took the two counter sections. I knew I wouldn't make as much money as them, but I didn't mind. Tables meant bigger parties, which meant larger bills, which usually meant bigger tips. Taking the bar usually meant single people or couples who didn't want to wait for a table. Smaller bills meant smaller tips, usually. But it was also easier work, and it occupied my mind with other things.

Taking the bar meant I spent less time running around. Since the bar wrapped around the grill — which was out front, unlike most restaurants — I had less distance to go to pick up food or put orders in. It was an easier section to work when you were feeling lazy or preoccupied, which I was.

It also meant that you usually weren't busy until later in the evening, once all the tables had filled up and people started opting to sit at the counter. So I had time to goof off or help the other servers with things; get drinks, make shakes, put fries in to cook. If you wanted to, you could make a lot of busy work when working the bar section. I've always found that busy work helps distract my mind from anything I need to be distracted from. This situation was no exception.

I was halfway into pouring a Mr. Pibb for Megan when I looked out the window into the parking lot. The sun had started setting, but it was still light enough out that everything outside was visible.

There, standing among all the parked cars, all the people driving around looking for spots, and the people walking to and from their cars, I saw a man standing perfectly still. It caught my eye as normally people aren't just standing in the parking lot. You park, get out of your car, and walk toward the mall. That's a pretty normal thing to do.

But he just stood there. Fifty, maybe sixty feet away, not moving.

He stood with his hands by his side, arms straight down. No swaying to his body, no motion in his hands or feet, it didn't even seem like he was blinking, though it was hard to see from how far away I was from him, even with my glasses and squinting.

He looked to be in his early 30s, dressed in a flannel button-down shirt, with a jean jacket over it. He wore ragged blue jeans, which were torn at the knees and looked to be a little too long for his legs. I could make out black shoes, but couldn't tell if they were sneakers or something else.

It felt like he was staring directly at me.

I hadn't realized how long I'd been looking at him until I felt the Mr. Pibb pouring out over the top of the glass onto my hand.

I instinctively pulled the glass from the soda machine and put it down, reaching for the towel I kept in the front pocket of my apron to dry my hand.

Once I'd put the towel back in my apron, I dumped the Mr. Pibb into another clean glass and handed it to Megan, who swung by on her way to the fry machine to pick up some fresh fries.

When I looked back up, he was gone.

The parking lot seemed normal again, though slightly darker.

Though strange, I tried to shake it off and get back to work.

It got busy enough by seven-thirty that I didn't give the parking-lot-man another thought. I was zipping around, helping my many customers at my two bar sections, dropping plates of fries, pouring ketchup left and right, topping off sodas, and ordering hamburgers like it was going out of style.

Sometimes, being that busy was a blessing. Not only did you make more money as a server, but the time went by much quicker. You get into a zone and don't think about anything but doing the best job you can for your customers.

The main part of the bar wrapped around the grill, as I mentioned before, but the other part of the bar was separate from the main bar, across a small walkway, facing out into the mall. It sat ten. It was usually empty, unless the restaurant was incredibly busy. It was just an awkward place to sit and most people seemed to prefer to not sit there. So it was empty most nights.

That night was different, though. I had a family of four sitting over there. The two kids, a boy and a girl, that were young, maybe ten or twelve. Nothing extraordinary about them, other than where they sat.

I heard Cisco call that there was "hot food", which is what the cooks always yelled when an order was up. There wasn't a bell or fancy pager system, it was just someone yelling "hot foot" and whoever wasn't busy would go get it and bring it to whichever table it was for.

I grabbed the four burgers for my oddball-window-sitters and swung around the counter to drop them off.

As I put the last burger down in front of the dad, I looked out into the mall. I often looked out there, across at Pizzeria Regina, just to people watch.

I didn't notice him at first. There were too many people walking in and out of the mall entrance at that time of night for him to catch my eye. But as I glanced back toward the main entrance to our restaurant, I saw him — the same guy from before. I turned around quickly and looked at the clock hanging on the wall by the grill. It was seven forty-seven.

It'd been two hours since I got busy enough that I hadn't thought about him standing in the parking lot.

Suddenly, he was standing just ten feet away from me on the other side of the glass. Staring at me again. It felt like he was looking directly into my eyes, making straight-on eye contact. This time he was close enough that I could tell he wasn't blinking. He stood there, expressionless, motionless. His hands never moving, just tucked neatly down by his side.

People walked past him in both directions, seeming not to even notice him. No one bumped into him or spoke to him.

I felt myself hovering over the shoulder of the guy who I'd just handed a burger to. I mumbled something mostly coherent about letting me know if they needed anything else and retreated behind the counter.

I had only turned my back for a moment, maybe fifteen seconds, to get back to the bar area. When I turned back around, he was still there. Though I was now at a different angle from where I was before, he still maintained eye contact with me.

I walked from one end of the bar to the other, near the cash register. He maintained eye contact without moving his body at all.

I picked up "hot food" and walked it to a table over in the far corner. I could feel his eyes on me the whole way there. When I looked back outside, he was still staring at me.

Perhaps I'd stood still too long. Perhaps something felt odd about my behavior. Perhaps my skin had gone pale. I don't know what happened, but Wendy came up to me and stood in front of me. She was short enough that I looked mostly directly over her head. I didn't notice she was there until she spoke. "Hey, you're in my way," she said.

"Sorry," I stepped aside, still locked eye-to-eye with the guy outside.

"What are you looking at?" she asked.

"That guy out there in the jean jacket."

"Where?" she asked.

"Right there," I pointed.

"I don't see anyone in a jean jacket," she said.

"He's right there, Wen," I insisted, still pointing.

She walked toward the window to get a better look. After a few seconds, she turned back to me and shrugged.

Did she not see him? Could she not see him?

"You see that guy, right?" I asked Jen when she walked by.

"Fuck. Not you, too," she said.

"What?"

"Dan's been telling me about some guy he's seen at his house all week. Some guy who he says keeps staring at him."

"Shut up," I said. "Did you see the guy?"

"No, I was over there the other night and Dan said he saw him out in the street, but I saw nothing. Are you guys teaming up trying to freak me out now?"

"I'm not, I swear. He's right there," I said.

"Wendy," she called across a table. "Mike's doing it, too."

"Stop it. It's not funny. There's no guy," Wendy yelled at me.

But he was there. I could see him. He was still standing there, staring at me. He hadn't moved at all. He still hadn't blinked. I hadn't taken my eyes off him, nor did he break eye contact with me. We stood there, locked together, eye to eye. It felt like days had gone by.

I made the silent decision to go out there and ask him who he was.

As I made my way through the line of people blocking the door, waiting for tables, I bumped into a woman who fell backward. I grabbed her arm to break her fall and helped her back to her feet, apologizing.

That tiny bump, those few seconds of helping her regain her balance, was all the time I'd taken my eyes off of him.

When I looked back, he was gone.

I ran out into the mall, looking down towards the main mall area, where our wing connected to the heart of the mall. Nothing.

I jogged the twenty feet out of the mall entrance to the parking lot. It was dark, but the parking lot was lit well enough. He wasn't there, either.

"He's fucking gone," I said to myself. "How?"

There was no way, in just a handful of seconds, that he'd disappeared. Even if he hauled ass down the mall or out into the parking lot, I'd have seen him. It was too quick for him to have gotten far enough away that I couldn't see him. If he'd ran, I'd have heard his footsteps. By the time I got out of the entrance of Johnny Rockets, he was less than five feet from me. I should have seen him, no matter which direction he went.

I spent ten minutes looking. I looked everywhere. I checked Pizzeria Regina across from us, I checked the hair salon next to it, and the shoe repair shop across from it. Suncoast Video. Mrs. Fields. Aldo Shoe. He wasn't in any of those places.

He'd just vanished.

And it seemed like I was the only one who'd seen him.

What the fuck was happening? How had Wendy and Jen not seen him? How had no one else seen him? Was he really there? I was starting to feel less like I was in a horror movie and more like I was losing my mind.

Thirteen

As soon as I left work that night, I drove to Dan's. Wendy and Jen got a ride home from Jessica, so I was off the hook to drive them home. I think, on some level, they both felt creeped out about my behavior that night, so they felt safer going home with Jessica. They used the guise of "girl time" and I let them get away with it.

"Okay, what the actual fuck?" I said as I walked into Dan's room.

It was after eleven and I normally wouldn't have gone to his house that late, but I felt like I needed to talk to him.

"Quiet. You'll wake Rachel or my parents," he said. "Let's go downstairs."

I followed him down to the basement, waiting for us both to sit at the table before saying anything else.

"You're not just fucking with Jen, are you?"

"About what?"

"The guy. She said you keep talking about a guy you're seeing outside."

"No. Fuck. She told you?"

"She had to," I said. "I saw someone tonight at work and mentioned it to her and Wendy. They thought I was faking it and trying to mess with them. Jen says you've been talking about it all week."

"I've seen him out in the street. I've seen him at Lil' Peach. I've seen him over by Brian's up the street. Every time, he's just standing there, still," Dan said. His eyes were red and his skin more pale than usual. I could see tiny, periodic shakes in his hands. He looked like he hadn't slept much.

"Why didn't you tell me about this?" I asked.

"You were so freaked out about the last time we went to Dudley Road, I didn't want to freak you out anymore," he said. I wasn't in love with how he said Dudley Road, but I skipped past it.

"If you tell me he's wearing a jean jacket and ripped jeans, I'm going to shit myself," I said.

His face turned white. He opened his mouth, but it seemed like he couldn't speak. He just sat there, mouth agape, white as a ghost.

"It is, isn't it?" I asked.

He nodded.

"When did you first see him?" I asked.

"Last week. That morning after you left. I took Rachel out back to play and he was standing across the street before we went through the gate to the backyard. By the Capone's mailbox."

"What did he do?"

"Nothing, he just stood there. He just stared at me. He didn't even blink. It freaked me out."

"Did Rachel see him?"

"That's the even more fucked up thing. No," he said. "She asked me what I was looking at and when I told her, she said 'not funny'."

"Neither Wendy nor Jen could see him tonight, either. I saw him twice at work. Once outside the mall and once inside the mall."

"Did you try to ask him who the fuck he was?" Dan asked.

"No. I finally decided to go do it and he vanished. Like, five feet from me, I looked away for a second and he was gone when I looked back."

"That's happened to me, too. Twice so far, I looked away and when I looked back, he was gone. The third time I saw him, at Lil' Peach, I had my eyes on him the whole time. A truck drove between us and then he was gone. Like some sort of special effect on a TV show or something. Truck zipped by for one second and he was gone. Just like you said, vanished."

"Christ," I said. "Fucking Christ."

"How is this a thing that happens in real life?"

"I don't know. I thought I was crazy," I said.

"I know. Me too. When Rachel said she couldn't see him, I thought she was mistaken. She's only five. When Jen said she couldn't see him up by Brian's house, I thought she was fucking with me."

"She said you were messing with her all week," I said, "but you were really seeing this guy?"

"Three times, so far."

"You think it's related to what we've been doing?"

"How the fuck?" he yelled, before quieting himself. "How the fuck can it not be? Some weird guy just starts showing up, staring at us suddenly? It's gotta be related."

"You're right," I said.

I was glad we were in the basement. If the creepy staring guy was outside, we couldn't see him.

If something like this were to happen today, I'd just whip out my iPhone and take a photo of him. I'd get some sort of photographic proof that I wasn't going crazy, that Dan wasn't going crazy. It couldn't be a coincidence that we both saw a completely made up person who didn't exist who just looked the same, behaved the same, and stood there staring at us.

After a few minutes of silence, Dan said, "We have to go back. There has to be more to this."

"I know. We have to find out more."

The thought never crossed my mind to go to the library and look up information about Dudley Road or the convent or the history of the area. It never was a thought to go knock on the door of the nunnery and ask them some questions.

Fourteen

It felt like the crack of dawn the next morning when I heard my mother yelling up from downstairs.

"Wake up. Dan's on the phone," she said, sounding irritated.

"What?" I yelled back.

"Pick up the phone. I've been yelling at you for five minutes!" The irritation seemed warranted.

"Got it," I said as I picked up.

"Get up," Dan said. "We've gotta get over there."

I looked at the alarm clock. It was 8:20. I don't remember what day it was, thinking back on it now, but I vividly remember 8:20 since that's my dad's birthday. I always found it easier to remember inane details if they correlated to something bigger in my life.

"Okay. I'm getting up. I'll be there in like twenty minutes."

"Good. I told Kevin and talked Brian into coming with us, too. See you in a bit," he said before I heard the receiver slam down.

I rolled myself out of bed and looked for the clothes nearest to me that didn't smell like the teenage boy I was.

I threw on my trusty cargo shorts and my And Justice For All Metallica t-shirt. I'd probably worn that combination more times than I could count, but that seemed unimportant.

As usual, my Mom didn't question me as I strolled out the door. She knew I just talked to Dan, and I wasn't wearing work clothes, so it was safe to assume I was going to Dan's. I didn't have a big group of friends and wasn't very popular, so the only place I ever went was to Dan's house. What we did after I got there was usually not something she concerned herself with unless I got in trouble. Which, frankly, didn't happen until I was older.

I honked as I drove away, up our road, heading to the adjoining road, which would take me over to Dan's house.

The entire ride over there — all of five minutes — I kept thinking about the jean jacket guy. Where'd he come from? Why was he just standing there? And, most important of all, where the hell did he go when he vanished?

"Good morning," I said to Kathy as I walked into the kitchen.

"Miiiiiiikkkkeeeeee," Rachel said, running up to give me a hug.

"Hey kiddo!" I hugged her back.

"Danny, Mike's here," Rachel yelled, unnecessarily loudly.

I heard his bedroom door close before Rachel finished yelling.

"Let's go," he said to me. "We'll be back later." He kissed his mom on the cheek and mussed Rachel's hair in one motion.

"Bye girls," I said, following him out the door, down the steps, and to my car. He was already buckling himself in by the time I even opened my door.

"Anxious, much?" I asked.

"Yeah, let's go. Brian should be waiting in the driveway."

And he was. As usual, he waited outside for us, rather than have us come into his house. The last time I'd been in the house was a few years before, back when we started our "band". We used to practice at Brian's house before I got a drum set. Once I did, we moved practice to my mother's basement. Anyway, there he was, waiting for us. I don't know why he always met us outside, but it'd been his preferred way to meet up with us since I got my license and a car.

"Hey guys." He climbed in behind Dan. "Why are we doing this? Again?"

I could tell he was nervous, but that wasn't too far from our status quo with Brian.

"I told you about the guy I've been seeing all week," Dan said.

"There's a guy. So what? He's creepy, big deal," Brian said, deflecting.

"I've seen him, too," I said. "He was at the mall last night."

"Oh, shit."

I made eye contact with him in the rear-view mirror. "No one else saw him."

"Oh, shit, oh, shit." He doubled down.

"Did you tell Kevin?" Brian asked.

"I did," Dan said. "But Mike hasn't."

"I didn't get out of work until late last night. I went right to Dan's to talk to him about it, but Janice would have killed me if I called Kevin at midnight."

"He's gonna freak out. He loves this stuff," Brian said.

"I know. I do, too, but this is getting a little too weird. Even for me," Dan said.

Kevin lived in the center of town. Tewksbury isn't huge, but it was still about a fifteen-minute drive from Dan's house to Kevin's. Dan and Brian lived on the south side, so we were about as far from the center of town as we could be. He was sitting on his front steps when we pulled in, playing his guitar, like he always was. He made his usual "just a sec" one-finger motion and ran back into the house to put the guitar down. Unlike Brian, who took meticulous care of his guitar, Kevin would just toss his on the couch or his bed, depending on which room he was in.

"Bye, ma," he yelled as the screen door closed.

"Dudes," he said, as he sat behind me, buckling himself in.

"Mike saw the guy Dan told us about," Brian blurted out, barely waiting for me to put the car in reverse.

"For real? Dan's not an insane person?"

"I am, just not for this," Dan said, laughing.

"He was at the mall last night, staring at me," I told Kevin.

"Did you go up to him and talk to him?" Kevin asked.

"No, I tried. I finally built up the courage to go do it and he just disappeared. Like, poof, gone."

"Creepy, right?" Dan said, not expecting an answer.

"Are we going there right now?" Brian asked.

"I'm starving. Can we eat first?" I said.

"Denny's?" Kevin and Brian said, at the same time.

"Denny's."

It was where we often went when we needed something to eat. It was open all night, so we usually found ourselves there late at night, when everything else was closed, but we didn't want to go home yet.

We drove to the Denny's on surface roads. Even though it was just down 93 in Woburn, we took the longer way to get there. Pressed for an answer now, I couldn't tell you why. We just did.

It must have been a weekday, because I don't remember waiting for a table for very long. They took us in right away and plopped the same sticky menus down we'd looked through a thousand times before.

"So, what's our plan?" I asked.

"I'm getting waffles," Brian said.

"Not about food, you fat fuck," I said, laughing. "The plan for today. Going there."

"Oh," Brian said. "That. Well, fuck you, I'm not fat."

The three of us who weren't Brian got a good chuckle out of it.

"I think we should wait until dark and try to sneak around the building. Not just around the woods," Dan said.

"Yes!" Kevin agreed.

"I don't know," Brian said. "I'm good with going around in the woods during the day, but what you're talking about sounds like trespassing."

"Don't be such a pussy," Dan said. In hindsight, he was always harder on Brian that I thought he needed to be. Or maybe Brian needed that as his motivation to disobey his strict mother and stepfather, or to face his fears and do something he wouldn't normally do.

"Fuck you," he retorted, "I'm not a pussy."

"You kind of are," Kevin said.

"Okay, focus. What are we doing?" I asked.

The server came over, interrupting our ragging on Brian, to take our order.

None of us spoke for a solid minute after she left. As if she was some sort of supernatural narc who was going to rat us out before we could even get there and do anything.

"I stick with going tonight and looking around that big brick building. It's a convent, right?" Kevin said.

"I don't know if it's a convent. I keep hearing it referred to as a nunnery, but I don't know the difference," I said.

"Whatever it is, the building. I want to snoop around. Maybe there's a way in, or maybe there's something else we'll find," Kevin said.

"I like your plan," Dan said, looking at Brian.

"What? Why are you looking at me?"

"You're the hold out. Are you coming or not?" Dan asked him, sternly.

"Okay, fine. I'll come. But if we get in trouble, my mother is going to kill me and all of you."

"Yes!" Dan said.

"Sweet," Kevin added.

"You really think there's something else out there?" I asked the group. "Something behind whatever that brick building is?"

"I don't know," Dan said. "But the stories all seem to stem from whatever that building is. Whether they're true, I don't know. Is there a convent somewhere? Is there a building where the nuns practiced witchcraft? Was there a rapist and a house? Damned if I know. But let's go try to find out."

"If there's something out there, we'll find it," Kevin said.

"I hope not," Brian added.

Our server brought our food and dropped it with little eye contact or words. We all seemed to take our time eating. I don't think it was because we were scared to go back to Dudley Road, but that it was still morning and it wouldn't be dark for many hours. We essentially had time to kill. Or, perhaps, on some level, we were scared.

Brian was right. Going out into the woods and snooping around was one thing. If anyone had caught us, we could just say we were out hiking. But snooping around on private property could be dangerous. If someone caught us, we could get into actual trouble.

Let alone if anything supernatural happened. Let alone if we saw anything that really freaked us out. Or, worse, if something happened to one of us.

Fifteen

I DON'T REMEMBER MOST of what we did the rest of that day to kill time. I remember going to Lil' Peach twice to get snacks and sodas. We stopped at Haffner's on Main Street to put a whopping ten bucks worth of gas in the car. We swung by Dan's house for a little while in the afternoon, mainly so Brian could call his mom from Dan's house to tell her he was right up the road.

Kevin sat in the same corner of the floor he always did, whittling away at a stick he'd picked up outside. His pocket knife was never far from his belt. I wondered if he planned to sharpen the stick to a point, to use as a weapon.

Brian, true to his personality, paced around the room. I could sense his anxiety. I could feel his sense of unease.

I took inventory of some items I'd taken from home; made sure the batteries in the flashlight worked, checked the compass to make sure North was still where it should be. I examined the two road flares I'd brought, even though I had no idea if they were good or not. Looking at them with my untrained eye surely didn't bring any certainty.

We more or less futzed around all day, just waiting for it to be just about nightfall. Watching the minutes tick by on the clock in the car while we drove around, burning gas, listening to Days of the New, Alice in Chains, Stabbing Westward, Sepultura, Stone Temple Pilots and Rage Against the Machine. Those six discs didn't leave my JVC 6-disc CD player most of that summer.

We were sitting in the parking lot at the Trahan School when the sun started to set. We'd sometimes walk there from Dan's house when we were younger, before I could drive. We liked to play on the jungle gyms, pretending we were John McClane, jumping from gym to gym, making sure not to hit the mulch beds.

"Twenty minutes until dark," Brian said. "Are we sure we're doing this?"

"Look, if you want to go home, we'll drop you and go without you," Dan said, turning around to look at Brian in the eyes.

"I'm just nervous, is all," he said.

"Don't be nervous," Kevin said. "It'll be fine."

I didn't believe him.

"Yeah," I added, "it'll be fine."

I'm not even sure I believed myself.

"I trust you guys. I don't know why, but I do," Brian said.

Though his mother and stepfather were always really strict with him, Brian was a good kid. We'd done nothing to get him in serious trouble. At least not up until then. After that summer? Sure. We did plenty to get his ass chewed out when we got him home. But up until then, we'd mostly just been out driving and having fun.

"Okay," I said. "Let's go."

I clicked my seatbelt in and waited to hear three more clicks before shifting into drive. In typical teenage asshole fashion, I tried to peel out of the parking lot. But since I was driving a Mitsubishi Galant, peeling out wasn't exactly something it did that often.

I'm sure it was entirely coincidental, but we pulled onto Dudley Road just as the sun had finished setting. It wasn't quite pitch black yet, but it was dark enough that we felt safe. We felt protected. Not from anything unnatural, but from humans seeing us, noticing what we were doing, and calling the police on us. We didn't know what to expect going out into the surroundings of the building, but we were on high alert.

I can't speak for Dan, but I kept looking over my shoulder the entire day, waiting for the jean jacket guy to show up. I was, on some level, hoping Kevin and Brian could see him, too.

I drove past the brick building intentionally.

"I'm going to go down to the turnaround spot and wait a little," I said.

"Let it get a little darker. Smart," Dan said.

"Right."

We pulled in, put the windows down, opened the sun roof, and I killed the engine.

My dad worked for JVC back then. It was the only reason I had a really killer stereo system in that car. I wasn't much interested in really loud music, but it was fun to blast music with the windows down. We always got odd looks when we drove down the main strip at Hampton Beach, blasting hard rock or metal. You'd normally only hear rap at the volume we played our music.

I bring that up because it's how we spent the next half an hour. The four of us sat on the car, listening to the Chaos A.D. album from Sepultura. I sat on the roof, controlling the CD changer with the remote control — yes, my stereo had a remote control in 1997, before they were integrated into the steering wheel of almost every new car years later — Dan sat on the other side of the roof. Kevin sat on the hood and Brian sat on the trunk, looking out behind us, in case anyone else pulled in.

As we usually did, we skipped to the last few tracks. They were all live tracks, and I just enjoyed them more, personally.

What I'd never done before — and something that freaked us out when we discovered it — was let the album play out after the last track. After "Amen/Inner Self" finished playing, there was silence. None of us noticed it, as we were all living in the moment. It was a gorgeous night, the sky was clear, the sounds of nature took over from the song naturally. It felt peaceful for a few minutes. None of us spoke. We just all sat on our respective parts of the car, listening to nature sing its call.

I didn't notice that the next CD hadn't kicked in by itself. One perk of having a multiple-disc CD player back then was that you didn't have to switch out the disc when you were done. The next one would just start on its own. After a few minutes of silence, of just nature, I heard a gunshot out in the woods. Quiet enough that it seemed far off, but loud enough that all four of us noticed it.

"What was that?" Brian asked, jumping off the car's trunk and coming around to the front where he could see the rest of us.

"It sounded like a gun," Kevin said.

"I heard it, too," I added.

"Me too," Dan said.

Then we heard it again.

I jumped down off the roof of the car.

"What the fuck?" I said, looking out into the dark woods.

"What is it?"

It sounded again. That time, we heard a click before it.

It was louder than the first two times.

Boom.

A fourth time. Louder than before.

"Is someone shooting at us?" Brian said, opening the back passenger door and jumping inside.

"If they are, Mike's car isn't going to protect you," Kevin said.

Boom. Again. Louder. Closer.

"What the fuck is it?" I yelled.

"Guys," Brian said, getting back out of the car. "It's the radio."

"What?" I said.

"It's the radio, the CD," Brian repeated.

I aimed the remote through the window and hit the pause button.

The sounds stopped. I skipped back some and pressed play. Again, the "gunshots" rang out in the woods.

"What the fuck is this song?" Dan said, climbing into the passenger seat.

Once the four of us were in the car, with the windows up and sunroof closed, I played "Amen/Inner Self" again, fast-forwarding to the end.

There it was, again. Faint, at first, but growing louder and thus sounding closer, as it progressed. It sounded like gunshots.

We listened to it a bunch of times that night, and many other nights after, trying to figure out what it was. I, to this day, maintain that it's the sound of an empty concert venue and a drummer is tuning his drums, or setting up his microphones.

Kevin insisted it was recorded gunfire, but couldn't explain why it would be as a hidden track at the end of the album.

Brian didn't care what it was. He was just glad no one was out in the woods trying to assassinate us.

Dan flip-flopped back and forth between tuning drums and recorded gunfire, depending on his mood when you asked him.

No matter what any of us believed, when we first heard that hidden track that night, in the turn around spot, it scared the shit out of us. Truly frightened each of us to our core.

I got out of the car and found myself not just pacing, but walking circles around the car. My mind racing. It seemed like everything was starting to scare me. Even things that wouldn't have even caught my attention before we started visiting Dudley Road.

"Well," Dan said, "now that we're properly fucking terrified, should we go exploring?"

Sixteen

"ARE YOU READY?" DAN asked in an ominous tone.

"Let's do it," Kevin said, first to exit the car.

I reached up and turned off the dome light before I shut the engine off and took the keys out.

I made sure the windows were all up and the sunroof and sunshade were closed.

I still remember this feeling of knowing we were doing something wrong as we started walking away from the car — this sense of someone watching me, watching us. I wouldn't call it a sense of dread, but it was an intense sense of terror.

We did our best to stay by the tree line, away from the house that stood on the corner of the driveway. I could see the flicker of a television on in one room inside. The rest of the house was dark, and there were no cars parked anywhere near it.

"You think that's part of the nunnery?" I asked, quietly.

From in front of me, Dan looked to our left and nodded. He put his fingers to his lips and silently shushed me.

The four of us crept along, in a single file line, along the perimeter of the parking area. It wasn't just a driveway, but a long and winding road of sorts. A chain-link fence, one of the tallest I've ever seen to this day, was in front of us. It had a gate that was easily fifteen feet wide, big enough for a large bus to drive through. On that night, we were lucky. It was open. Almost inviting us in. The pavement lead along the right-hand side of the building, maybe a hundred or hundred and fifty feet from the road. It veered off farther to the right and eventually turned into parking spots. A small path from the parking spots seemed to lead around the side of the building. It was dark, but I could still make out the outline of the building.

I followed Dan, not saying a word until I was confident no one was out there.

I felt Brian very close behind me. His big oaf feet clumping along, literally the only thing any of us could hear. Flomp flomp flomp on the pavement.

I stopped for a second to turn around and look at him.

Saying nothing, I made eye contact and gestured a sort of "are you fucking kidding me?"

He shrugged silently.

Kevin pushed him from behind, to nudge him to keep moving.

Once we transitioned from the pavement to the gravel path, I felt somewhat safer. We were easily a hundred feet from the building, but still on the property. We'd gone through the chain-link fence gate and were inside the property now. The nunnery. The convent. We still didn't know exactly what it was, but we were on their property now, creeping around outside. I don't know what we were looking for, but we kept pressing forward.

Dan had gotten too far ahead for my liking. When I diverted my eyes from the brick structure to him, he was at least twenty feet ahead of me.

"Hey!" I whisper-yelled.

He turned around and looked at me as if we were the ones who were the problem. He wasn't going too fast, we were going too slow.

By the time I caught up to him, Brian and Kevin were still behind us. I had a moment to stop worrying so much about the noise I was making while I walked to look at, and truly appreciate, the building.

It stood tall, likely three stories on the inside, and was red brick everywhere. There were windows, all of which were covered from the inside. I saw no lights on anywhere, no movement from the inside of any kid. On the outside of the building, I saw one external door. It sat about fifty feet farther up than we were. Above it, a single light fixture, like the kind next to the back door that your mom would leave on for you as a kid, so you could get in the house after dark. It was on. It was the only source of light we could see from our position.

It was, aside from the stories of the area, an unremarkable building from this angle.

Kevin and Brian caught up with us and we moved on.

The back of the building was a sharp ninety-degree turn, but more of the same. Bricks everywhere, taller than seemed necessary. We made the left and kept going.

I think we felt safer once we got around to the back of the building. At least I felt safer from anyone who might see us from the road and call the cops on us.

We followed the back of the building closely. We had been close to the building and were only walking for a few minutes when Dan held up his hand for us to stop.

"Are you a military commander?" Kevin said, a little louder than I'd have liked.

"No, shut up. Look," Dan said, pointing diagonally to our right.

There, about fifty feet away, was a separate building. A single story building, not connected to the brick building at all. It looked older and run down.

"Is that..." Brian said. I could almost hear him gulp, like some sort of cartoon character. "Is that the convent?"

"It has to be," Dan said.

"We found something no one else has talked about," Kevin said. "No one that I've heard talk about this place has said anything about a building back here. They just talk about the nunnery being out in the woods."

"It's been hiding right here the whole time," I said in awe. "Maybe it's not been hiding. Maybe no one has ever thought to come look here. Everyone's out looking in the deep woods, by the turn around spot." d

"You're right. It's almost too simple," Dan said. "Come on."

He didn't wait for any of us to agree to go check out the building. He was just off.

Trying to stay as close as possible, I followed right behind him. I was scared. I wouldn't have admitted that back then, if I were pressed. But, now, all these years later, I can admit that I feared that other building.

There were windows along the side of the building that faced us. They were old and dusty, covered in years of filth, so we couldn't see through any of them. Had you walked up behind us at that exact moment, you'd have seen the four of us spread out, each looking in a different window, a few feet apart. We were the worst Goonies. No one watching guard, no one listening for footsteps. We all had our noses pressed against the glass, our hands shielding our eyes from any light from the main building.

In between the four windows, right in the middle, was the only door we saw.

Dan, being Dan, started approaching it first.

"What if there's someone in there? Don't." Brian said.

"There's no light on, there's no one in here," Dan said.

I had wondered if Dan's persistence to keep coming back, to keep exploring, resulted from how many times the jean-jacket man had visited him. Maybe he thought if we understood it, the visits would stop.

"You don't know that. I'm not going in there. Don't open that door," Brian had said in one big blur of panic.

"I'm in, let's do it," Kevin said.

While silent, I followed the two of them to the door.

With his hand on the doorknob, Dan stopped and looked at Brian, still standing a few feet away.

"Either you come with us or you wait out here by yourself," he said.

"Fuck, fine," Brian said, hurrying over to us.

The door opened with no fuss. It hadn't been boarded up from the inside or abandoned for too long. The hinges weren't rusted shut. They didn't even squeak. I expected a long, drawn out, terrifying squeak as Dan pushed the door open. It was, well, very unsatisfying.

The four of us hurried inside, closing the door behind us. We were in a room that was approximately forty feet by twenty feet. The drop ceiling tiles had mostly fallen. There were four more windows on the opposite wall from the one with the door we'd just come through. To our left, was a hallway leading away from the room we were in. To our right, another wall with two windows. It faced back in the direction we'd just come walking from. The wall to our far left had a small cutout in it, approximately two feet wide and three feet tall. In it stood a statue of Mary. Her hands extended out, palms up, as if she was waiting for someone to hand her something. It was a smaller version of the statue out in front of the main building.

"Creepy room," Dan said.

"What's down that hallway?" Kevin asked, not expecting us to answer his question.

I followed him in that direction and could hear Dan and Brian start to argue in silent voices, trailing off behind me.

A ladder was lying on the floor near the statue of Mary. As if someone had been in here working, perhaps recently, trying to restore the ceiling tiles. Perhaps it was too much work, and they gave up. It seemed odd that the ladder was just laying there to me. If this building had been abandoned, why leave the ladder? Did the nunnery have enough ladders already that they didn't need this one?

Kevin made the left and disappeared from my view for just a second as I caught up to him.

"Holy fuck," I heard him say. "Guys, get over here."

I quickly hurried my steps and heard Dan and Brian do the same.

As I turned down the hallway, I could see Kevin looking at something. He was ten feet in front of me, standing still, his hands both up by his face, holding something.

"What is it?" I asked as I approached.

"It's, I think, it's a funeral card. One of those little cards they hand out at funerals with a prayer, telling you about someone's life."

As I got close enough to see it, I thought he was right. It was a funeral card dangling from the ceiling by a piece of twine.

"Who is it?" Dan said, as he got closer.

"It's fucking Jesus," I said. "Why is there a funeral card for Jesus hanging from the ceiling?"

"A bigger question is why are there more of them?" Brian asked.

I looked up to see him pointing down the hallway. Every four or so feet, another one hanging from the ceiling; the same card, the same drawing of Jesus, and the same prayer on the back. The twine was all roughly the same length, dangling from the drop ceiling. I could see ten of them down the hallway. The last card hung directly above a turn to the right.

On the right and left of the hallway were small rooms with old bed frames. The old bed frames you'd see in a movie about an abandoned mental hospital.

"This has to be it," Dan said. "This is the convent. Look, that's where the nuns slept." He pointed into one of the rooms.

Kevin wasted no more time. He scurried off and was gone around the corner before any of us could say anything else.

"Fucking Kevin," Dan said, running off behind him.

"This is fucking weird," Brian said.

"Why Jesus?" It was all I could think to say. Of everything weird we'd seen at Dudley Road so far, the fact that Jesus' funeral card was hanging from the ceiling was the thing I focused on being the most out-of-the-norm.

"There's more," I heard Dan say.

I grabbed Brian's arm before making my way down the hallway. Not to pull him along with me, but as if to tell him it was going to be okay, and I was right there with him. He grabbed my hand with his for a brief second before we rounded the turn to the final hallway.

That hallway we'd turned down, like the other, had windows along the side. And it, too, had cards dangling from the ceiling, similarly spaced to the last hallway. It was a shorter hallway, though, only about twenty feet long. At the end of the hallway stood a large and very old-looking door. From the inside, it seemed clear that someone didn't want anyone coming into this building through that door. It had four separate deadbolts on it. Two were the kind you turn with your hand and two were much older looking, the kind you slide from behind the door to the little latch on the frame. All four were locked. The lock on the doorknob itself was also locked.

"They don't want anyone coming through that door," I said aloud, quietly to myself.

"Why?" Brian asked.

"This is weird," Dan said. "This entire building is weird. But this is clearly the convent. This is either where the guy raped some nuns or where nuns were witches. Depending on which version of the story you believe. Either way, some shit happened in this building."

"We need to get the fuck out of here," Brian said. "Something locked that door from the inside. Something doesn't want us here."

I could see his eyes tearing up. His hands we visibly shaking.

"It's okay, Bri," I said, trying to calm him down.

"It's not okay," he said much louder than any of us had spoken in the hour since we got out of the car. "It's not fucking okay. Let's fucking go already."

"Fine, fine, okay," Kevin said. "Let's go."

We took one last moment to examine the door. I pulled on the handle to make sure it was really locked. As if I'd feel better, somehow, if it wasn't.

I was the last to turn away from the door, as my friends had already started heading back to where we'd come into the building. When I turned around, the three of them stood there, completely frozen with fear.

"How?" Kevin asked. "How?"

"How what?" I said, taking a few steps forward to join them.

"This card is blank," Kevin said.

Dan, who'd walked up to the next one, said, "this one, too."

"Were these blank when we came into this hall?" I asked.

"No. I looked at every one of them on the way to the door," Brian said. "I wanted to see if they were any different."

"Were they all the same?" Dan asked.

"They were identical. Now they're blank."

"Like someone erased Jesus from them," Kevin said.

"Like Jesus left this building," I said. I had wanted to make a joke to lighten the tension, but I was honestly too scared.

"Let's go," Brian said. "Let's go now."

We walked to the end of the hallway, quickly confirming that the other cards in the final hallway were blank before making the left onto the hallway with the tiny bedrooms.

It didn't take long for me to realize that the ten cards hanging from the ceiling in that hallway were also blank. Every one of them. They were just empty sheets of cream-colored paper — no faces of Jesus. No prayers. No writing of any kind.

I don't remember making the last right into the room with the statue of Mary. I knew my feet were moving on their own, my brain trying to block out any thoughts of panic or concern. I just knew we needed to get out of that building.

I paused as we exited the door, looking back, waiting for Kevin to close the door behind him, since he was the last one out. I tried looking past the building we'd just emerged from, trying to see if there was anything else that may lie out in that direction.

"Back to the car. No more exploring," Dan said matter-of-factly.

Seventeen

Something seemed different about the grounds once we'd left the secondary building. As we walked back along the brick walls, the ground itself seemed softer. The sky darker, but clearer. I felt a sense of calm, even though I was freaking out about what had just happened.

We walked in silence, doing our best to each individually pretend that we were okay. Acting as though we weren't terrified and confused and worried. I led the group around the corner to the side of the main building with the single door still illuminated by its solitary light. Brian followed closely behind me, with Dan and Kevin taking their time holding up the rear of our convoy.

Immediately after making the right around the corner, I noticed it. As if the light above the door was shining down, revealing its presence.

"That wasn't there before," I said to Brian.

"What wasn't? What are you talking about?"

"That," I said, leading him toward the door.

"What are you doing? It's just a door."

I didn't know if he just couldn't see it or if he didn't want to. But I saw it, and it was calling to me.

On the ground, to the right of the door, was a heart. I couldn't initially tell what it was made of, but as I grew closer, it was obvious. There were two sticks that were bent together to form a heart. It wasn't professionally made. It was simply bent together and held with three carefully placed pieces of tape. It looked like it could fall apart at a moment's notice.

"What is it?" Kevin asked, as he and Dan crept up to the door.

"It's a heart," I said. "It wasn't here when we walked by earlier."

"That doesn't make any sense. It's nighttime," Dan said.

"Yeah, why would someone come out and put this out here after dark?" Kevin asked.

"I don't know," I said. "But it wasn't here when we walked by earlier. I know for a fact."

"You're sure?" Dan asked.

"I'm fucking positive," I said. "I know it. I have the memory of an elephant, you know that."

"Why would it be here now? It's just some cheap home crafting thing?" Kevin asked.

"Is it glued? Maybe someone put it out here to dry the glue?" Brian said, ever the logical one.

"No, it's just taped together," I said.

"Well, don't touch it," Dan said. "We've already had enough weird shit for one night."

I don't know what compelled me. What unseen force told me it was a good idea. I don't know what came over me, but something drew me to that stick-heart. Something made me see it and then need to explore it more. I don't know what tripped up in my brain, but I picked it up.

"Dude, Jesus fucking Christ," Brian said.

"I... I just... I don't know," I said. "I have to hold it."

"Okay, you held it," Brian said, walking away. "Now put it down."

He was just about back to the car when I stopped following him with my eyes. I turned to Dan and Kevin. "I know it wasn't here before, but it is now," I said.

"And it's going to stay here," Dan said. "Put it back and let's go."

"I will." I said, holding it a little closer to my face, trying to examine it for any unusual markings or materials.

"I'm going to the car with Brian," Kevin said.

"Me too," Dan said.

They'd all left me alone there, standing under the only light in the immediate area, holding this made-by-someone heart constructed of sticks and tape. All three of them were gone from my field of view, presumably waiting by the car for me to unlock it. I just stood there, as if I was comatose or possessed, clutching this heart. First, I held it up to look at it, but found myself clutching it to my chest. Hugging it. Just holding it near me.

It gave me a sense of peace and calm. It made me feel like everything that had happened so far was over, and that I was going to be okay.

It made me feel safe. It made me feel like I was at home and I belonged there, at that time, at that place.

It made me smile, and it made me feel warm.

I did the only thing I could think of right then. I took it. I brought it back to the car and convinced the guys that it needed to come with me. That I needed it to be mine, but I couldn't explain why. I unlocked the doors, instructed everyone to get in, and put the heart in the trunk.

We drove off that night feeling scared and unsure of everything we'd seen happen. We left with more questions than answers. We left with four friends and a heart made of sticks. I left feeling amazing, positive, and safe. I left feeling like I could do anything. I hadn't felt that way since the first time I kissed a girl. That feeling that rushes into you where you feel invincible. That sense of being bulletproof.

Eighteen

I WOKE UP IMMEDIATELY when I heard the phone ringing that night. It felt like it was ringing louder than I'd ever heard it before. I didn't bother looking at the clock before picking it up. I knew it was late. Someone was calling and I knew they had something important to say.

"Hello?" I tried to keep my voice low, to not wake my mother or sister up.

"He's back." It was Dan. He was whispering.

"Who's back?"

"Him. The guy."

"Fuck. Jean jacket guy?"

"Yes. He's standing in my backyard."

This concerned me more than the other times. Dan's entire backyard was fenced in. You couldn't get back there without opening the gate, which made a lot of noise. The gate was also right outside Rachel's window.

I looked over at the clock, rubbing my eyes. It was just after two in the morning. I'd only been asleep for a couple of hours, but it felt like the whole night had gone by.

"What's he doing? How'd you know he was out there?"

"I just finished playing Tetris. I got up to put the Gameboy back on my desk and saw a shadow through the blinds."

"What's he doing?" I repeated.

"Just standing there, as usual."

"How far away is he?"

"He's by the fence, over near the clothesline."

I knew that meant he was pretty close to the house. Maybe fifteen or twenty feet from Dan's window.

"Is he… is he staring at you?"

"Doesn't he always?" Dan said, yelling. Anger was rising in his voice.

"Stay put. Keep an eye on him. I'll be there in ten minutes."

"What are you going to do?" Dan asked.

"I don't know. I'll figure it out on the ride over."

I threw on the clothes I'd worn that day and ran downstairs, not really caring if I woke anyone up. After grabbing my keys and wallet, I jumped in the car and sped out of the driveway. I did not know what I was going to do once I got over to Dan's, but I knew I had to do something.

Dan's driveway was a little weird. Since he lived at the end of one street connected to another, their property formed a triangle. So you could get into the driveway from either end, which usually meant Kathy and Charlie's cars would be nose to nose. Kathy would come into the driveway from Pringle Street, Charlie would come in from Hill Street. As I always had done, I pulled in from Pringle, behind Kathy's car. I did it on instinct. I did it out of habit. I did it not realizing that, perhaps, my brain picked that side of the driveway knowing it was farther away from the backyard than the other side of the driveway.

I went straight into the house, which was unlocked, as usual, and tip-toed to Dan's room. His door was closed, and no light was shining under the door. I wondered if he'd had the lights off or turned them off to hide in the shadows. I gently nudged the door open.

"Jesus fuck!" Dan screamed before immediately putting his hands over his mouth to quiet himself.

"Sorry. You should have known it was me," I said, entering the room and closing the door behind me.

"He's still out there. What are we going to do?"

"Let me see," I said, walking over to the sole window in Dan's room. I pulled the blinds to the side, just enough to see through. There he was, standing by the fence. His face seemed more ragged than I remembered from seeing him at the mall. He had pock marks all over, though it looked like he was trying to grow a beard to cover them.

The streetlight out on Hill Street was almost directly behind him, illuminating his entire face better than I'd seen it, even in the middle of the mall.

There was something empty about his eyes. Something lifeless. Something I couldn't put my finger on. His eyes didn't move. He didn't blink. Every time we'd encountered him, he'd just stood motionless, staring at us.

No less than a minute after I'd been eyeing him up and down, the door to Dan's room opened silently.

"Jesus fuck!" Dan yelled again. "What the fuck are you doing?"

It was Brian. He'd walked down the street and was standing in Dan's doorway.

"I saw him," he said. "About twenty minutes ago. I heard a noise outside, so I looked outside and he was just standing there in our driveway."

"Yeah, well," Dan said, "he's in my backyard now."

"His face seems different this time," I said. "Weathered."

"I noticed that, too," Dan said.

"I really thought you guys were fucking with me," Brian said. "I didn't think he was real until now. I had to tell my mom I needed to borrow something from you to come down here."

"He's real. But why is he here? Why is he showing up for the three of us now?"

"I don't know," I said. "But he's here."

"What do we do? Should I wake my parents up?" Dan asked.

"No. I doubt they'll be able to do anything," I said. "I'm going to go out there."

"What?" Brian yelped. "Are you insane?"

"Look, it's just a guy, right? A freaky guy, sure. But it's just a guy."

"Just a guy who could have just a gun and just shoot you in your just face," Dan said.

"He's following us," I said. "There's got to be a reason, so I'm going to find out."

I took the bat Dan kept by his bedroom door and walked out of the room. I could feel, and then hear, the two of them closing the door behind me and rushing back to the window.

It never took me so long to walk the five steps down the hallway and turn towards the kitchen before. Every step I took was like dragging my feet through the thickest mud you can imagine. I don't know if I was just terrified or if it was because it was almost three in the morning. Or, maybe, some combination of both.

I could see Rachel sleeping in her toddler bed through her door's slight opening as I made the turn at the end of the hallway, then again turned to my right to exit through the kitchen door, into the three season porch and down the stairs.

The gate to the backyard was just a few feet away from where I stood. I took a moment to compose myself, ready the bat on my right shoulder, hold my breath for just a second or two, and count to ten. My nerves were as calm as they were going to be when I reached for the handle to the gate.

That handle had always creaked when we opened it, which is why we rarely closed it. But in the wee hours of that morning, it creaked louder than any single rusty hinge had ever creaked in the history of humankind. It made so much noise that I worried about waking up Dan's family and their neighbors. I also worried it would scare away the guy I was going to confront.

"Where would he even go?" I asked myself. The only other entrance to the backyard was through a much larger gate in the fence, about twenty feet farther into the yard than he was standing when I left Dan's bedroom. That gate was chained and padlocked. In over four years of going to Dan's house almost daily, that gate had never been unlocked, let alone opened. If I scared him, there was nowhere else for him to go, except through the gate I was standing at, holding the latch in my bat-free hand.

I counted to ten again before pushing the gate open.

It squeaked as I slowly opened it, pushing it with my left hand, still clutching the bat with my right. I didn't know what I was going to do with the bat, but I was glad I had it in case I needed to defend myself.

"Just do it," I told myself as I pushed the gate the rest of the way open.

I took two steps into the backyard, stepped aside, and closed the gate behind me. In hindsight, I don't know why I closed the gate. It would have made for a faster getaway if I needed to run if I left it open. But I closed it and made sure the latch clicked into place.

I never took my eyes off of him.

He never took his eyes off the window to Dan's bedroom, but I knew he knew I was there. I was only twenty feet away from him and I made enough noise opening the gate to wake the dead. There was no way he didn't know I was there.

I stepped closer, two steps at a time, pausing for just a moment, waiting for him to turn and look at me as I took each step.

When I got within ten feet of him, I called out. "Hey. Hey you." I didn't care how late it was, or who I woke up. I needed to be assertive and make sure he knew I meant business.

Almost instantly, he turned his entire body to face me as I'd finished calling out to him. He didn't first turn his head, he just lurched to his right, in one fast motion. He was staring directly at me.

I heard Dan say, "Jesus fuck!" from the house, through the closed window.

"What are you doing here?" I yelled, taking another step. "Get the fuck out of here!"

He took a step toward me.

We were now just a handful of feet apart. I was close enough that I could see his chest rising and falling with each breath. I could see his eyes up close. They were still unblinking. They felt dead. It felt like the person behind them wasn't a person. It was just a shell of a man. The pock marks I'd seen from a distance weren't pock marks. They appeared to be scars. Half-inch long scars, covering almost the entirety of his face.

He took another step toward me. I took a step back and readied the bat from my shoulder, now gripping it with both hands, holding it out in front of me as a buffer between him and I. As if I could use it to keep him back if he suddenly lunged at me.

"Stop right there!" I yelled. "Don't come any closer! Who are you? What are you doing here?"

I heard the screen door slam shut and the sound of two people coming down the stairs from the house.

Dan and Brian were coming to my rescue.

He took another step.

"Back the fuck up!" I was screaming now.

I saw a smile flash on his face. He was enjoying this.

He took another step and reached out with his left arm, touching the bat. He swatted it, but I held it steady. I wouldn't let him push it away.

"We're coming!" I heard Dan yell from the driveway.

"I'm going in your trunk," Brian said. "Tire iron."

They were looking for things to arm themselves with in my trunk. I heard it pop open on the other side of the gate.

The moment it did, I heard the voice from the forest again.

"No!" it screamed. "No!" I heard it over and over again. The voice came from nowhere. The man's mouth didn't move. It wasn't him. It was a woman, but he heard it, too. For the first time since seeing him, his eyes closed. He didn't blink. He closed his eyes, as if he was listening intently.

The voice grew louder. The yelling continued. Pleas for "help". Begging for it to "stop".

I saw no one other than the man in front of me. His eyes were still closed.

He was listening to the same cries for help I was.

It no longer seemed like he cared I was there. His back was to me when he turned around. He then turned a bit to his right, then to his left. He was trying to track where the voice was coming from.

The ground surrounding him spun. I saw one of those tiny tornados you would see on a windy day, where a cloud of dust would blow up, spin around, and disappear in a matter of seconds. It was swelling around him. He continued to look in all directions, trying to pinpoint where the source of the screaming was coming from.

I knew only the three of us and he could hear it. No one else heard this screaming. He kept spinning around, faster and faster. The earth beneath him swelling higher and higher, engulfing his entire body.

I jumped back, making more room between the two of us. He was surrounded by dust and dirt covering his entire body. His eyes still closed. His movements became more and more frantic as the cries continued.

The trunk to my car slammed shut just as Dan opened the gate to his back yard and rushed through. I turned and saw Brian was just a few steps behind him.

No sooner did the trunk close did the screaming stop.

I turned back to look, and the man was gone. The wind swirling around him, causing the dust storm disappeared. The yard was immediately silent and empty except for the three of us.

"Where'd he go?" Dan asked.

"He was just here," I said. "Literally just here. I turned around to see you guys coming in the gate and then he was gone."

"I didn't see him when I came in the gate," Brian said.

"I did," Dan said. "He was there. I saw him for a split second."

"What the fuck?" I said, almost silently to myself.

"I'm going home. Fuck this," Brian said, handing Dan the tire iron he'd taken from my trunk before walking back off through the gate.

"Everything stopped when the trunk closed," Dan said.

"You're right. I heard Brian close the trunk, and then the yelling stopped. Everything stopped," I agreed.

"How?"

"I don't know," I said. "I don't know."

"What the actual fuck?" Dan said. "Who the fuck is this guy and how'd he just vanish?"

"I didn't hear him move," I said. "There's no way he, like, jumped over the fence. And even if he did, you'd have seen him. You were facing that way."

"We'd have a heard him running off up the road, too," Dan said.

"Wait," I said, thinking out loud.

"What?"

"The screaming started when the trunk opened."

"Did it?" Dan asked.

"Yes. You guys came out and he was just standing there. He kept coming closer to me. But there was no screaming."

"And it started when we opened the trunk?"

"Yeah," I said. "He had just come closer to me and tried swatting the bat out of my hand when you opened the trunk. What did you take from the trunk?"

"I grabbed the first thing I saw," he said, holding out a shovel.

"Why did I have a shovel in my trunk?"

"I don't know. That's not the point," he said. "But I grabbed it and came to the gate immediately."

"Brian grabbed the tire iron and shut the trunk. That's when it stopped," I said, still thinking out loud.

"Right," Dan agreed.

"Let's go back in the house," I said.

I took a moment to look back around the yard, really looking into every dark nook and cranny, even all the way at the back where Dan's dad, Charlie, would rake the leaves to compost. Just to make sure I wasn't missing jean-jacket-guy hiding somewhere out there.

My eyes scoured every inch of that yard. I stared at every single thing that made a nose for the next few minutes until I could figure out what it was.

I followed Dan through the gate and up the stairs into the house.

We were both somber and silent, not understanding what the hell had just happened.

We went down the hall, around the corner, and back into Dan's room, slowly, quietly, half-heartedly thinking to ourselves.

It wasn't until I put the bat down back by Dan's door that I noticed it.

"It's burnt," I said, picking it back up.

"What?" Dan asked.

I handed him the bat, butt-end first.

His mouth dropped as soon as he saw it. Right at the end, near the Louisville Slugger logo, was a burn mark, shaped like a grown man's hand. It was right where jean-jacket-guy had swatted the bat trying to knock it out of my hand.

I didn't know what to say at that point. I just stood there, in shock, before I sat down on the bed next to Dan.

"Well, I think that rules out 'just a guy'," Dan said. "I don't think it's a guy anymore."

There, at almost three-thirty in the morning, on his bed, I was speechless. I opened my mouth to talk, to say anything I could to agree with him, but I couldn't. I just sat there, still and quiet, with no words to express how utterly terrified I suddenly was. What had started out as just some random — albeit creepy — guy following us around, now seemed to be something else, something perhaps supernatural.

What he was, whatever it was, he was gone for the time being. I didn't know how long he'd be gone for, but in that moment, I was happy enough to fall asleep on the floor in Dan's room, as I had so many other times.

We both barely slept, jumping up at every sound for the next three hours until Rachel got up and immediately came to get us. Every noise I heard was the end of the world. Every sound, every creak, every squeak was the guy coming back, entering the house and burning us alive. I had some of the worst dreams of my life that night. Some of the most terrifying, yet vivid, nightmares I've ever had.

Nineteen

EVERY TIME I CLOSED my eyes for days, I relived that night. I didn't just see it, but I could feel it. The wind whipping around, the sky pitch black, the sense of sheer terror. It was there every time I closed my eyes, no matter if it was day or night.

It seemed to change the more I experienced it. The more I felt the night again, the more it felt like I could almost navigate around within the memory. I could, somehow, see things I didn't remember seeing when it happened in real time. As if I had some sort of playback control like a sports announcer. I could pause the memory, but still explore around within it.

I had drifted off on Dan's fold-out chair. It was three days later, and though it was mid-afternoon, his house was quiet enough that we'd both fallen asleep. There, in that memory — that dream, I guess — I seemed to leave my body. I was floating, like when someone dies on a TV show and they have an out-of-body experience. I felt that, in this dream memory, even though it didn't happen that night. I didn't die, though I felt like I came pretty close to death.

As I floated above Dan's backyard, I saw the conclusion of the evening. I saw, over the fence and around the corner of the house, Dan and Brian open my trunk. I saw them rummaging through the things within, and I saw them each wield their choice of weapon.

It seemed like I was fifteen or twenty feet in the air, looking down on the whole thing. I saw Dan come through the gate to the fence. Right then, for the first time, I saw myself. Jean jacket man was not far from me, closing in on me, reaching out. It was then that I heard Brian close the trunk, but from this angle, I could see something I didn't notice then, or even in any of the reliving of the memory; I noticed him look up at the sky and open his mouth. Jean jacket man, from the angle I was looking down on him, appeared to be trying to call out, either in pain or in pleasure, as the trunk closed.

There was no sign of him after that. Once I blinked, he disappeared. It was the same every time I relived that part of the memory. I blink. He disappears. Every time.

This time, though, it was different. Once he disappeared and the dust all settled, I stayed floating. From below, I could hear the three of our voices talking to one another.

Then, just as it had happened, I watched Brian exit through the gate, make a right to head towards the end of the driveway, and then make the right up Hill Street, heading home.

With no input or control of my own, I floated out over the fence, onto the road, and stopped in the middle of Hill Street, looking toward Brian's house.

His jacket reflected just enough of the streetlight that I could see him, clearly, down the street. He didn't walk very quickly, but his house was only a few up the road. On a normal day, it was less than a two-minute walk.

Just as he turned to his left to enter his driveway, I heard him yell. Not a word, not a cry for help. Just a yelp. As if he'd been hit on the head or in the face.

Try as I might, I could not fly my way up the street to see what had happened. I think, in my memory, I couldn't control that part of it, as I hadn't actually gone up the street that night. I know what you're thinking; I didn't fly overhead, looking down on the whole event, either, I know. But, this memory was bizarre.

As I started floating down to the ground, I heard another yell. Barely audible over the sound of my own heavy breathing. I heard Brian's voice, clear as day, as if it were whispering in my ear.

He said "help". He didn't yell. He didn't scream. He just calmly said "help".

I jolted awake, quickly realizing where I was.

Dan must have heard me sit upright, because he was sitting up within a second.

Before I could even say something, he asked, "Have you talked to Brian since the other night?"

"No, have you?"

We both looked at each other and for just a split moment, I felt like he'd just seen the same thing I had. As if we were, somehow, connected in that memory I had while I was dreaming.

Dan picked up the phone from his nightstand and dialed Brian's number.

His mom answered.

Though I could only hear half of the conversation, I could tell that Brian wasn't home. From what I could hear Dan saying, it sounded like he'd left a note on the kitchen table — as Brian usually did when he was with us — and that she expected him home later today.

"And he said he was camping in my yard?" Dan asked.

I saw him nodding, as if everything were all right.

"Okay. Yep. Yes."

He hung up.

He stared at me, mouth agape.

"Well?" I said, not able to wait anymore.

"Brian is not home."

"I gathered that from your conversation," I said.

"He's here."

"What?" I didn't follow.

"The note he left the other night. He said he was camping out with us and that we were going to work on some songs, like usual."

"But he's not here."

"No shit, Mike," Dan said. "Obviously he's not here."

"So where the fuck is he?" I asked.

Dan paused before answering. He looked at me hard and long in the eyes, not breaking eye contact.

"What is happening right now?" I asked.

"This is going to sound weird," he said.

"Nothing sounds weird to me anymore."

"I just had a dream. About the other night," he said. "And in the dream, I was flying. I saw the whole thing from above."

"Holy shit," I interrupted. "I just had the same thing happen."

"Did you see Brian make it home? I know that's weird, because we never saw him after he went out the gate. But did you, like, fly up the road and see him get home?"

"Kind of. In my dream, I went over the fence and watched him turn into his driveway. Then he..."

"He whispered 'help' to you, too?"

"Fuck," I said. "Fuck, fuck fuck, fuckity fuck."

"And now he's not home. Janet thinks he's with us, and clearly he's not with us."

"So, again, I ask. Where the fuck is he?"

Visions of everything that had ever scared me started flashing through my head; Chucky, Freddy Krueger, Candyman, mom threatening to hit me with that wooden spoon every mother in the '90s had. I don't know what triggered those images to run through my head, but it gave me the creeps. I tried to shake them off, but they kept coming for a number of minutes, before disappearing entirely.

Twenty

Perhaps it was a gut feeling, or perhaps it was just not knowing what else to do. But something had us driving over there, to the road. As soon as we knew Brian was missing, we knew we had to go try to find answers, even if it meant putting ourselves in more jeopardy.

We had called Kevin before leaving Dan's to first make sure Brian wasn't somehow with him, but also to brief him on what had recently discovered. Kevin already knew about the jean jacket man, but had known little about what had happened the other night, other than the bits and pieces we'd told him the next morning.

"Hey," he said, jumping in behind Dan. He reached over and tapped us each on the shoulder, as he did virtually every time he'd gotten into my car.

"Hey," I said.

"Yo," Dan said.

"So, what's the plan?" Kevin asked.

"I don't know," I said. "I just know we need to go there. Like he's going to be there, or something."

"How would he even have gotten there?" Kevin asked. "You're the only one of us with a car and a license."

Logic didn't seem to matter. I knew what he was saying, but it didn't register in my head. My gut told me Brian was there, or at least had answers to what happened to him.

"It's only three, so we have plenty of hours of daylight to look around the woods before it gets dark," Dan said.

"Should we go back to the outbuilding once it gets dark?" I asked.

"I think we should. What if we missed something last time?" Dan said.

"I think so, too," Kevin said.

"All right. I agree."

We left the center of town, heading over to Dudley Road, as we'd done a handful of other times. We sat in silence, listening to that Days of the New CD we just couldn't get enough of. I kept the volume low, not because I thought any of us were going to talk along the way, but it just felt better. It felt more calming.

We were just leaving Tewksbury when Dan spoke. "What did he need help with?"

"I don't know," I said. "But I definitely heard a thud before he asked for help. Like someone hit him."

"Is that what you heard?" Dan asked. "I couldn't tell what it was when I heard it. I knew it wasn't normal, whatever it was. But I couldn't see his driveway to know for sure."

"Do you think someone grabbed him?" Kevin asked. "Like, kidnapped?"

"I don't think so," Dan said. "There would have been a struggle. We would have heard something more that night. We were outside long enough, weren't we?"

I thought about it for a minute before answering, "Yeah. We were definitely outside long enough for him to have gotten home. We took at least that long to put the shit back in my trunk. He'd have gotten home. If there was some sort of struggle, we'd have heard it that night. Not just in the memory dream."

"So, where could he have gone?" Kevin asked.

"Drinks?" I asked, pulling into the Lil' Peach in Billerica.

The three of us jumped out of the car, heading into the store.

We grabbed snacks and Cokes, our usual. I paid, since I was the one with the job.

"Eleven fifty-one," the clerk said, reaching out for cash.

I handed him a ten and two singles, waiting for my change.

As we left the store, I noticed something by my door, on the ground. I bent over and grabbed it before getting back in the car.

"What's that?" Dan asked.

"A scratch ticket." I held it up to show him.

"Five-dollar one, nice," Kevin said from the back, cracking open his Coke.

"Scratch it," Dan said.

"Why was it just sitting there on the ground?" I half-mumbled to myself.

I put my Coke in the cupholder and dug a dime out from the change holder in the center console.

Over the years, I'd always loved scratch tickets. My mom would get them for my sister and me for birthdays and Christmas, and my grandfather on my mom's side was a big scratch ticket lover. He'd buy an entire book of one-dollar tickets, knowing he'd at least double his money if he got a winning book. Thinking back, I missed those times. I missed feeling normal. I missed the time when my entire existence wasn't taken over by what was happening to me.

This time was no exception. I jumped right in, first scratching off the ten numbers that I'd have to match my two numbers to.

5, 11, 12, 15, 19, 11, 5, 7, 4, 2, 9.

I knew from seeing the five and eleven twice that it meant I'd won something. When you scratch enough of them, you know how they work. Later in life, I'd learn to just look for the three-digit-code between the numbers to see if I'd won anything.

"I think we got something," I said, mostly to myself.

I scratched the two numbers under "Your Numbers" at the top.

A five and eleven.

I quickly scratched off the prizes under the two fives and two elevens.

They were each one hundred dollars.

"Four hundred bucks!" I yelled. "Holy shit!"

"Nice find, Mike!" Kevin said.

"Wow, good luck!" Dan added.

"Yeah, aside from our friend being missing and all," I said.

"Aside from that," Kevin said.

We had a moment of happiness then. Well, maybe not happiness, but a moment of feeling like things were okay with the world. If Brian had not been missing, it would have been a pretty good afternoon. Had he been there, the four of us would have gone in, cashed in the ticket, and gone somewhere fancy for a nice dinner together. Something we'd done so many other times. The four amigos. My three best friends.

I couldn't help but blame myself for Brian having gone missing. Had I not brought up the story I'd heard to Dan, he'd have probably never heard it himself. We'd probably never have ended up going there. Brian would be with us, celebrating our newly found money.

Twenty-One

THE REST OF THE ride over to the turnaround spot had me feeling pretty good. Brian kept slipping in and out of my mind, though. That last ten minutes or so, I kept hearing his voice. His whispering "help" in my ear. I knew Dan had heard it, too, but it didn't seem to bother him much, if at all. The more I thought about — and felt — Brian, the more the feeling of happiness from winning the money faded.

It was a pleasant afternoon, not too hot, not too humid. We were approaching the end of June, so the humidity would kick in soon enough. I remember pausing for a moment in the turnaround spot, looking down the trail into the woods. I don't know what I was looking for or what I was hoping to find. Was I, even a little, hoping Brian would just come walking down the trail and wave to us?

"I think we should go past the house remnants," Kevin said. "Go further than we have before and see what else is out there."

I didn't love that idea, but I couldn't pinpoint why.

"Yes," Dan said. "Let's do that."

"But we need to stick together," I said. "We can't get separated at all, even for a minute. And stay in constant communication."

All three of us closed our doors at the same time. It was so in sync that only a single door closing could be heard echoing out through the woods.

I turned around and faced the trail first, making the first strides into the woods.

I'd love to tell you we found Brian out there. I'd love to tell you that we walked right past the skeleton of that old house and we saw him sitting there, waiting for us. I wish I could tell you how he told us he'd just wandered off that night and found himself out in the woods. But none of that happened.

We walked around aimlessly for hours, on the trail and off, wading through — sometimes — waist high shrubbery and brush. The whole time talking to one another, calling out Brian's name. I'd wondered if anyone had found us out there in the woods that day, what they'd have thought. Crazy kids? Maybe. Missing friend? Probably.

Less than an hour in, I knew our search was pointless. There was no reason to keep walking around. Brian wasn't out there. But I let us keep doing it because it felt like we had to do something. Our purpose, at least for that day, was to at least look for our friend. Our friend who no one thought was missing, except for us.

We tried to make a game of it. To see how far we could get from one another, but still maintain a line of sight and still be able to hear each other. Though we were worried about our friend's wellbeing, we tried to do our best in keeping our own spirits high.

Twenty-Two

WE LOOKED IN THE woods for about three hours. We would have beaten an entirely fresh path if we kept at it. He wasn't out there, and part of me knew he wouldn't be. It was unlikely, a shot in the dark. But we tried anyway.

The sun had just set, and the sky was a milky pink, bright and vibrant through the trees. I could just make out the moon overhead as we silently returned to the turnaround spot.

"I knew he wouldn't be out there," Kevin said.

"Mhmm," I muttered, agreeably.

Dan was silent. I knew it was hitting him harder than Kevin and I. He and Brian had been friends much longer than we'd known either of them. I don't think he felt responsible, per se, but he definitely was bothered by his lifelong friend going missing.

As we sat in the car, I took my time starting the engine, knowing where we were going next. I wasn't in too much of a hurry to go back sneaking around the nunnery. I knew we had to at least go look, but I was scared of what might happen once we got there. I feared that we'd get caught by someone who lived there, or one of the neighbors, or some rent-a-cop walking the perimeter.

"What do we do if we find him?" Dan asked in a somber tone.

It was a question I hadn't even thought of. I had just assumed that if we found him, we'd grab him and bring him home.

"What do you mean?" Kevin asked.

"What if he's, like, a hostage or something?"

"Who's holding him hostage?" I asked, turning the key and bringing the car to life, along with the radio, which I'd forgotten to turn down. It scared me more than it should have.

"I don't know," Dan said. "But he's clearly not able to get home or get back to us."

"Maybe the ghost nuns got him," Kevin joked. He made a childish "boo" sound that seemed to rub Dan the wrong way.

"Look, fuck you, okay?" It was Dan's go-to response when he didn't know what else to say.

"I'm sure he's fine," Kevin said. "We just need to find him."

The reverse lights illuminated the parking lot behind us as I backed up. I opted to go out the peaceful side of Dudley Road that night, so when we got back around to where we'd park, we were on the right side of the street where the car would be properly hidden from passersby.

Everything along the ride seemed calmer, darker. Houses only had their porch lights on. It seemed like, collectively, the whole street wasn't home. It was so peaceful, yet so eerie.

As we drove along, I felt this sense of calm come over me. Sigh after sigh came out of me involuntarily. I wasn't hyperventilating, though it felt like I was breathing much heavier than I should have been.

"You okay?" Dan asked.

When I looked over at him in the passenger seat, I could tell he was more upset than he'd been since we realized Brian was missing.

"Yeah. I'm just worried about him," I said.

Kevin was looking out the window, not paying attention to us. His reflection in the rear-view mirror was dimly lit as the night sky took over from the afternoon sun, but I could still see him trying to make out shapes or a person or something as we drove down the road.

Once we made the left back onto Dudley Road, the sense of calmness disappeared. Almost immediately, I felt dread. This dark feeling of overwhelming sadness hit me right in the chest, like a bully hitting a much smaller kid. I let out an "oomph", without realizing it.

The same sound came from both Kevin and Dan, just a second apart from one another. They felt it, too.

We parked the car, made sure it was off the road enough where no one would think anything about it, and ventured down the driveway.

Like last time, the gate was open. This time, it was fully open, the entire width of the driveway. We didn't have to sneak past the house we thought was a guard house this time. We just sauntered in like we owned the place. Thinking back on it now, I don't think we even tried to keep our voices down. Perhaps something subconsciously felt like, if we didn't seem scared, we wouldn't be scared.

Dan led the way along the tree line, keeping us away from the building. Even as we approached the door where the stick heart was the last time we came, I still felt the sense of dread. I kept trying to tell myself that nothing would happen to us and that there was a reasonable explanation for what happened to Brian. My internal dialogue kept trying to convince my brain that we'd just find Brian somewhere and take him home. At no point did I try to explain where he was, or why he was there, or how he got there. Over and over again, as we rounded the corner at the back of the building, I told myself that everything was going to be okay.

Kevin ran ahead of me. He and Dan were side by side, leaving me just a few feet behind them. Though I could tell they were talking to one another, I couldn't hear their conversation.

Something about the sky that night seemed brighter than the last time we were there. The last time we stood in front of the door leading to the outer building. The two windows flanking each side of the door seemed dirtier than I remembered.

"Let's do this," Kevin proclaimed, attempting to push the door open.

"You ready?" Dan asked.

"Let's go," I said, avoiding his question. I wasn't ready, but I knew I had no choice.

"It won't open," Kevin said. "It's stuck."

"Is it locked?" I asked.

"I don't think so," he said. "The knob turns. It just won't open."

Dan took a step forward and leaned his shoulder into the door, joining Kevin in his attempt to push the door open.

On their third joint attempt, the door moved a few inches. Though I'm sure it was just the old wood creaking, I swear I heard the building groan for a split second.

My two friends pushed harder together and got the door fully open. I rushed to close the door behind us as we hurried inside. It made me feel a tiny bit safer knowing that nothing could sneak up behind us if the door was closed.

Kevin took a few steps to the right, to where the door would have been, if it were still open.

"Why was is so hard to open this time?" he asked himself.

He knelt down and reached out, touching the ground.

"What is it?" Dan asked.

"It just... it doesn't make sense," Kevin said. "There's dirt and dust and a bunch of crap here, piled up behind the door."

"So?" Dan said.

"Think about it," Kevin said. "We opened this door the other day."

"I still don't get it," Dan said.

Though it took me a second, once I knelt down next to Kevin, I got it.

"If we opened the door the other day, all this shit would have been pushed back in the door's path," I said.

"Right," Kevin said. "It would have opened easier than it just did."

"Look," I said, holding up a handful of the debris. "This has been here for years. You can just tell it's old."

"What if someone was working in here and made a mess?" Dan asked.

"You mean after we were last here, someone came out here and did what?" Kevin said.

"I don't know," Dan said. "I'm just saying it's possible."

Kevin got up and walked to the middle of the room, facing the statue of Mary on the far wall. He seemed to think about something else.

"What is it?" I asked.

"It's nothing. Just weird that the door we came in the other night now suddenly is like we were never here."

"Nothing surprises me anymore," Dan said.

The rest of the room seemed unchanged. It was just as we'd come in the other night. The ladder still lay on the floor. The drop ceiling tiles still seemed to hang down, ready to fall. To me, it didn't seem like any other living person had been in this room, or even this building, since we were here the other night.

Kevin knelt again, still in the center of the room. Dan and I were still by the door, somewhat puzzled at what Kevin was doing.

After only kneeling for a moment or two, he jumped up. He went straight to a standing position and leaned toward the hallway at the end of the room.

"Did you hear that?" he asked. "It's Brian."

He started making his way toward the hallway. A brisk walk at first, then a jog, then a full-on run. He was out of the room before I could look at Dan and confirm that he didn't hear anything.

"Kevin, wait!" I yelled. "Stick together!"

Dan and I ran off after him. We got to the entrance to the hallway, just as Kevin rounded the corner into the far hallway, with the locked door at the end.

"Guys, come on, he's here!" he yelled.

Dan ran ahead of me by just a few steps, so he rounded the corner before I did.

Just as I entered the doorway, turning right into the last hallway, I knew something was wrong. I stopped where I was, turned around and looked behind me. The hallway ended right behind the door I'd entered. The far end still had the door with all the locks on it.

Dan stood in front of the door, his arms both outstretched, and his palms both flat against the door. His breath was elevated. I could see sweat forming on the back of his neck from where I stood.

"Brian's not here," he said.

And neither was Kevin. Much like Brian disappeared turning into his driveway, Kevin disappeared somewhere in the split second it took Dan and me to get from one end of the hallway to the other.

Despite his fun and light-hearted nature, I knew that this wasn't a prank Kevin would have normally played. There was nowhere for him to have gone in that hallway. It was maybe ten feet wide and about twenty feet long. There were only two ways in or out of it. The door Dan and I had come through, where we would have seen Kevin, had he left that way. And the door with all the locks on it. The locks were still locked, so there was no way he got out that door and then locked all the locks from the other side. It wasn't possible.

I stood there, hands on my hips, catching my breath, waiting for Dan to turn around. Hoping he'd have some sort of answer, or that together we could figure out what to do.

Time seemed to stand still. Neither of us could say anything, but we were both thinking the worst.

"Wherever Brian is," Dan said, turning to face me, "Kevin is with him now."

The fact that Brian wasn't alone anymore, wherever he was, whatever supernatural thing had clearly happened to him, made me feel a little better. No matter what was happening to him, knowing Kevin was there with him took a bit of weight off my shoulders.

We stood in the hallway, double-checking to make sure there was no other way out; no trap door that could have popped open to reveal Kevin beneath it.

With no words, Dan walked past me, only stopping in the doorway. He turned back to me. "Can we get the fuck out of here?" he asked.

"Yes, let's fucking go," I said. I knew staying there any longer would not help us figure out what happened to Kevin or find Brian.

As I took my first step towards Dan, a light from the main building turned on. It shone through one of the windows on the side of the hallway nearest the main building, illuminating one of the funeral cards hanging from the ceiling.

It only took a fraction of a second of the light, hitting it just the right way for me to see it clearly.

Jesus' face was still gone, as it was the last time we'd looked at those cards. But this time it wasn't blank. An almost lifelike photo of Brian was on both sides of the card. The one closest to me dangled in the still air, spinning around, as if someone had just rushed past it. As it spun, the string wound itself up to where it couldn't wind anymore, then began spinning back the other way.

Dan had seen it, too. He stood, silent, in the door leading to the hallway. He didn't need to say anything, but I knew it was time to high tail it out of there.

I ran over to him and walked, side by side, down the hallway, doing our best to ignore the funeral cards with Brian's face on them.

As we made the right back into the main hall, Dan stopped for a second.

"He's not dead," he said. "He's not."

"He's not," I agreed.

The same groaning sound I'd heard when Kevin and Dan opened the door rang out again. Louder that time. Clearer.

"You heard that, too, right?" I asked Dan.

"It sounded like the building groaned," he said.

"Sometimes I don't know what's real and what's not. I feel like I'm going crazy," I said.

"I feel that way all the time lately," he said.

With our backs to the statue of Mary, we walked twenty or so feet to the exit. I reached out and pulled the door open. It was completely silent and easier to open than earlier.

Dan exited first, after peeking his head outside to make sure no one — and nothing — was outside, and turned back to face me.

Once I'd gotten outside, I reached back in to grab the door handle, to pull it closed.

I almost threw up immediately. A white light flashed in front of my eyes. I felt a coldness fall over my body.

There, on the wall, to the left of the statue of Mary, was written I WILL TAKE THEM ALL in huge, red letters. It was written with someone's hand, not a brush or marker or another utensil. I could make out the fingerprints, even from twenty feet away.

From where I stood, it looked like it was written in blood.

I hoped, I even silently prayed, that it wasn't the blood of my missing friends.

Before Dan could ask me what was taking so long, I pulled the door closed, not letting him see what was written on the wall.

It seemed like the right thing to do. While it made me almost pass out from sheer terror, I knew that there was no reason for Dan to suffer those same feelings.

"Let's go," I said.

I don't remember walking back to the car. I don't remember driving back to Dan's house, or walking inside, or anything else that night. Every time I closed my eyes, I flashed between seeing that writing on the wall to reliving the night in Dan's backyard.

Over and over again, those two memories kept haunting me. I kept reliving both moments every single time I closed my eyes.

I wasn't sure what the message on the wall meant, but I knew it couldn't have been any good.

Twenty-Three

As I DID SO many nights over those years, I spent the night at Dan's house. As we'd gotten older, we'd started sleeping in the basement, rather than in his room. I'm not sure if it was our desire for more freedom, our desire to make more noise without bothering anyone, or our desire to be farther away from Rachel as she got older.

I still don't remember how we got there. I do, however, remember getting out of the car in his driveway. As I always did, I parked behind Kathy, since Charlie would leave for work earlier and Kathy could then pull straight out of the driveway, instead of me needing to move my car.

We silently tip-toed down the stairs. Dan grabbed the cordless phone from the wall by the bathroom door before he closed the door behind himself.

I would normally walk down the stairs into the darkness without waiting for the lights to flicker on. They sometimes took longer to come on, probably because of how old they were. They were those old-looking, long tube lights that are embedded into the drop ceiling. The kind you remember from elementary school. Those that come on, then flicker a bit, and make that "hoummmm" sound as they warm up.

Not that night, though. I waited, scared, I suppose, halfway down the stairs for the lights to fully come on. I waited for the blinding white light to illuminate every corner, every crevice, every single item Dan's family stored in their basement to be lit before I took the last step down into the basement.

"Hey," Dan said, as he stepped downstairs, phone to his ear. "We're at my house."

I figured he was talking to Jen. I mouthed her name to confirm, and he nodded.

"Okay," he said, then paused a second. "She's three-way calling Wendy."

As I often did, I sat on the daybed, facing the table where Dan sat.

It wasn't often that he'd call Jen as soon as we got to his house, but I understood why he was doing it at that moment.

"I'm here," he said after a few minutes. "Mike is here, too."

He pulled the phone away from his ear and pressed the button to enable speakerphone. Jen's voice was the first I heard, just catching the end of her saying, "what's up?"

"We just came back from Dudley," Dan said.

My brain tuned out the telling of the entire story. I sat there staring at Dan from ten feet away, knowing everything he was saying, but couldn't actively listen to the words as he spoke them. I just zoned out completely. As if something inside me told me there was no reason to listen to what he was saying, since I already knew the gist of it.

Every so often, I'd zone back in to hear some sort of reaction from either Jen or Wendy. A gasp. A groan. Some question about why or how or the like. Then I'd zone back out. My vision fading from blurry to normal. Dan was in focus, then out of focus.

My mind had been playing tricks on me for days, maybe weeks. I'd been hearing things I knew weren't there, seeing things I knew weren't real. Jean jacket man was real, I knew that for a fact. I was skeptical at first, but after the burn hand print on the baseball bat, I was convinced that he was real. I wasn't yet convinced he was human.

The sound of footsteps upstairs snapped me back into reality virtually instantly. I blinked a few times to get my eyes to focus again. Dan was still sitting across from me at the table, phone in hand.

My eyes lifted themselves to look at the ceiling. It was after eleven, so everyone else who lived in that house had been asleep for at least an hour. It seemed unlikely that it was Kathy or Charlie, or even Rachel.

Thump. Thump. Thump.

Small steps, growing louder than when I'd first heard them.

Dan looked up at the ceiling as well. He'd heard them the second time.

"Hold on," he whispered into the phone before putting it down on the table.

He looked at me and pointed up, shrugging, as if to ask me what I thought it was.

My shoulders had barely finished shrugging when a third set of thumps echoed throughout the basement, even louder than before.

Thump. Thump. Thump.

"I have to go," Dan said, hanging up without waiting for a response.

He nodded to me, using his head to gesture toward the stairs. He silently said "let's go" and got up from the chair.

It only took me a second, but I was right on his heels, ready to go upstairs and find out what — or who — was up there.

Dan took a deep breath, let out an unnerving sigh and bound up the stairs, two at a time, not even being careful about being quiet. I followed suit.

We paused a second at the top of the stairs before opening the door. Dan turned and looked back at me. "You ready?" he asked.

Though I tried my best to say no, to turn around and run back down to the safety of the well-lit basement, I couldn't. I nodded and let out a faint "mhmm".

The door burst open and Dan jumped to the left, taking just one step away from the door to make room for me. Once I'd gotten clear of the door, I closed it behind me.

From our position, we could see most of the house. It wasn't a huge house and the tiny hallway connecting the kitchen and the bedrooms made it so you could see almost everywhere. Everywhere except the hallway to the bedrooms, which stood right behind me.

Dan took a tiny step toward the kitchen and poked his head around the corner of the door. He looked to his right, first, into the galley kitchen where the door was to enter the house.

"Nothing," he said.

He then looked left, through the eating area, into the living room. It was dark, with just a slit of light from the streetlight outside passing through the blinds, illuminating half of Charlie's chair and the floor in front of it.

Before he moved any further, I took two steps forward, aligning myself to his right. The darkness of the living room seemed overwhelming, but I squinted, hoping to see something, but also hoping to see nothing. In my head, I counted to fifty before my night vision kicked in. The bright fluorescent bulbs in the basement had really done a number on my ability to see clearly at that moment.

We were thirty, maybe forty, feet from the far end of the house. From the living room and all of its unknown inhabitants. I nudged Dan with my arm to see if he'd move forward at all.

That did the trick, and we were both off to venture into the living room to see what else we could find.

The entryway was large enough that we didn't need to go one at a time, so we walked in together, side by side.

I held my breath, as if that was going to protect me from anything malicious that was in there.

Dan seemed to hold his, too, as he reached for the table lamp by Charlie's chair, clicking it to life.

Though not very bright, it illuminated the room well enough for us to see there was no one in there. No malicious person or being. No jean jacket man. No one or nothing of any kind out of the ordinary. Just a bunch of Rachel's toys in the middle of the floor.

The opposite end of the hallway leading to the bedrooms was to our left, opening up right in front of Dan's parent's bedroom, with his room in the middle, and Rachel's at the other end, by the basement door. From the top of the stairs, we couldn't see that hallway.

If there was someone in the house, that was the only place left, aside from in Dan's bedroom, that the person could be where we wouldn't have seen them yet.

I grabbed Dan's arm, and saying nothing, took the first steps toward the hallway. I crouched, trying to give myself the element of surprise, expecting to find a person standing there, waiting to ambush us. Step by step, I crept through the living room, making it to the edge of the hallway.

with no thought about noise, I jumped from the living room the final step into the hallway, ready to "aha!" and catch someone.

But there was no one there. No shadows. No person. No item. No object. Nothing.

I motioned for Dan to come before moving into his bedroom.

He caught up with me, standing next to me, as we started venturing to his bedroom, just a few steps away.

Like the living room, it was dark. Even more so, as there were no street lights in his backyard to slide through the blinds. I reached in and flipped on the light switch before stepping in.

Nothing seemed out of the ordinary. Everything in its place. His bed was neatly made, as Kathy had done every day of his life.

Stepping in, I looked around further. Behind the door. In the closet. Nothing.

Everything was as it should have been.

We both stood in the center of his room, silent. I suppose we were waiting to hear more footsteps. More noise of any kind. But none came.

Ten minutes passed.

Fifteen.

Twenty.

Neither of us moved. Neither of us spoke. We just stood, waiting.

Dan finally broke the silence.

"There's nothing here," he said. "But I fucking heard someone walking around up here."

"It wasn't your parents," I said. "We'd have heard their door open and close."

"No."

"Let's go back downstairs," I said. "I'm fucking exhausted."

The two of us walked out of Dan's room and back down into the basement. The lights were still on, gleefully humming their fluorescent tune.

We spent between midnight and one in the morning just sitting, listening. Waiting for something else to happen.

"What did the girls say?" I asked, sometime around 12:30.

"They're freaked out. Wendy asked if we told Brian or Kevin's mothers or called the police."

"Are they even missing?" I asked. "Like, actually missing, according to the law?"

"I don't know. But I also don't think the police can do anything," Dan said.

"Jen said she wants to go to the woods tomorrow and look around some more."

"Did you tell her we already did that?"

"Of course, didn't you hear me?"

"I zoned out," I said. "I wasn't listening."

"Oh. Yeah, I told her everything we did. How Kevin just vanished from the room by the door in the outbuilding."

"This whole thing is so fucking weird."

That was the last thing I remember saying before I fell asleep. I dozed off into a dreamless sleep. A hard, but peaceful sleep, where nothing seemed to bother me or encroach on my night.

Footsteps woke me up early in the morning. Footsteps walking past me, close enough that I felt a breeze.

Without moving, I popped my eyes open, scanning the room from the daybed. Dan, still asleep on the floor in the sleeping bag. Nothing else out of the ordinary from my vantage point.

Down by my feet, by the door to the laundry room, the piles of boxes with Christmas and Halloween decorations stood undisturbed. The door partially open, as it usually was.

Without hesitating, I turned and sat upright in one motion, looking towards Charlie's office.

Scanning from my right to my left quickly, I saw nothing. All the books on the bookshelf were in order. Dan's punching bag in the corner of the room was in place.

No amount of convincing could tell me otherwise; I heard footsteps in the room. Then, I felt a breeze blow by me and wake me up.

"Dan?" I said, quietly at first. "Dan. Dan. Wake up." I pleaded.

He rolled over, facing away from me, towards the table on the other side of the room.

Then it happened.

The door to Charlie's office opened slowly, creaking. The overhead lights, still on from the night before, started sweeping into the small office.

As the door opened more, the light illuminated more of the room.

The desk where Charlie's computer was became visible.

The chair where Dan and I took turns playing "King's Quest" and "Space Quest" on the computer a million times before became illuminated.

The door continued to open, moving quicker.

"Who's in there?" I said, yelling.

It slammed shut as soon as I said something.

Then the door to the laundry room slammed shut, twenty feet away.

As I looked toward the laundry room, waiting for someone to come out, the door to the office opened again.

Faster that time. Opening immediately.

Before I knew it, a figure emerged into the doorway, partially lit from the shoulders down. But the face was somehow still in the shadows.

"Dan!" I yelled. "You can fucking wake up now!"

But he didn't. He ignored me.

The figure took a step forward, fully into the light.

His pock-marked face was immediately recognizable.

He took another step toward me, stopping just shy of where Dan's head lay resting on the floor. Just a foot or so away.

"I warned you." His voice was raspy, as if he had gone days without speaking aloud. I could feel the warmth of his breath from where he stood, though he was four or five feet from me.

I cowered and slipped back against the wall, putting another two or three feet between us.

He raised his arm, stretching it out toward me.

"Put it back," he said, pointing at me. Though his voice remained calm and relatively quiet, I could feel his anger.

It was the first time I'd been that close to him. It was the first time he'd spoken to me and the first time I'd had more than a few seconds to study him.

Though I was more scared than I'd ever been in my life, I took the time to really look him over.

His hand showed charring. It was burnt, but not the typical burn you'd see on a person where the burn is blistered or bubbling or scarred. His hand was mostly black, like a burnt piece of wood would be. It didn't seem to affect him as he lowered his hand back to his side.

"Put what back?" I asked.

"Put it back," he repeated.

"Dan, wake the fuck up!" I yelled so loud it hurt my throat.

He stepped closer. "This is your last warning."

"Dan! Dan! DAN!"

But Dan didn't move.

"Dan cannot help you," he said. "Neither can Brian or Kevin."

His voice was still quiet, but less calm now. He was approaching a whispering yell.

"DAN!" I tried one last time.

"Put it back. I will take your girls. I will take him. I will take you."

He leaned down and in close to me. A few inches from my face now.

"Put it back!" he screamed. His voice echoed throughout my head: the basement, the house, probably the whole neighborhood.

I closed my eyes, cringing against the sound. A sound so loud, so powerful, that drops of blood fell from my ears. I felt my eardrums vibrating, possibly ruptured. Pain erupted throughout my head as he continued his exhale, holding onto the last word he said, still screaming.

As his voice faded, crackling and with a gargling sound, I opened my eyes.

He smiled and cocked his head.

"Or else," he said, opening his mouth.

More gargling erupted from his throat. A buzzing sound followed.

Before I had could think about anything else, bees started coming out of his mouth. First one, then another, then a third. They flew around his head, circling him a few times before flying off into the room.

He opened his mouth one last time, and an entire swarm of bees flew out. Hundreds of bees, flying at unnatural speeds. They were everywhere before I could even process what was happening. They surrounded him, then me. None of them stung me. None of them even touched me. They just flew, buzzing, everywhere.

"Dan!" I yelled again, "wake the fuck up, right fucking now!"

I closed my eyes and grabbed the pillow from my left, trying to swat the bees away. Trying to protect myself, in case they tried to attack.

"No!" I yelled out at nothing.

I swatted five times with the pillow before opening my eyes.

Dan stood in front of me now, rubbing his eyes.

"What the fuck are you doing?" he asked.

My eyes jolted around the room. The door to Charlie's office was open. The door to the laundry room was open just a crack, like Kathy always left it.

"He's gone," I said. "He was here."

"Who was?" Dan asked.

"Jean jacket man."

"Fuck you," Dan said.

"He was here. He talked to me," I said.

"What did he say?"

"He wants me to put it back."

"Put what back?"

"I don't know," I said. "I asked him, but he just kept repeating 'put it back'."

"Did he say anything else?"

"He said you couldn't help me. And Brian and Kevin couldn't, either."

"How does he know our names?"

"I don't know. But he said he'd take the girls, too."

"Take them?"

"I think he is holding Brian and Kevin somewhere," I said. "I think he's going to take Wendy and Jen and you if I don't put back whatever he wants me to put back."

"Did we take anything from the forest?" Dan asked.

"I don't think so, right? We just poked around in that old house."

"Maybe one of the girls took something? Maybe Kevin or Brian?" Dan asked.

"I don't know. I don't think anyone did. They didn't tell me," I said.

"Why is he telling you to put it back? Why wouldn't he tell whoever took it?"

"Bees came out of his mouth."

"What?"

"Bees. They came out of his mouth. That's what I was swinging the pillow at."

He looked around the room. "No bees here now," he said.

"I know. And he vanished when I closed my eyes. Like, he knew you were going to wake up and didn't want you to see him, or something."

"Let's go get the girls," Dan said. "This is all too fucking weird to not talk about in person."

"Whatever we do, let's get out of your house for a while," I said.

The two of us walked upstairs without a word to Kathy or Rachel, who were in the living room, got in my car and drove straight to Burlington to pick Jen and Wendy up.

Twenty-Four

DAN HAD TALKED TO Jen earlier, so we knew she was over at Wendy's. The two of them just hung out after getting home from work. As I always did, I honked when we pulled into the driveway. And, as usual, Wendy's dad turned the porch light on, opened the door, then pushed the screen door open to look at who was honking. I'm sure he knew it was us, as Wendy would have told him we were coming, but he always checked anyway. Just to be safe, I'm sure.

He nodded. I nodded back.

"Wen," I heard him yell as he pulled the screen door shut, "the guys are here."

"Bye daddy, home later," she said, pulling the door closed behind her, tailing Jen.

Jen jumped in behind Dan, Wendy behind me. As usual.

"Did either of you take anything?" Dan asked as soon as we pulled out of the driveway.

"Take what? Like drugs?" Wendy asked.

"We don't take drugs," Jen said.

"No, you dipshits," Dan chortled. "From Dudley. Did you take anything?"

I looked back in the rearview mirror and made eye contact with Wendy for a second.

"No," she said, "and I don't like the way Mike just looked at me."

I held the silence for just a touch too long, I think.

"What the fuck?" Wendy shouted. "What happened?"

"Spill it," Jen said, reaching around the headrest and mockingly choking Dan.

I told them everything that had happened since we last saw them. I tried to recount every single detail of the last couple of days, every painstaking and terrifying detail. I held nothing back.

The only sound in the car for a full thirty seconds was the sound of the blinker, signaling our turn. Click. Clack. Click. Clack.

Neither of them spoke.

Dan remained silent, letting them process what I'd just told them.

Click. Clack.

"Wait," Jen said. "You're not going there right now, are you?"

I didn't reply.

"Mike?" Wendy asked, eyeing me in the rear-view mirror.

Click. Clack.

I turned the wheel and made the right onto Middlesex Turnpike. The road that would lead us to the road which connected to Dudley Road.

Even twenty minutes away, they could tell that's where we were heading.

"We have to go out into the woods and figure out what's missing," I said, trying to remain calm.

"Why?" Wendy asked. "Why now?"

"It's escalating," Dan said. "It's getting more..."

"Angry," I said. "Not stronger. Not more powerful. Whatever it is, it's getting more angry with us."

"We have to figure out what's missing, so we can put it back," Dan said.

"Well, I didn't fucking take anything," Jen said.

"Me either," Wendy added.

"We didn't take anything, either," Dan said. "All we found out in the woods was the remains of that house."

"Did we even move anything there?" Wendy asked.

"I mean, I poked around at stuff. I moved some stuff," I said. "But I didn't take anything from there."

Something told me we shouldn't be going there right then, not after dark. We had enough eerie experiences during daylight in the area. I knew something worse could happen at night. Knowing that jean jacket man had threatened to take the rest of my friends, I had to be careful. But, at the same time, I had to figure out what he wanted back.

"He said he'd take us all?" Wendy asked, barely audible.

"Yeah," Dan said.

"Wait," I interjected. "No. Not all of us. He specifically said 'the girls' and 'Dan'."

"That's all of us, stupid," Dan said.

"It's not," Wendy said. "He didn't say he'd take Mike."

"Why?" Jen asked.

"I don't know," I said.

"No," I interjected. "He said he'd take me. But only after he said he'd take you three."

After careful consideration, I decided to pass the end of Dudley with the Nunnery and drive down to the nicer end to get to the turn around spot. Driving by all the horse farms at night felt easier that night. It felt as though not driving directly past the building would make a difference.

"I'm going to park in the turnaround spot," I said. "We'll go the rest of the way on foot."

"We should go out into the woods, back to the old house and take another look," Dan said.

"How many flashlights do we have?" Jen asked.

"I have two in the trunk," I said.

No matter how many times I'd driven down that road, from either end, the point where the newer pavement turned to older pavement creeped me out. The trees seemed to get lower, and the road narrowed all at once. The beautiful horse farms disappeared instantly, replaced by trees and low visibility in every direction. Nothing about that transition ever sat easy with me, even when I tried to tell myself that it was "just a road". We were so far from the nunnery there, it truly was just a road. It is a dark, narrow road with houses and residents on it. People lived there — modern people. Even so, no matter what, it was a scary drive.

The headlights seemed to linger a moment or two after I shut the car off, illuminating down the path in front of us, and showing us every nook and cranny for a blink of the eye.

And then, total darkness surrounded us as the lights from the dashboard shut off.

My eyes automatically squinted for a moment, adjusting to the darkness before getting out of the car.

As no one spoke, I assumed the others were doing the same. Or everyone was just too afraid to be the first person to open their door.

Once I felt comfortable being able to see in the dark, I grabbed my door handle.

"I guess let's go," I said.

The door swung open in a calm silence. The only sound I could hear was nature; crickets chirping, an occasional bird call, the flapping of what I thought was a bat. Everything was normal at that moment.

Dan exited next, meeting me at the back of the car right before I opened the trunk to get the flashlights.

Jen and Wendy had just opened their doors when I put the key in the trunk lock to open it.

As soon as I opened the trunk and the light came on, a loud, unmistakable scream echoed through the woods in all directions around us.

There were no words. It wasn't a cry for help. It wasn't anyone's name. It was just the sound of someone in pain. Someone hurt. Someone being hurt. It was so loud that it felt like it would knock me over. I felt a breeze blowing gently in my face, probably coincidentally timed with the scream, but on some level, it felt like the scream caused it.

Dan pushed me aside, shuffled through all the things that amassed in my trunk, and fished out the flashlights. He handed one to me and quickly trained the other one down the path, then in the opposite direction. He was trying to find a person screaming.

I aimed my flashlight back and forth to the left and right of the turnaround spot. The dense trees and brush made it hard to see in either direction.

"Hello?" I yelled out. "Where are you?"

"Shut the fuck up!" Dan yelled at me. "What the fuck are you doing?"

"Someone's out there and is hurt," I said. "we have to help."

"We're going to get hurt if you don't shut up," he said. "We'll look, but do it quietly."

As I stepped back to the trunk, I reached to close it, making sure we had the only two flashlights there were in there.

The screaming continued at the same volume as it started. It was deafening.

"We have to help whoever that is," Jen said.

"Please!" Wendy begged.

I slammed the trunk shut and motioned for Dan to head toward the trail.

Within a second of shutting the trunk, the scream stopped. The breeze died down.

A handful of seconds later, all the sounds of nature returned. Once again, the crickets chirped, the birds made their calls. Everything returned to how it was before the screaming started.

"The fuck?" Dan said. "What just happened?"

"I don't know," I said. "Let's get in there, though. The sooner we go look for whoever that was, the better."

Dan grabbed Jen's hand and pulled her in behind him, heading down the trail.

Using the flashlight as a pointer, I signaled for Wendy to follow them in.

"I'll stay at the back with the flashlight," I said.

We walked as a collective, peering through the woods, trying to illuminate anything we saw that could be a person in need of help, while still trying to retrace our steps from the previous visits, trying to notice if we'd taken anything before.

Flashlight beams zipped back and forth from fifteen feet in front of me. Other than the light we'd brought into the woods with us, it was pitch black. A night darker than any other we'd spent out there. I knew Wendy was just in front of me, as I could hear her footsteps crunching on the leaves and dirt. But I could see nothing other than a silhouette of her tiny frame. Had I not known it was her, I wouldn't have been able to tell.

Once we'd gotten about halfway to where the old house remains were, I felt a presence behind me. As if someone was coming up the trail, gaining ground on us.

I stopped for a moment, letting the others walk ahead of me a bit, and turned around. Looking down the trail, I saw nothing at first. I closed my eyes and listened intently for a minute. All I could hear were the footsteps of my friends, getting further away from me. Step. Crunch. Crunch. Branch snapping.

I kept my eyes closed for another minute, hearing my friends getting further away from me, but not hearing anything else.

The sense of someone's presence grew stronger. That feeling of someone getting closer to you, an indescribable feeling like someone in your personal space.

But there was no one anywhere near me when I opened my eyes.

"Mike," I heard Dan yell-whisper. "Come on."

Turning back towards my friends, I saw something I'll never forget.

Two flashlights.

Pausing for a moment to gain my composure, I looked down at my hand, wondering if perhaps I'd dropped the flashlight I was carrying and maybe Wendy or Jen picked it up and kept walking. Perhaps the two lights I saw were our own flashlights.

Forcing my eyes shut for a second, then pushing them back open, I hoped I was just seeing double in the dark. I squinted, hard.

Two lights still present.

Flashlight still in my hand, I sprinted the thirty yards to where my friends were.

"Turn the light off," I said. "Quick."

"What? Why?" Dan asked.

"Just do it," I said, shutting mine off, and reaching for his.

"Okay, fine, I'll do it," he said, shutting it off.

"What's happening?" Jen asked.

I took her hand, and reached for Wendy's in the darkness, pointing their bodies down the trail, further away from the entrance.

The light was still there. A hundred or so feet away. Motionless.

"What the.." Wendy yelped, jerking her hand out of mine and covering her mouth with both hands.

"Should we.." Dan started asking, "Hello?" he said loud enough that whoever held that flashlight should have been able to hear him.

The light went out immediately.

It didn't die down and fade out like a flashlight does. It just immediately went dark. Completely dark.

At the same time, I realized I could see the backs of my friends. They were faint, but lit up.

Holding my hand up to the back of Dan's head, I could see my hand.

Then I realized what was happening. I turned around and saw it behind us. Another light. Another motionless light, hovering around waist high.

Stepping toward it, I yelled, "Who are you? Hello?"

A whoosh of air hit me as I felt my friends turn around, facing the same direction I was.

The light stayed on for another second, then went out. It vanished the same way the other one had.

All four of us stood still, silent, in the dark. Only a moment passed before the light on the other side of the trail turned on.

We stood in the middle the of trail, the four of us, trapped. Something on either side of us, holding us where we were.

"Hello?" Dan said, "Come closer."

"What are you doing?" Wendy squealed. "Don't invite it here!"

Darkness again.

Dan turned to face me. I could tell he was looking over my shoulder, but couldn't see his face.

Then the light behind me turned back on. I saw Dan's face. He looked excited, almost. It seemed he enjoyed what was happening.

"Do it!" he yelled, though I still don't know what "it" was.

Darkness.

I continued to face him, looking behind him. Wendy had stepped closer to me, pushing herself against me, as an effort to gain protection. She grabbed my free hand and squeezed it. I could see Jen similarly grabbing onto Dan. He and I continued to face in opposite directions, watching over each other's shoulders.

The light behind him came on again. Shining directly in my face.

It bounced. Up and down, about a foot.

Again, it bounced.

It only took me a split second before I realized it was bouncing because whoever was holding the light was now running toward us.

"Stop!" I yelled.

Darkness.

Then Dan's face lit up again. The light behind me was on again.

"Come on!" Dan taunted it.

His face went dark, then was lit again. This happened four times in a row.

The light behind me was also coming closer to us.

"Pussy!" Dan yelled, "Come on!"

Darkness from behind me.

The light in front of me came back on, still bouncing, getting closer. Maybe fifty feet away now. Bouncing faster, picking up speed.

"Stop!" I yelled, as if we were playing Mother May I from childhood. As if telling it to stop somehow would keep it away from us.

Dan's face lit up, then got dark. The bouncing behind me was continuing.

"Is it getting closer?" I asked Dan.

"Not close enough!" he yelled, still taunting.

"Dan, stop it," Jen said, "I'm scared!"

The light went out.

For a solid minute, maybe more, neither light came on. We stood in darkness and complete silence. The sounds of nature had stopped entirely. All I could hear was Wendy breathing heavily, still squeezing my hand. The only feeling I had was fear. The only physical part of my body that I could feel was my heart beating. Thumping wildly in my chest.

Mustering up every ounce of courage I had left in my body, I flicked the flashlight on and aimed it over Dan's shoulder, down the trail.

Turning around, I shined the flashlight down the trail behind me, back toward the trail's entrance.

"There's no one," I said.

Dan turned his flashlight on and did the same thing a number of times.

"What the hell?" he said.

"Can we go?" Wendy asked.

"Please," Jen added. "Let's get out of here. We'll come back tomorrow, when it's light out."

"Good idea," I said. "Let's go, Dan."

I knew he would be the only one of the four of us that needed coercing to leave.

"No, no," he said. "You're right. Let's go."

As I turned to head back to the car, the flashlight in my hand flickered. I smacked it a few times, as was the common fix for those older flashlights. Sometimes the battery connections didn't connect properly and a good whack usually fixed it. It flickered again, then went dim.

Dan's light from behind me seemed to do the same thing. As his dimmed to barely usable, mine went completely out.

Wendy grabbed my waist, clinging in the darkness.

Then, about twenty feet down the trail, a light came on again.

As I turned to Dan to ask him what we should do, I saw the light behind him come on as well.

Back and forth, I flipped my head, seeing both lights at the same time.

Both lights started bouncing. Their holders now making strides toward us, running, getting closer by the second.

Fifteen feet and closing. Bouncing faster and faster, getting brighter, closer.

I held my breath, my eyes frozen open. The anxiety in my chest hitting me like a heart attack. A drop of sweat fell from my forehead, stinging my left eye.

At ten feet, both lights stopped bouncing, but continued to get closer and closer to us, flying along above the ground.

Dan and I shined our flashlights back and forth in both directions, yelling nonsense and obscenities, trying to make it stop.

I dropped my flashlight and grabbed Wendy, trying to shield her from whatever was about to happen.

"Fuck you!" Dan yelled as the lights got within reach.

Not knowing what else to do, I dropped to the ground, pulling Wendy down next to me.

Looking up, I saw Dan and Jen standing, holding each other, expecting the worst.

The light on Dan's side of the trail arrived first. It flew right through the two of them, close enough now that I could see it clearly. It looked like a small, round ball of light. It was not attached to anything, but floated freely in the air. There was no person holding it, no arm attached to it. It just floated along, passing first through Dan, then Jen.

It flew up toward the sky for a moment. Then, directly above my head, it stopped in mid-air, hovering. It illuminated all four of us clearly, like a very full moon on a clear night. I could see everyone's face as I looked around, all four of us puzzled, fearful, confused.

The second light arrived a spilt second later, meeting up with the first one.

They hovered, inches apart, above Wendy and I. Floating.

Both lights went out for a second, then came back, just as bright as they had been.

Again, they dipped and came back.

It was like they were a pair of eyes, blinking.

Twice more they blinked, still hovering.

Dan reached out to touch the one closest to him, seemingly no longer fearful of these lights.

"Don't," Jen said.

"I think it's okay," Dan said.

I stood and helped Wendy up. She was still clinging to me as we stood just off the trail, watching the lights float.

As his hand approached the light, the scream in the woods started again, louder than before.

This time, it yelled "no", over and over again. Getting louder and louder. The accompanying breeze turned to wind, blowing leaves around the trail and making the trees surrounding us creak.

As Dan got within an inch of the ball of light, it blinked rapidly, then disappeared.

The other light vanished at the same time.

Once both lights went out and Dan's hand fell, seemingly unsatisfied, to his side, the screaming stopped.

I picked up the flashlight I'd dropped, grabbed Wendy's hand and pulled her in the car's direction. Neither of us said a word. Neither of us looked back, but hoping Dan and Jen were right on our tails.

No one said a word until we were in the car and had driven out of Dudley Road.

We took the horse farm route out, opting not to pass the nunnery, so we'd feel safer.

As I made the right onto North Road, I felt the car suddenly jerk to the right and a loud pfooosh sound rang out in the night air.

Quickly pulling over, I got out of the car, flashlight again in hand, and walked around to the passenger side of the car.

Both tires were flat. Not just flat, but sort of exploded. As if we'd run over something enormous and the tires just erupted. Both of them.

When I went back to the driver's side to get in, I noticed those two tires were blown as well.

Not knowing what to do, I looked to the sky and mouthed "why me?" but said nothing aloud.

Leaning in the door, I made eye contact with Dan. "You will not believe this."

"What happened?" Wendy asked.

"All four tires are blown out."

"What?" Jen asked. "Did you hit something?"

"I don't think so."

The intersection of Dudley Road and North Street, at that end, was illuminated fairly well by an overhead streetlight. I traced the short drive back to where we'd turned, looking for anything in the road, but saw nothing.

Despite not wanting to go knock on a stranger's door in the middle of the night, I knew I had to.

Thankfully, the man who lived on the corner was awake and offered to call the police for me. When they arrived, they arranged for a tow truck to bring the car to the Sears Auto Shop at the Burlington Mall, and gave the four of us a ride home. It was, to this day, the only time I've been in a police cruiser. And, thankfully, I got to ride in the front.

When the service advisor from Sears called me the next morning, he joked saying "rough night?"

Not in the mood for small talk, I pushed him to tell me how much it would cost for new tires.

He presented my options, and, being a poor teenager, I went with the four cheapest tires they offered. With installation and alignment, my total came to $399.79.

Twenty-Five

WHEN MY ALARM WENT off the next morning, I had no recollection of how I'd gotten home. Its incessant buzzing, growing louder, only added to my confusion. The usual sounds were buzzing around the house. I could hear my Mom in her room, but it didn't sound like she was getting ready for work. The television in there was on. The news.

My head felt groggy, but I couldn't remember why. Had I gotten into a fight last night? It sure felt like it.

As I smacked the alarm clock, I glanced over at it. A minute after nine. Why did I set an alarm? Did I have to work today? I must have.

"It must be Thursday," I thought to myself. If my Mom is home and I have an early shift at the restaurant, Thursday is the only day it could be.

"Mom?" I called out.

No answer.

"Mom?" I called again.

Footsteps thumping down the hallway toward my closed door.

"What?" she said from the other side.

"Is it Thursday?"

"Yes, I'm going to Market Basket shortly."

"Okay," I said, "thanks."

The blinding pain in my head was getting worse the longer I was awake. When I sat up, I almost threw up.

"Do you need me to take you to get your car?" she asked.

"Yeah."

"I'm leaving in ten minutes. If you're ready, I'll take you now."

The momentum of swinging my feet over the side of my bed just about made me fall over. Something was off with my balance. It felt like my equilibrium was off.

Before standing, I sat for a minute. Some clean laundry was at the foot of my bed, within reach, so I was able to get dressed without having to stand.

My shoes were tossed on the floor by my nightstand, also within reach.

"I'm leaving in two minutes," I heard my Mom call from downstairs.

"Coming," I yelled.

The first time I stood, I fell back on the bed. I shook it off and tried again, finally able to stand up.

Shaking my head a few times helped clear the cobwebs, and I got downstairs without falling again.

Most of my teen years — well into adulthood, come to think of it — my Mom worked in the Burlington Mall. She took the same route to and from the mall every day she worked. She either worked the morning or night shift. Either 10-6 or 2-10, depending on the day. I'd ridden with her on that same route many times before I got my license, as I had a number of jobs in the same mall by that point.

We pulled out of Pinewold Road and made the right onto Shawsheen Street, heading toward the intersection of Route 38, where we'd make a left onto Main Street.

She could probably do the drive in her sleep or with her eyes closed, she'd done it so many times.

"What are you going to do today?" she asked as we passed Boudreau's Auto, heading up the hill toward Wilmington.

"I have work," I said, curtly.

"Then what?"

"Probably go to Dan's."

"Something weird happened this morning."

That caught me off guard. I panicked.

"What?"

"Brian's mother called the house. She thought he might have been staying here. He hasn't been home in a couple of days."

"Oh," I panicked more. "No, he's at Dan's. They've been working on a new song." The lies just flew out of my mouth.

"Why does she think he's at our house?"

"They were all supposed to stay over so we could work on a new song when you're at work," I said. It wasn't uncommon for us to wait for her to leave the house to have band practice in the basement.

I knew she wouldn't call Kathy to check. She knew we all spent nights at each other's houses for most of our friendship. I figured lying was the only way that was safe for me to explain Brian being missing without launching into a tirade about haunted places and how some paranormal psychopath had abducted my friends.

"When is he going home? In case his mom calls again."

"Not sure," I said, looking out the window. "I think tomorrow"

We made the right on South Street, heading along the South end of town.

As we drove along, I couldn't help but think to myself about where Kevin and Brian actually were. I wasn't into science fiction enough to wonder if they were in some other dimension, underworld, or something. I just knew they weren't where I was anymore. We couldn't see them.

I wondered if the jean jacket man was just a regular person. Maybe there was an explanation for everything we'd experienced with him. Perhaps he was just some guy who was pissed off at us for being dumb kids.

There had to be an explanation for who he was and where my friends were.

We passed my high school — Shawsheen Tech — and made the left down Bicknell Road, where my mother would undoubtedly honk her horn at her friend Joyce's house.

She did.

Throughout the entire ride, I tried to not focus too much on how I'd have to hand over almost four hundred dollars to Sears once we got there to get my car back. As annoyed as I was with the whole situation, I tried to tell myself that it was found money. It wasn't coming out of my pocket. Just a few days ago, I'd won $400 on that lottery ticket we found outside of Lil' Peach. So, I was breaking even and would have four brand new tires on my car.

As we made the right on Route 62, I felt something odd. The dizziness and grogginess came back. My vision got blurry for a brief second and the radio seemed to change stations by itself.

Once again, I shook my head, trying to tell myself that nothing was wrong, and I was imagining it.

At the intersection of Route 62 and Route 3A, I saw him. Jean jacket man. Standing on the far side of 3A, by the Presbyterian Church.

There was no mistake, no doubt about it. It was him. Standing. Motionless. Like usual.

But why was he there? We were in Burlington, miles away from the Billerica line, even further away from Dudley Road.

Trying not to cause too much suspicion, I closed the window I'd had open. It made me feel safer than having it halfway open.

He knew it was me. Even though I was in my Mom's car, he knew.

Once the light turned green, we made the left on 3A and passed him. His head turned from his left to center as he made direct eye contact with me. I could feel his anger from ten feet away.

The car in front of us suddenly stopped, putting us directly in front of him. I looked straight ahead, trying to not turn to my right and look at him. I did my best, but something compelled me to look. Something overwhelmed me to see what he was doing and to figure out why he was there.

Slowly, I turned my head and looked out the window.

He'd stepped closer to the car, about five feet away now, just standing on the curb. He raised his arm and extended his hand, pointing at me.

If I had a single doubt before that moment that he knew it was me, that doubt was gone. He was just as sure of my presence as I was of his.

Traffic cleared up, and we moved along, my Mom none the wiser of what had just happened.

I turned my head and looked out the back window. He still stood there, his long pointer finger still aimed at me, following me slowly up the road.

"What's with all this traffic?" my Mom said, startling me.

"Looks like construction up ahead," I pointed out.

Like usual, we took her "shortcut" down Church Street and connected to Lexington, which brought us out by the Kohl's, across from the mall.

Still a bit frazzled, I jumped out of the car at Sears, thanked my Mom for the ride, and ran inside to pick up my car.

At that point, I still had no idea what time I had to work, but it wasn't unusual for me to show up early for a shift, punch in, and get some extra hours. The restaurant didn't open until eleven and it was just after ten, so I had time before I had to get over there, anyway.

Twenty-Six

"Hey," Jen said as I walked in the back door of the restaurant. "Did you get your tires fixed?"

"Morning. Yeah, I just picked the car up from Sears."

Wendy must have heard me and came out back through the swinging double doors. She did the same thing she did every time she saw me at work. She gave me the biggest hug her tiny frame could muster. It's strange the things you remember about people you haven't seen or spoken to in a long time. Wendy's hugs are definitely the thing I remember most about her.

"You okay?" she asked.

"I'm fine. We're all fine," I said, brushing past her to look at the schedule posted on the wall near the manager's office.

I'd lucked out, I was working the morning shift. Well, lunch shift, really. It was just the three of us waiting tables that morning, Francisco working the grill, and Oscar washing dishes out back. That was a fairly common crew for a run-of-the-mill lunch shift.

I debated telling the two of them what had happened on the ride to the mall and what had happened at Dan's house the other night. The idea of filling them in made me worried about what they'd think about everything. They'd already been more involved than I'd wanted them to be, but I felt like there was no turning back by that point. Dan's relationship with Jen being what it was, he'd probably already told her what happened at his house.

Rather than blurting out what happened, I played it cool, letting them tell me if they knew anything more. Oscar's English wasn't very good, so I felt comfortable enough out back discussing everything.

"Thirty minutes," Debbie, the general manager, said on her way out of the office. "Morning Mike."

"Hey Debbie," I said, making my way to the time clock to punch in.

"So," Jen said. "Screaming at you?"

That didn't take long.

"Dan told you, huh?" I asked.

"Yeah, and of course I told Wen."

"You thought I was scared before?" Wendy said, half jokingly.

"This has all gotten insane," I said. "And now my mother's asking where Kevin and Brian have been."

"When did she ask about them?" Jen asked.

"This morning, on the way here. She's up at her store right now."

"Have you talked to either of their moms?" Wendy asked.

"I haven't, but I think Dan talked to Janice the other day. I don't remember if he actually told me that or if I dreamed it."

Wendy motioned toward a bunch of ketchup bottles she'd just finished filling, silently asking me to grab them and help carry them out front. The two of them had gotten through most of the opening shift prep duties before I got there, which made it easy for me to space out before we opened the doors. Even though we technically opened at eleven, customers rarely started coming in until half an hour later or so. Lunches were never usually that busy.

While the girls finished prepping the soda station, getting clean silverware — I never understood why we had so much silverware, most of what we sold were finger foods — filling napkin dispensers, I did the stuff they didn't enjoy doing. I checked the bathrooms to make sure they were clean and stocked. I counted the money in the one register we used and made sure the one we didn't use was empty, checked with Francisco so make sure he didn't need any help to prep.

But I mostly just gazed out into the parking lot and into the mall. My eyes darting around, looking at the people walking around out in the mall or making their way in from the parking lot. The foot traffic was picking up, since the mall opened at ten, even at the end of the wing we were on.

People were coming and going, oblivious to the world around them, and my life and what was happening in it. They didn't know who I was, what was happening, where my friends were, or even that I was sitting in a giant plate-glass window, looking out at them.

You could ask me what I was looking for until you're blue in the face, but I couldn't tell you. Was I looking for him? Did I think he followed me to the mall? I don't know. It's hard to say what I had hoped to see out there that morning, but I looked. I looked hard and long.

Nothing caught my eye. No one jumped out in front of me with a demon face. No one flew through the open air of the mall's tall ceilings. No one vanished before my eyes. Nothing happened until Wendy came up behind me and tapped me on the shoulder.

"Jesus!" I said. "You scared the shit out of me."

"I'm sorry! What are you looking at?" she asked.

"I'm not really looking at anything."

"What are you looking for, then?"

"Nothing. I guess. I don't know."

Jen came over and sat on my right. Wendy plopped down on the bar stool to my left. The three of us looking ahead, out the window.

"Do you think we'll find Kevin and Brian?" Jen asked.

"I hope so," I said.

"Me, too," Wendy added.

"What if we don't? What if something happened to them?" Jen asked.

Pausing for a moment to think, I replied, "I'm not worried that we won't find them," I trailed off.

"What are you worried about?" Wendy asked.

"I'm not sure you want me to say," I said.

"Tell me," she said, putting her hand on my arm.

"I'm worried if they're hurt, and about who's going to disappear next."

Twenty-Seven

As usual, after lunch died down, Debbie asked if anyone wanted to go home early. Our shifts were usually ten to five, but almost the entire wait staff would get sent home around two, even on the weekends. I used to think waiting tables was an awesome job. You had generally short hours, made pretty good money for a teenager, and usually got to go home early unless you were also working the night shift.

It wasn't uncommon for me to volunteer to be the one to stay behind, so I did what I'd normally had done and let Wendy and Jen head home.

Sometimes one of them would argue that I should go and they'd stay. Sometimes they'd both argue over it. But not that day. They both hugged me and made a bee-line for the time clock to punch out and get out of there. I didn't mind most of the time. There were very few tables in the afternoon, especially on a Thursday, so it was mostly just hanging out and waiting for the night shift.

Most afternoons, Francisco and I would just hang out and do nothing. Sometimes we'd have to prep for the dinner rush, but that was rare. That day was a day where we just got to hang out. I suppose if then were now, the two of us would have been on Facebook or Instagram or some other social media app. But given none of that existed then, we were forced to just hang out and talk. He was an interesting guy, and I always enjoyed working with him and learning from him. Most of the conversational Spanish I know — to this day — comes from working with those guys in that kitchen.

"Oh, good, you're still here," Debbie said, emerging from the back.

"I let Jen and Wendy go home," I said.

"I figured you would. Jess and Megan just called in sick. Together. Again," she said.

"For tonight?"

I knew where this was going already.

"Yes. Do you want to make some extra money? If not, I can call Andy or Tim or Melissa in. They're all off tonight."

"I don't mind. But I want the corner."

The corner was the one big booth we had in the restaurant. There were only twelve tables in the whole place, but they turned over quickly. Getting the corner meant you had a good section with the biggest table, which meant you'd get the bigger parties. Which, in theory, would get you the bigger tips, because of the size of the party.

"Deal," she said.

Of all the managers I worked with or under at that job, Debbie was always my favorite. She asked a lot of me, but also seemed to appreciate me more than anyone else. She also understood that location better than anyone else. The owner often sent his son and daughter — Kay and Mitra — in to work at the various locations he owned, so he could get some first-hand insights into how each store was running. They were very strict and I remember so many louder-than-they-should-have-been conversations with both of them.

Debbie popped back through the swinging doors to the back, saying something in Spanish to Oscar — likely telling him he could punch out and go home.

The night shift flew by, thanks to an unusually busy night. Nothing out of the normal happened, which was a colossal relief.

I was happy to have what many would consider a normal day at work.

Since I'd been there so long, Jazmin, who came in to relieve Debbie sometime late afternoon, let me be the first one to leave after the dinner rush died down.

"You sure?" I asked. "I don't mind staying and helping close."

"It's nine thirty," she said. "You've been here long enough for one day. Now go or I'll put you in my trunk and bring you home with me."

That type of weird thing was par for the course with Jazmin. I never figured out if it was her way of flirting or a cultural thing where she didn't know what to say and just said whatever she wanted. So many times, she'd say something weird like that.

"Ok, you're the boss," I said, heading to the back.

Many of us, myself included, would just take our cash tips and shove them in the front pocket of our apron throughout the shift. Since customers paid at the register, we never needed to worry about making change, unless a customer asked us to break a twenty so they could leave a tip. Part of the end of shift routine was standing out back by the office, sorting, straightening and counting the cash you made that day.

Technically, you were supposed to keep track of it and report it at the end of the week, so you could be taxed on it. No one ever did that, though. We'd all just make up some random number on the paperwork and say we made a hundred bucks or something. In reality, we made more than that.

For some reason, I remember the exact amount of money I made that day. My double shift earned me $251. Not a ton, but not terrible, either.

Once I'd tossed my dirty apron into the hamper, unrolled my sleeves, and punched out, I said my goodbyes and headed out the back door into the loading dock area. It was common to head out the back of the restaurant, an easier way to the parking lot than going back out through the front.

Inside my car was cool and dark, only illuminated by a streetlight thirty feet away. The steering wheel felt colder to the touch than it should have been. Even though it was dark out, it was still relatively warm.

Most nights I'd have gone straight to Dan's, or even picked him up and gone to one of the other guys' houses. Most nights we'd go out and have fun. Drive around and blast music, stopping at Lil' Peach or Market Basket, thinking we were much cooler than we actually were.

Most nights I'd have not looked over my shoulder walking to my car. Most nights, I wouldn't have gotten in and immediately locked all four doors. Most nights, I wouldn't be afraid to start the car in fear of the stereo blaring. Most nights were normal. That night was anything but normal.

The stop light at the mall was barely in my rearview mirror when I noticed it. A car racing up behind me. Its high beams flashing, repeatedly. It got within inches of my rear bumper, then backed off a few car lengths.

Adult me would have pulled over or turned onto a side street. I would have gotten myself out of that situation as quickly as I could and let the car pass me.

Teenage me did what teenage me did. He sped up.

"Fuck you!" I yelled into the mirror. "What the fuck are you doing, asshole?!"

I yelled as if, somehow, the person driving the car behind me could hear me.

My hands motioned to go around me.

My finger flipped him off a number of times.

My mouth continued yelling, continued its profanity-laden word vomit.

His lights flashed more. His bumper close to me, then backing off.

As I pulled up to the intersection at the center of Burlington, I'd normally have made a left to go home down 3A. I'd made that left hundreds of times before. He was right on my ass, still, so I moved over into the right lane at the last second. I figured he wanted to go left, since he was behind me. By moving over, I opened the left turn only lane for him. He had free rein to make his left and be on his way.

Part of me hoped that as he pulled up next to me, I could see who it was. I could see that it was someone I knew playing a joke on me. Maybe I'd see it was someone from work trying to tell me I'd forgotten my wallet. Maybe there was a reason for it.

He didn't pull up next to me. I didn't get any look at him. At the last second, he pulled into the other lane behind me.

As soon as that happened, I realized it wasn't someone who I'd pissed off by driving too slowly. It wasn't someone trying to get me to let him pass. It wasn't someone who was in a big hurry and needed to get home.

They were following me. Whoever it was.

I turned the radio off. As if the silence would help me concentrate on driving better, making more sound decisions.

The only sound I could hear was the engine-revving behind me. The high beams still turned on, blinding me in the rear and side view mirrors. The lights were so bright I couldn't even make out what kind of car it was. All I knew was whoever was driving it was intentionally following me. And they were not following me to give me one of those big Publisher's Clearing House checks. They had malicious intent.

Immediately, when the light turned green, I floored it. The engine of my Mitsubishi Galant roared to life, flying through the intersection, from zero to fifty in, well, way longer than would be an acceptable number to brag about.

Tires screeched from behind me. Distance between my rear bumper and his front bumper grew to four or five car lengths. I'd caught him by surprise. He wasn't expecting me to take off so quickly.

His high beams turned off. He was falling farther and farther behind me as I made the left around Burlington Common, heading back toward 3A, making sure to slow down as I passed the police station.

My eyes were pinned to my rear view, wondering if he'd make the same left I did. Wondering if he'd follow me down this road, past the police station.

The radio turned itself on. Deafeningly loud.

"Fuck," I screamed as I realized that the person behind me wasn't just any normal person. It was him. It was jean jacket man. There may have been other people who could follow me so aggressively, but none of them could turn my radio on. I still don't understand what supernatural ability he had to connect to my car like he did, but he used it to his advantage.

Silence filled the car as I flipped the radio back off.

His lights behind me grew closer as I merged onto 3A, too far from the mall to go back, but still very far from home.

High beams popped back up as he merged. Flashing. Over and over. Repeatedly getting closer to me, then backing off.

The radio came on again, louder this time. Impossibly loud.

I reached and turned it off, still checking the rear-view mirror behind me. His car was closer than it had been before, his headlights not even visible in the mirror. His engine roaring, almost moaning, as if it were a child crying to be fed. Its sound was the only thing I could hear.

Something compelled me to slam on my brakes. To see if I could scare him off by getting closer to my car than he'd have liked to.

His brakes screeched. I could smell burning rubber, even with the windows closed.

The radio came on a third time.

The station changed immediately, pausing for a moment, then changing again. As if he were in the car with me, trying to find a station playing a song he liked. The volume went up and then down.

My hazards turned on. The sound was barely audible over the blaring radio. The newly flashing light illuminating from my dashboard catching my eye.

The car backed off. Its lights turned completely off, coasting down the hill toward the gas station I'd stopped at dozens of times before.

Never did I even think about stopping. The only thought I had was to get home. To keep going. That I'd be safe when I got home.

All I saw behind me was a small faint silhouette of his car. Ten car lengths behind me. No lights on the front of it at all.

Cars driving the other direction began flashing their lights to notify the driver that his lights were off.

The intersection I'd make a right on came up quickly. I made the turn fast, but not fast enough that I had any inclination to lose him. He knew where he was going. He knew where I was going.

As I made the left onto Prouty, he was right on my tail again. His lights were back to flashing. High beams, them low beams, then off, then repeating.

"What do you want?" I yelled. I pleaded to him, knowing full well he couldn't hear me. "What did I do?"

I flew over the hill I remember intentionally speeding over many nights, trying to "get air" (they put a stop sign there in when I was about 20. Too many car accidents from kids trying to do the same). I rounded the bend and hit the stretch of road with no houses and no street lights.

He sped up and pulled up next to me. His headlights were now halfway up the rear door, gaining ground, inch by inch.

The engine roared louder.

My radio flipped back on, the stations scrambling to static, to noise, growing louder and louder.

I focused all of my effort on ignoring it, ignoring the sounds his car was making, ignoring everything but the long, dark road ahead of me. I fought with all my might to keep the car straight, wondering if he was going to ram me off the road into a tree.

He gained on me, pulling up just about next to my door. Just a few more inches and I could see his face. Just a bit more and I'd know for sure it was him. I'd know that my suspicions were right, and it was the jean jacket man.

Without hitting my brakes, I lifted my foot off the gas pedal, just enough to slow my car's acceleration. I was going sixty. He must have been going just a touch faster. As soon as I let up on the gas, he was next to me.

Part of me expected to look over and see him staring at me. Part of me expected he'd try to throw something at me or shoot me. Part of me didn't want to look.

I forced myself to turn to my left and look. As we sped down the dark stretch of road, all I could see was his face, lit by the lights from the dashboard of his car. He didn't look at me. He didn't turn to acknowledge that he was next to me. He did not show me he saw me.

But I saw him. I made out every feature of his face in a way I'd never seen before. The lights from his dashboard lighting him from a lower angle, shining up from below, highlighting every creepy, marked feature of his face.

He suddenly sped ahead of me. I looked down and saw I was slowing down and was going just over fifty. He must have sped up to seventy or more, because he got quite a way ahead of me in the blink of an eye. I thought, just for a second, of making a left on any of the side streets along the road, or pulling into someone's driveway and knocking on their door. Just for a moment, I thought of ways to get to relative safety.

The radio still loudly switching stations. His brake lights were the only thing I could see ahead of me.

Suddenly, his car stopped in the middle of the road. He pulled to his right, blocking off both lanes. There was no way I could get around him. There was nowhere for me to go — no roads between me and him. Only one driveway I could pull into.

He got out and stood by the back of his car. By the rear bumper, the only place I could even try to get around him. His eyes glowing in the night, reflecting my headlights. Like a wild animal in the woods when someone is approaching with a flashlight. He was unfazed. He stood his ground until I got within a couple of car distances.

Thirty. Twenty. Ten. I slowed to a crawl, wondering what his next move was.

The radio flipped off.

My engine was now the only sound, as his was off.

All four windows in my car went down simultaneously.

I turned the wheel hard to the left, to avoid hitting him or the car.

"Put it back," I heard him say. Not a yell. Not even a regular speaking voice. But a whisper. A whisper so loud that I could hear it from the ten feet away that he stood from my car. A whisper so potent that it echoed through the night air, flying in through the windows that I knew he'd somehow opened.

My foot instinctively jammed on the brakes, and the car came to a halt just inches from his hip.

He stood just outside my passenger window. His waist in clear view. But he did not bend down. He didn't pop his head into my window and reiterate his message to me. He did not try to do anything at that point. He just stood there for a few seconds.

Time seemed to stand still. The seconds felt like eons. The air was still and quiet. The houses to my left were all dark. The road was empty, except for us.

"Two days," he said. "Two days and I take someone else."

"I don't know what you want me to put back," I pleaded. "What did I take of yours?"

"Two days," he said again, walking back toward the driver's side of his car.

"What did I take, you motherfucker?!" I yelled, opening my door.

"You took something that doesn't belong to you," he said, opening his door to get in.

"What did I take of yours?"

"Not mine," he said. "But not yours. Two days."

"What happens in two days?" I said as he sat down in the car.

"Someone else joins Brian and Kevin," he replied as he shut his door.

"I don't know what I took," I yelled as he started driving away.

"I don't know what I took," I said to myself, over and over again.

I had two days to figure it out, or he was going to take someone else. Maybe Wendy. Maybe Jen. Maybe Dan. Maybe me. Maybe all of us. I didn't know, but I knew I had to figure it out.

Twenty-Eight

My car was still in park and I was still shaking as I saw his tail lights make a left at the end of the road. My hands trembled in fear and anxiety from what had just happened. My eyes were growing cloudy, making it hard to see anything, even the dashboard right in front of me. Was I crying? No, surely I couldn't be. My vision was just weird because I was so scared of what I'd just gone through.

Instinct took over, and I made the right down Pringle before I even knew what else had happened. I drove there in complete silence, except for the occasional ticking of my turn signal. The radio stayed off. The windows stayed up. The rest of the drive was completely normal.

No memories exist of parking or going into the house. I don't remember anything before getting into Dan's room and closing the door behind me.

It was after ten, but it wasn't uncommon for me to show up at their house after work. Most nights, if she knew I was coming, Kathy would have told Charlie to make some extra dinner for me, just in case, and left it on the counter for me to find. I don't remember if that happened that night. I don't recall even walking through the kitchen. I was just there, in Dan's room, shutting the door.

He sat up on his bed and pulled his headphones off, putting his Discman down next to him.

"Hey," he said, "I didn't know you were coming over."

I just launched right into everything that had happened. I told him everything. I felt myself shaking the entire time. It was the first time I'd felt really, truly scared of jean jacket guy. He'd been tormenting us for weeks now, but that drive home was the first time I felt like I was in actual danger.

It was also the first time Dan had no words. He looked at me blankly, trying to find the right thing to say. I could see him churning over what words to choose. I could feel him trying to make sense of it all.

"I," he said, "I uh. Well. I."

"I know," I said. "I didn't know what to say, either."

"I saw him tonight, too," he said.

"Wait? When?"

"About two hours ago. I went to take the trash out and he was across the street, but Steve's mailbox."

"What did he say? What did he do? I need to know everything."

"Nothing. He just stood there. He didn't say or do anything," Dan said.

"He didn't approach you or talk to you?"

"Not at first, no. He just stood there. Then, when I was about to head back into the house, he stepped toward me. I froze and couldn't move. I just waited for him to make another move, but he didn't. He just took another half step, so his feet were together. Almost military-like, like he was standing at attention. I could feel him staring at me from across the street. He stood motionless for a few seconds, then I saw the street light reflect off of his teeth as he opened his mouth."

"What did he say?"

"He took a second to speak, but then he said 'your girlfriend is next'."

"Fuck," I said. "Fuck. He told me I had two days to put it back. That's all he kept telling me."

"What does he want you to put back?"

"I don't know," I said. "I tried to get him to tell me and he wouldn't. He just kept repeating himself."

"I didn't tell Jen yet," Dan said. "I don't know if her knowing will do any good or not."

"You can't tell her," I said. "She'll freak out."

"I know. That's why I haven't said anything."

"And obviously we can't tell Wendy. She can't keep a secret to save her life."

"I know that, too. And she's so scared she'll immediately go tell Jen."

"Fuck," I said again. I didn't know what else to say.

"Let's go," he said.

"Go where?"

"Dudley. Maybe if we go there again, we'll remember what we took that he's so pissed off about. Did he say anything else?"

"No. Just that whatever we took isn't ours. He said it wasn't his, but it's also not ours."

Normally we'd have snuck out of the house that late, but Kathy was just getting home from work and we passed her on our way out.

"We're just running to the store. Be back in a bit," I told her. The lies just flowed out of my mouth like a seasoned professional.

"Be safe, boys." She'd always called us boys, even well into adulthood.

"We will, Mom," Dan said, shutting the passenger door quietly, to not wake Rachel, sleeping just inside.

I waved as we backed out to the driveway. She'd gotten halfway up the stairs before she was out of sight.

The lights were all on at Brian's house when we drove by. I could sense they were worried about him, but neither Dan nor I had anything to offer to help them at that point, so we kept our distance. I knew that we had no way of bringing Brian back, or Kevin, for that matter. So we kept focusing on what would help.

"Did you go there without me?" Dan asked.

"When?"

"Any time. At any point?"

I ran back through my memory and Dan was there every time I'd gone to Dudley Road. Every footstep around the woods, every minute sneaking around the buildings, he was there. There'd never been a time where I went there without him.

"No," I said. "I never went without you."

"You're sure? Did you take anything? Did I take anything?"

We got to Billerica faster than I think we ever had before. We parked where we'd always parked and jumped out of my car, making our way down the long driveway, through the fence that never seemed to be closed, and along the side of the main brick building. Everything seemed much more peaceful than the last time we walked along that same route. Every cricket chirping seemed happy, every bird flapping along the tree line seemed to be content. We were the only two people who felt afraid. After what I'd been through earlier, I think I had every right to be scared of jean jacket man.

The door that had previously been lit by the single light above it was dark. Had I not remembered the door was there, I don't think either of us would have seen it. We'd have just kept walking along, hiding in the woods, away from the building and its windows. The night sky was just as dark as last time we'd walked along there, but the lack of that single light bulb made the whole side of the building feel like an abyss.

Neither Dan nor I spoke as we walked toward the back. Our footsteps were the only sound that could be heard besides nature itself. Everything perfectly silent, perfectly perfect.

I stopped for a brief moment, pausing to look at the building to our left. I wanted to stop, to focus on really remembering what we'd taken from here, to use my energy not on staying silent and unseen, but to really remember.

My memories flashed back to the out-building with the funeral cards, the locked door, Kevin disappearing, and Brian vanishing into thin air. I thought about Jen and Wendy both clinging to me for dear life as we walked through the woods. Had we unknowingly picked something up from the trail? Did we take anything from the ruins of the house we'd found before?

"I just figured it out," Dan said.

"What? Tell me." I whispered.

He pointed to the un-lit door. The only exit on the side of the building we were on. "That," he said.

"The door?"

"No. You took the heart thing by it."

"What heart thing?" I didn't remember what he was talking about.

"The stick thing," he said. "It's in your trunk, remember?"

"That can't be it," I deflected. "It's just some sticks."

"Did you take anything else?" he asked.

"No, I don't think so."

"Then that's it," he said. "That's the thing we have to put back."

"Are you shitting me? The stupid twigs?"

"It seems stupid, but obvious, now that I think about it."

Nothing about that made sense in my head. Why would a couple of sticks taped together matter to anyone? Who cared about that?

"I'll go get it," I said. "You want to stay here?"

"Fuck no," he said. "I'm coming with you."

I nodded, and he followed me back out to the car, parked where we'd left it, nothing out of the ordinary.

The trunk opened with a flook sound and there it was, the heart, sitting in my trunk.

I reached in and grabbed it, holding it up to the trunk's tiny light to illuminate it, looking the heart over to make sure it wasn't damaged.

A voice let out a scream from deep within the woods. A scream that sounded like it was in pain, but happy at the same time.

Dan and I looked at each other, but didn't speak. It seemed we'd found the thing we needed to return, so I closed the trunk and followed Dan back down the driveway toward the door.

The crunching of leaves under my feet felt louder than before. It felt, somehow, angry. As if I was crushing tiny parts of Mother Nature herself and she was mad at me for it.

As usual, we stuck to the tree line, just out of sight, should anyone come walking around the corner in our direction. Dan was a few paces in front of me.

When we arrived at the door, the light above it was on. From as far away as I was, I couldn't tell for sure, but it seemed like the door was open, just a tiny bit. As if someone had just come out or gone back in and the slow moving hydraulic hinge was taking its time closing.

It stopped me in my tracks, but Dan didn't notice. He kept moving forward, close enough to be next to the door. He was fifteen feet ahead of me by the time he stopped.

Another, louder scream came from the woods, echoing around us.

When he looked back at me, I motioned with my head toward the door. It still seemed like it was ajar from where I was.

He shrugged and pointed, as if to tell me to go put the heart sticks back.

I never told him, but I'm telling you now. That was the most scared I've ever been in my life. Everything up to that moment had paled in comparison to running the fifty feet from the shelter of the woods to that door to put the heart back. I ran faster than I thought was possible, not caring about any potential noise I would make along the way. I ran like my life depended on it, which, for all I knew, could have been true. I ran like doing it quicker would make it less scary.

When I finally got over to the door, I saw it was open. I could see a dark hallway inside, but couldn't make anything else out. For a moment, I thought about ignoring my tremendous fear and going in. I thought about quietly opening the door the rest of the way and having a look around. That only lasted a brief second before I came to my senses.

I popped the heart back on the ground, roughly where it was when I took it. Just to the right of the door, on its side.

Nothing happened right away. One last scream that seemed to die out before it matured. No flashes of light. No jean jacket man showing up to thank me or kill me or take me or anything. Just more silence, more crickets chirping. An owl hooted from over near Dan. I don't know why I was surprised that nothing happened, but nothing did. I had given little thought to what should happen when we returned the thing that the jean jacket man had wanted put back, but as I stood there looking across the field at Dan, barely visible in the woods, I thought about it. Would this bring our friends back? Would this stop him from taking Jen? Would this be the end of it all?

And then, in a quick flash of light, I saw movement in the woods, to my right, behind Dan. Just a flicker of something reflecting the moon at just the right angle. For just a split second, I saw something move. I raised my hand and pointed in the direction, trying to get Dan to turn, look, be aware, and be cautious. I tried flailing my arms to get him to look at what I'd just seen. But he didn't notice me. He didn't seem to notice anything.

I blinked a few times, hard, to get my eyes to clear up. Maybe I had been seeing things. Maybe all the adrenaline from the run from the woods to the door was causing me to imagine things that weren't there. Maybe it was the energy of the building causing me to hallucinate. Maybe it was in my head.

I blinked twice more and then focused my eyes on Dan, who seemed to be frozen. He seemed to be stuck in some sort of deep thought. He wasn't moving. He wasn't acknowledging me, trying to get his attention. He just stood there.

"Dan!" I yelled out as quietly as I could, but still loud enough that he should have heard me.

And then I saw it. I saw him. Jean jacket man. He was standing right next to Dan, about a foot or so behind him, likely just out of Dan's peripheral vision.

"Dan!" I yelled as loud as I could. "Run!"

But it was too late. Jean jacket man's arms flew up from his side and covered Dan's mouth. Dan's eyes bulged from his head, seemingly from surprise, though not from pain. His arms flew up to fight his way free, but it was a futile effort. Jean jacket man was too strong.

Without taking my eyes off the two of them, I started sprinting back across the field, toward the woods. The fifty feet that had previously taken just a few seconds to cross seemed to take an eternity on the run back. My feet felt heavy. The grass under them felt like mud. I felt like no matter how hard I tried, I couldn't move fast enough.

Every step I took to get closer felt like it was too slow. It felt like there was no point. I felt hopeless.

I watched Dan slowly disappear back into the darkness of the woods, a hand still over his mouth, an arm also wrapped around his torso, holding his arms down, lifting him slightly off the ground. I watched the two of them melt into thin air, sliding back into the darkness and sanctity of the woods.

By the time I got to the tree line and my eyes adjusted, they were gone. No sign of either of them. No sign of a struggle. No sign that Dan had even been there just a few seconds ago.

I huffed and puffed, trying to catch my breath from my run. My capillaries starving for oxygen, my eyes killing me from the transition to darkness. I fell to my knees and grabbed handfuls of dirt, grass, and pine needles. I grasped at anything.

Then I heard him whisper.

It sent shivers throughout my entire body.

"Put it back."

I turned and looked back at the door, at the heart. The door opened slowly. When it got halfway open, I saw the silhouette of a man standing inside it. A man much larger than jean jacket man. A man that I could feel was not a friend.

The door slammed shut, its sound echoing throughout the woods, my body, and everything I could feel at that moment. It slammed so hard that the light above it went out and the heart fell over.

"Put it back," I heard, faintly, from the other side of the door.

I mustered up the courage and crept back to see if I could open the door, talk to the person inside, and reason with him.

It took a minute for my eyes to adjust before I tried to open the door, but it wouldn't budge. It was locked, and it was solid.

I bent over to pick the heart up and put it back against the building.

It had broken. It was no longer two sticks bent together to form a heart. It was a handful of sticks, laying on the ground, shards of what they used to be.

And then, I knew, despite putting the only thing I'd taken — we'd taken — back, jean jacket man was still not satisfied. And, despite telling Dan that Jen would be taken next, he'd taken Dan. Like Brian and Kevin before him, he'd been taken right before my eyes.

Twenty-Nine

I FELL TO THE ground, shaking from head to toe. I could feel my heartbeat in my fingertips and the balls of my feet pulsing, throbbing, fueled with anxiety and adrenaline.

My fists balled themselves up and starting hitting the ground on both sides of me, unknowingly smashing the remnants of the heart to my right. The light above the door remained dark, the sounds of nature quieting around me. Silence soaking in from all directions.

The thumping of my heart was all I could hear, all I could feel. Nothing else existed but me. No one else around. No other sounds. No thoughts, but fear rummaged through my head. I felt nothing but emotional pain.

No plan I made in my head made sense. No amount of willpower made me get up and go running through the woods to find Dan. None of my thoughts were clear, except for one. I needed to get to Wendy and Jen. I needed to protect them, somehow, from whatever was next.

There was more time than I should admit between when I had that clear thought and when I got up off the ground. There were more tears than there should have been, too. My three closest friends were gone now, leaving just me and the girls. I still did not know where they were, or if they were safe. I had no idea why the jean jacket man took Dan, even after I'd put the heart back. And who the fuck was the guy in the doorway? Why was this all happening to me?

Then, as I rose to my knees, another thought occurred to me. Had this happened before? To someone else? Had jean jacket man done this all before?

Everything I knew about him seemed supernatural. He seemed like he had abilities beyond human. He definitely could do things humans shouldn't be able to do.

As I walked back toward my car, alone, something else popped into my head. He drove a car. Could a supernatural being drive a car?

None of it made sense.

Once I'd gotten in my car, I took a few moments to calm myself, wipe the tears from my eyes and really focus on what I would do next.

I left Dudley Road that night, terrified, anxious, and worried.

As I drove up Middlesex Turnpike toward Burlington, so many other thoughts creeped into my head.

Why had the heart being returned not put a stop to everything?

Why did the other man slam the door so hard that the heart broke?

Were my friends still alive? Had he killed them?

If they were still alive, were they hurt?

Who was that other man?

I'd pulled onto Jen's road without even noticing, instinctively parking under the same tree I always did. Normally, I'd just honk, Dan would come out and I'd take him home from there. But, that night, I got out of the car and knocked on the door.

"Hey," Jen said. "Where's Dan?"

"I need you to just trust me and come with me. Maybe bring some clothes with you."

"Why? Where are we going?"

"Just trust me, please," I begged.

"Where's Dan?"

"We need to go, please."

She asked me where Dan was three more times before retreating into her house to grab a bag with some clothes in it.

"We're going to Wendy's next," I said. "Jean jacket man took Dan."

"What?!" she screamed.

"I'll fill you in when we get there."

Wendy's house was on a quiet street and I felt like we'd be safer there than at Jen's house. And I knew my mother wouldn't love the idea of two girls coming over and maybe not leaving for a couple of days. I knew Wendy's dad saw me as harmless, so I didn't think he'd mind if we all crashed in their living room for a few days while we figured everything out.

"Hi," Jen said, walking into the house without knocking.

Wendy was sitting in the living room by herself. I'd only been in her house once before, when a bunch of us came over to watch Scream when it came out on VHS. I didn't see her family anywhere, so immediately told them had happened.

I covered every detail. I talked about why we went there, how we'd figured out what thing I needed to put back, how it didn't work, and last, about who the new mystery guy was standing inside the doorway that night.

Jen cried. Wendy swore a lot.

The two of them lectured me on how what we'd done was stupid, on how immature and irresponsible we were for opening whatever can of worms we'd opened, how we were so childish.

They were right. I don't know what we had done to cause all of that to happen, but it was stupid that we did. We were never the type to leave well enough alone, but this was all a new level of crazy, even for us.

"Listen, I know," I said. "I know what we've done here is moronic, but that doesn't change the fact that my friends — our friends — are missing, and we need to figure out how to get them back."

"Where do we even start?" Jen asked.

"I don't know," I said. "But I know that I need to stay here with you two for as long as I can to make sure you're both safe and unharmed."

I hadn't previously thought about it, but the concept of Wendy and Jen being taken meant there was no one else. Had he taken them, who would he move onto next? My family? Co-workers? Other friends? Me? Who would be next? Or would there be someone next?

"Is he taking people who were there?" I asked aloud, but mostly to myself.

"What do you mean?" Wendy asked.

"Well, Kevin, Brian, and Dan were all there with me at some point. Either in the woods or in the building, right?"

They both nodded.

"And you were both there, too, at some point. Which is why he said he'd take you."

"When did he say he was going to take us?" Wendy asked, perhaps forgetting I'd told her about that already.

"Irrelevant, he said it. My point is, if he takes the two of you, would he take anyone else? I've not brought anyone else there."

"Did you tell anyone else about it?" Jen asked.

"No. Nobody."

"So what if he takes us? Then he takes you, and that's it?"

I thought about it for a solid minute before answering.

"I don't think he'll take me," I said.

"Why the fuck not?" Jen asked.

"Think about it," I said. "If he takes me, there's no one left."

"Isn't that kind of the point?" Wendy asked, motioning with her hands toward Jen and I.

"I don't think it is," I said. "If he takes the three of us, there's no one left to do whatever else he wants from us, from me."

"Right, and?" Wendy asked.

"Right, and there's more to this. He took Dan after I put the heart back where I took it from."

"I see what you're saying," Jen said. "If he takes you, you're not here to torture anymore."

"Exactly," I said.

"I get it," Jen said. "But what else does he want?"

"I don't know. I thought it was the heart, but that wasn't it."

"And who's the new guy? Jean jacket man's boss? His friend? An accomplice?"

"I don't know that, either," I said. "Maybe I was seeing things. Maybe there wasn't someone there."

"But you said the door closed and locked, right?" Wendy asked.

"It did. I know that for sure."

"This is terrifying," Wendy said, reminding us she was scared.

"I know. I'm sorry."

I spent the next half an hour reminding them how sorry I was. How sad that the whole thing made me. As they each fell asleep, I covered them with a blanket, propping their heads up on the pillows, one on each couch. They looked peaceful as they slept.

As tired as I was, my fear outweighed the exhaustion. I stayed awake all night, until morning, where I had breakfast with her dad before he went off to work. I told him how we'd watched a scary movie and they were too scared for me to leave. He didn't seem to mind.

Most of the night, I'd stayed awake, trying to figure out answers to my questions. Trying to figure out why things were happening, who those people were, all of it. But I couldn't figure anything out. I was, for lack of a better word, stuck.

Thirty

"HELLO?" I SAID, FUMBLING for the receiver, as it rang me awake.

"Oh, hi, honey." It was Kathy, Dan's mother. She always called everyone "honey".

Immediate panic set in. I knew she was probably calling to see where Dan was.

"Hi, Mrs. P.," I offered as little as I could.

"Is Danny with you? He didn't come home last night."

My teenage ability to tell a convincing lie kicked in. "Yeah, he's here. Didn't he leave you a note when we left last night?"

"A note? I didn't see one," she said.

"Maybe he forgot. I told him to leave one on the counter."

"I'll look again. Can I talk to him?"

"Talk to him?" I gulped.

"Yes, I need to tell him something."

"Oh. He's... he's in the bathroom. What is it? I can tell him."

"He's always pooping, isn't he?" She giggled like a little girl. "Just tell him to not forget he has a doctor's appointment tomorrow at four."

"Okay, I'll tell him when he gets out of the bathroom."

I didn't know how much more I could lie to her. Kathy knew me well enough to see through my bullshit most of the time, but I'd hoped I was pulling this off. A small spec of happiness made me glad that Brian and Kevin's mothers hadn't checked in on where their kids were.

"Ok, honey. Thank you. Are you boys coming over to the house later?"

"I'm not sure yet. I think I might have to work today and Dan mentioned wanting to go to Kevin's."

The lies kept flowing like water from an open spigot.

"Well, have him call me later, please."

"You got it. Bye." I said, hanging up, not realizing how I'd just suspiciously cut the conversation off.

I decided to preemptively get out ahead of the ball and called Kevin's house.

I knew no one would be home. His mom worked during the day, which benefited me.

The answering machine picked up, and I left a message.

"Hey Kev, it's Mike. Just wanted to confirm I was picking you up at 11 for band practice. Don't forget to tell your mom you're staying over this weekend so we can practice."

We got away with a lot under the guise of band practice. Most of our parents let us pretend we had a shot of becoming famous musicians and supported us practicing whenever we want.

Then, when she got home from work, Kevin's mother would hear the message, assume Kevin heard it when he woke up, and then got picked up and was at my house. If nothing else, it bought me a few days of Kevin being at my house where his mother wouldn't be calling around looking for him.

A similar message got left on the answering machine at Brian's house. Thankfully, no one answered there, either.

In hindsight, I'm not sure if either message even got listened to, or if I'd just thought I was being clever.

In either case, neither of their mothers called around looking for them after that day. My plan to trick them into thinking everyone was at my house must have worked.

Thirty-One

"No matter what happens, we stay close to one another," I told the girls, as we got out of the car in the turnaround spot, in broad daylight.

"Why are we doing this?" Wendy asked. "This is insane."

"I'm not one to be scared, but I agree with Wen, this time," Jen added.

"It's the middle of the day, we have plenty of time before the sun goes down," I said, as if it being light out would make trekking through the woods any less scary, given all that had happened to us.

"What are we looking for?" Wendy asked. I could tell she was more scared than she had been before.

"We're going back to that old house we found."

"What? Why?" Jen asked.

"We need to see if there's something out there that's missing. Jean jacket guy keeps telling me to put something back, but we put back the only thing we took. What if something else is missing, and we didn't take it? What if he's confused and thinks we took something we didn't?"

"What do you mean?" Jen asked, clutching Wendy's hand as we started up the trail. They were both behind me, but just barely.

"Well, we can't be the only people fucking around out here, can we?"

"Oh my God!" Wendy yelped. "You're right! Someone else took something and we're getting blamed for it."

"I'm getting blamed for it," I corrected her. "Just me."

"But what about Dan and Kevin and Brian?" Jen asked.

"They're just bait. No, not bait. What's the word I want? They're a tool for him to get what he wants. A means to an end."

"Jesus, Mike, don't say end," Wendy said. Their voices were getting more faint, so I stopped to look behind me. They were five or ten feet back. I stopped to wait for them to catch up. It's likely I'd been walking faster, subconsciously, to get out there, look around, and get out of there.

"I'm scared," Wendy said.

"Me fucking too," Jen added.

"That makes three of us," I said. "I'm scared shitless here."

We got to the location where we could see the house off to the left and veered off the trail, pushing past the brush we'd gone by before, making our way over to the remnants of that house.

The girls were both behind me by a step or two, the sound of leaves crunching under each step the only sound I could hear.

"It's quiet," I said. "I don't hear any animals or anything."

It was eerie and struck me as odd. We should have heard something.

The house was a handful of feet ahead of us, getting closer and closer. For some reason, I expected something to happen. Someone to jump out. A voice to yell. Anything.

But nothing did. I could feel the silence throughout my entire being.

Everything was as I'd left it the last time I was there. A few fallen branches, and some leaves were added to the otherwise undisturbed house.

"Everything seems the same," I said, kicking some leaves out of frustration.

I kneeled in the corner, looking to see if anything seemed out of place, or had been taken since the last time I was there. But nothing jumped out at me. Everything seemed the same.

"Are you done now?" Wendy asked. "Can we go?"

"Yes, this was a waste of time," I said. "Let's go."

I led them both out of the house, heading back to the trail. I'd made it just one step before I heard a branch snap to my right. Before I saw him, I made it a second step.

"Oh. Hello there," he said, as if we'd startled him.

He was older, I'd guess fifties, tall, with very broad shoulders. He had the same salt and pepper hair that I'd known my dad to have my entire life. His face was clean-shaven. He wore a plaid shirt — red and blue with black — and blue jean overalls. His boots were covered in mud.

"Sorry," I said, instinctively, as if we were in the wrong.

"For what?" he replied immediately.

"I," I muttered, "I don't know. I'm just sorry."

"Nothin' to be sorry about," he said. I detected an accent not from New England, but couldn't place it. It sounded southern, but not too far south.

"We were just leaving," Jen said.

"Don't rush on my account," he said.

"No rush. We're just heading home." I tried to sound confident, but I was scared.

"Find anything good in there?" he said, pointing to the house a few feet behind us.

"Just junk," I said, reaching back to grab Wendy's hand. Her other hand was holding on to Jen already.

"Okay then," he said. "Have a great day."

He stepped to his left, moving out of our way, as if he were granting us permission to go. We were off the trail, but I still felt the need to take a very wide berth from him, as if he was going to reach out and grab us or something.

As we passed, I made sure we were out of his reach.

We got a few steps toward the trail before he spoke again.

"Weren't you here last night?" he said, pointing toward me.

"Last night? No," I said.

"Sure you were. I saw you over by the building. You were with your friend."

"I don't think so. I wasn't here last night," I said, turning my back to him.

"You sure? You look awful familiar," he said.

It must have been him in the doorway. It hit me like a bully in a pillow fight with a pillowcase with a shampoo bottle in the bottom. It was suddenly so obvious. The dark shadow standing in the door right before Dan was taken. It was him.

"I'm sure. We've gotta go, mister," I said, not able to think of any other words. I pulled Wendy's hand and thus Jen in tow, and made sure they were walking directly next to me as we scurried back to the trail.

"Okay then. Bye." I heard him say, just about out of earshot.

Thirty-Two

"WHO THE HELL WAS that?" Wendy asked, once in the safety of my car.

"That was the guy in the nunnery last night. I'm ninety-nine percent positive."

"The guy who saw Dan get taken?" Jen asked.

"Yes. I'm pretty sure he saw that whole thing."

"But he seemed so..." Wendy said.

"So human?" I asked. "So does jean jacket guy, right?"

"There's definitely something not right about both of them," Jen said.

"I agree."

The car jumped to life as I backed up, doing a three-point turn to get us out of the turnaround spot. I made a right, opting to head the nicer way out of Dudley Road, by the farms and horses.

"Why was he there?" Wendy asked.

"Not sure," I said. "But he seems to have no problem being out in the daytime. Jean jacket guy seems to prefer night."

"I'm so worried about Dan," Jen said. She paused for a moment and added, "Kevin and Brian, too."

"I get it," I said. "Dan is your priority. It's okay to be worried about him."

"We have to get him back. All of them," Jen said.

"We will. I'll figure it out," I said.

We drove in silence back to Wendy's house. I'm not sure if none of us had anything to say or if we were just scared. My thoughts continued to race, trying to figure out what thing was missing, and most importantly, who the new guy was.

Thirty-Three

Wendy's dad pulled into the driveway right before us, barely getting out of his car before I parked.

"Hey Dad," Wendy said, running up to him. She hugged him.

"Hey Mr. T," I said, getting out of the car, waiting for Jen to get out. She took a beat to herself in the back seat. I assumed she was trying to regain her composure.

"What have you all been up to?" he asked.

"Just the usual," Wendy said. "Can we go inside?"

He unlocked the door, and the girls followed him in. Jen held the screen door open for me.

"I'll be back in a while," I said. "Stay here. Stay inside. Don't let Wendy's dad go too far out of your sight. Stay close to him."

She came back outside and got closer to me.

"Where are you going?"

"I don't know. But I need to figure some stuff out," I said. "I'll be back in a couple of hours to check on you. I promise."

She stepped down the two remaining stairs and hugged me, a tight hug that felt almost suffocating. It stuck out in my mind because Jen wasn't a hugger. Come to think of it, I don't remember more than a handful of times that she'd ever hugged me.

"Be careful. Please."

"I will."

I left there, truly not knowing where I was going or what I was going to do. But I felt obligated to do something, to go somewhere.

As if, perhaps, my not being there would lead jean jacket man and his friend somewhere else, so the girls would be safe.

Thirty-Four

THE ENGINE WAS STILL warm; the radio had yet to turn itself off, but I'd been sitting in the car for almost half an hour. My gut brought me back to the woods, back to Dudley Road. I'd been over the woods way too many times. I'd thoroughly looked through that old house just a couple of hours before. I'd called out to my friends until my throat hurt. But something brought me back there. Some unnatural force told me I needed to be there, to do something, to look at something, to talk to someone or something.

Without getting out of the car, I looked around at my surroundings. Through the windshield, through all four windows, through the back window. I caught my reflection in the rear-view mirror at one point and wondered if, maybe, I was the problem. Was I the thing that needed to be put back?

The surrounding woods seemed to be illuminated by something extra. Sunlight shined in from every direction, showing me every leaf, every stick, every branch, every drop of dew on every blade of grass. Everything was still, nothing rustled, no breeze blew through the trees.

I told myself I was taking a lay of the land, but honestly, I was just terrified of getting out of the car. Some amount of hope was left in me, telling me I'd be able to accomplish something by being back there again so soon. But no amount of hope outweighed the fear I had filling my entire body.

From head to toe, I felt scared. The dread of leaving my car and going back out into the woods was almost too much to handle.

The radio shut itself off. I'd been sitting for a full half an hour. The sudden silence made everything more real.

As I finally opened the door and stepped out, I heard Dan's voice. Quiet, very quiet, but I was certain it was him.

"Mike," he said. "Mike, you have to do what they say."

He repeated himself over and over again. It's all I could hear.

Intently listening didn't help. I couldn't tell where it was coming from. Was his voice even real? Or was I hearing it in my head? Was it subconscious?

"Dan?" I called out, then again in another direction. "Dan, talk to me."

But nothing.

He'd repeated what he said five times, and that was it.

I waited. I hoped he'd say something else and I could narrow down where his voice was coming from.

Then I heard Brian's voice.

"Do what they say," Brian said.

He repeated it four more times.

Then, Kevin's voice.

"Do it," he said.

He said it four more times.

The world started spinning around me. My vision became blurry and my senses seemed to be numb. Nothing made sense. Where were my friends?

"You should listen to them," a voice came from behind me.

I spun around, barely past the front bumper of my car, and there he was, again.

"You came back," he said.

I was stunned by what was happening and couldn't speak.

He stood closer to me than I'd have liked. Close enough that I could smell his aftershave, a dense-smelling musk I've never forgotten.

As he took a step closer, the dirt beneath his boot made a crunching noise.

"Where are your ladies?" he asked.

"They're," I stumbled backward, falling, "they're not here."

I didn't want to say they were at home. I didn't want to give anyone an idea of where they could be at that moment.

"Oh, that's too bad," he said.

I took another step backward.

"Who are you?" I spat out.

"Me? Oh, don't worry about that," he said. "I'm just a guy in the woods right now."

The way he said 'right now' made it seem like there was more to it than that, as if he had some plan I wasn't aware of.

"Why are you bothering me?"

"Bothering you? Don't be silly," he said. "I'm just trying to help you."

"Help me? Help me how?"

"I know," he said.

"You know what?"

"I know everything."

"Everything?"

"Yes," he said. "Everything."

"Who is he?"

"He being whom?"

"The man with the jean jacket who keeps taking my friends?"

He laughed.

"We're being honest now, are we?" he asked.

"What do you mean?"

"You haven't been honest with anyone outside of your group of friends for quite some time now, have you?"

"I'm trying to protect people," I yelled, a little louder than I intended to.

"I can respect that. I'm just trying to help everyone get back to being happy. And get back what's rightfully theirs."

"So who is he?"

"Joseph? He's mostly harmless."

"Harmless?! He took my friends!"

"I know he has. And I will scold him for that, I assure you. But he's felt like he has no other options."

"Are they?" I had intended to ask if they were okay or unharmed, but he interrupted me.

"Are they dead? Heavens no."

"They're not?"

"No. Joseph won't hurt them unless he has to. And he hasn't had to, yet."

His use of 'yet' sent shivers up my body.

"What does he want?"

"What do you think he wants?" he asked, stepping closer.

"I don't know. I've been trying to figure it out."

"And what did you discover?"

"I don't know. I thought it was the heart stick thing I took, but that doesn't seem to be it."

"Isn't it?" he asked, smiling.

"Is it? I put it back last night. If not that, then what is it?"

He seemed to pause for a moment, contemplating how I'd said I put the heart stick thing back the night before.

"I could tell you, but what's the point in doing that? It'll be better if you figure it out on your own."

"I've tried," I begged. "I've tried to figure it out, and I just don't know."

"You better hope Joseph doesn't find your girls. I know he's been rearing to take them next."

"Why not me? Why take my friends and not just take me?" I asked, ready to give up.

"You're not what he needs right now. You're the only one who can put it back."

"You know so much, but you won't fucking tell me what it is!"

"Now, now, Michael, let's calm down."

He knew my name. Not only that, but he used my full name, as if he were one of my parents punishing me.

"I can't fix what I don't know. I can't undo something if I don't know what it is."

"You have another day to figure it out."

"What happens in another day?"

"Joseph goes on the hunt."

"You have to stop him. He's insane."

"Oh," he said. "I know he is. But I can't control him. Not anymore. Not now."

"So what am I supposed to do? What do I do now? Where do I go?"

"You're close to figuring it out. So, were it me, I'd suggest keeping at it."

"You're no goddamn help!" I yelled, pushing past him to get in my car.

"Be careful, son," he said. "Time isn't the only thing that's running out. So is our patience."

'Our'. He said 'our'.

As I slammed my car door shut, I realized that perhaps Joseph and overalls man were working together. Maybe they were a team, and this guy was playing good cop to Joseph's bad cop.

He stood there in front of my car as I backed away. He waved, a gentle, friendly wave that felt so ominous I just about puked.

I flipped him off as I sped away, heading out toward the safe end of the street.

"What the actual fuck?" I said out loud. "Now there's two crazy people to deal with."

A tiny fragment of relief flew through my mind. My friends were alive. I had no idea where they were or what was happening to them still. But at least, now, I knew they were alive.

Although nothing good had come of my returning to Dudley Road, I learned who the jean jacket guy was. Not that it helped me any, but now I knew he had a name. Should I head to the library to try to look up someone named Joseph from the area? Should I keep trying to figure out what the thing was that I needed to put back?

I did none of those things. I did, however, pull over to the side of the road, once I'd cleared the woods, and stopped the car. I sat there for a few moments, watching two horses run around in their pen. I watched them frolic and play and enjoy their lives. I watched them, jealous of how little care they had about anything other than themselves. I watched them, knowing I had no idea what I was going to do, which frustrated me beyond belief.

I sat in complete silence, except for the sound of the horses' occasional neighing and the sound of their hooves galloping. My body sat idle while my brain raced. I sat, wondering what my next steps would be and if I should tell the girls about my second encounter with overalls man.

I'd laid my head in my hands for a moment or two before the radio turned on and startled me.

As it tended to do, on its own, it changed stations before settling on white noise. The volume began to increase, louder and louder. I tried turning it off, but it wouldn't go off. The sound of static filled the car and slowly grew to a volume so loud that my ears hurt.

It wouldn't turn off, so I was left with no other choice but to turn the car off.

Thirty-Five

ALL NIGHT, I TOSSED and turned, flipped and flopped. I pushed my blanket off and pulled it back on. Over and over.

Every noise I heard was terrifying. Every sound the house made or a tree branch creaking outside my window caused my eyes to pop open, darting around my room, looking for answers, trying to find out what it was.

It was one of the worst night's sleep in my life, even before I'd fallen asleep.

The last glance at the clock on my headboard showed 2:35 am, before I remember my eyes closing for more than a handful of seconds.

I don't know how long I was asleep for, but I was woken up in a way I'd never forget.

Footsteps coming up the stairs, loud, thumping, determined.

I sat up immediately, turning to look at the clock. 3:51 am. No one should be walking around the house at that hour. Maybe my sister was coming home from a late night out? Maybe her best friend Allyson had a fight with her parents and was coming to crash on my sister's floor?

No. Neither of them would thud up the stairs so loudly. They both would at least try to be quiet. My sister knew better, and Allyson was too nice to wake my mother or me up in the morning.

More thuds. More thumping. I counted six after I'd sat up. If I had heard the very first step, whoever it was would be halfway up the stairs. If I hadn't woken up right away, they could be at the top in the blink of an eye.

Seven.

Thud.

Thump.

Eight.

Thump.

Nine.

Whoever was coming up the stairs was getting close to the top. Although my door was closed and locked — something I constantly did in my late teens, for "privacy" — I didn't feel safe.

Ten.

Thud. Thud.

They stopped.

The double thud was both feet hitting the landing individually.

They were at the top.

Silence came from the hallway, but I knew that just eight feet down the hallway from my door was someone. Someone who didn't care about who they woke up climbing the stairs.

If it were my sister, she'd have made her way into her room by now and I'd have heard the door close.

If it were Allyson, she'd have already taken a step or two toward my sister's room, maybe stopping to knock on my door to see if I was awake, something she'd done more times than I could count.

But I heard nothing, except the rustling of leaves in the field behind our house.

For a moment, I contemplated calling out. Quietly yelling through the door, hoping a friendly voice would answer.

For an even shorter moment, I knew who it was, and why he was in my house.

Thump.

A single step. He'd taken a step away from the stairs. Did he know which room I was in?

So many things flashed before my eyes. My mom was in her room. My sister was probably in her room.

Fuck.

Was he there for me or one of them?

I had to get up. I knew I had to go see what was happening.

Just as I swung my feet around and off the edge of the bed, I heard him come closer.

Thump. Thump. Thump.

My doorknob jiggled, slowly and quietly.

It wasn't my sister.

And my mom knew better than to come into my room at almost four in the morning.

It was him. Or the other him. Or, worse, them.

The knob jiggled harder, louder.

"It's," I said, "it's locked."

No response from the other side.

My eyes started adjusting while I contemplated getting up and opening the door. I didn't think whoever it was would leave on their own.

"Open it," a quiet voice said from the other side. I recognized it as Joseph's voice.

"I can't," I said to myself, but loud enough for him to hear me.

"You can. You will. You must."

It took more effort than it should have to force myself to stand. I knew it was him from his voice, but I didn't know why he was there or why he was there at four in the morning.

I'd normally have no problem maneuvering around my room in the dark, but that time, I fumbled.

The doorknob didn't seem to be where it was supposed to be. I stood there, in the pitch black, fumbling for it, reaching for where I knew it should be, sliding my hand up and down along the door, along the wall to its left.

I finally gave up and found the light switch, which turned on the overhead light.

It was blinding.

He was in my room not even a second after I'd opened the door. He closed it behind himself and re-locked it.

Now we were in my room, together, alone, and I felt so unsafe. I felt so exposed.

"I don't think you understand the severity of the situation you're in," he said, getting right in my face.

"Listen, Joseph," I said. "I do get it. But I've asked you a number of times to tell me what thing I took you need me to return. And you won't tell me."

"Don't think because you know my name that you have a leg to stand on," he said.

What the fuck did that even mean?

"You have twelve hours left or I take Wendy and Jen."

"I can't tell you any more times. I don't know what the thing is. The only thing I took was the heart and I've returned that."

He scoffed and snarled a bit.

"You have twelve hours to figure it out."

He got very close to my face, our noses virtually touching. I could taste his breath. Even at four in the morning, it was worse than mine.

"If you've thought all this time that I'm the bad guy, you're wrong. I'm not even remotely as terrible as he is."

He must have been talking about overalls man.

"I do what he tells me to, because I'm afraid of him, too."

"What?"

"I've taken your friends because he's told me to," he said. "Not because I want to."

"Are they okay?"

He didn't answer right away.

"Are they okay?" I asked again.

"They are. For now. But he says things are going to get worse for you if you don't put it back. Jen is next. Tonight."

He took a step back, turning away from me. He reached for the light switch, putting his other hand on the doorknob before turning the light off.

"Twelve hours," he said, flipping the switch. "Twelve."

I had to squint to see anything once the light went out. I didn't see him leave my room, but I heard the door shut and then him thumping down the stairs.

No other sounds once he'd gotten downstairs. No sound of him leaving through a door. No sound of him doing anything else down there. He just got to the bottom of the stairs and seemingly disappeared.

"Mom?" I called out. "Mom?"

I must have not been loud enough for her to have heard me.

Part Two

Thirty-Six

I MUST HAVE FALLEN back asleep at some point, because the next thing I remembered was waking up in a cold sweat. My pillowcase, sheets, and blankets were soaked through and I felt the cold puddle of sweat under the small of my back before I'd sat up.

There must have been some small part of me that was convinced it was a dream. Some small iota of my being that felt like what had happened couldn't have possibly been real. I rubbed my sleepy eyes, and saw the clock on my side table. It read 8:59am.

As my vision started clearing, I noticed a ray of sun fluttering through the shade covering the window on the back side of our house, allowing a small bit of light to hit just right on my desk. Part of me felt like it was some sort of sign, like I needed to jump up and run over to my desk to find a clue illuminated by the ray of sun.

But I knew better. My life wasn't a movie. It wasn't a book. It was real life and life didn't work like that. Not in the real world.

I stretched my back, twisting left to right, trying to shake the proverbial cobwebs from my head. My eyes opening and closing as I crossed paths with the sun again and again.

"Just about seven hours left," I mumbled.

I had just seven hours before Joseph would take Jen, and possibly Wendy.

Still, I had no idea what I needed to return to Joseph, or the other guy was. And, from what I'd seen the last couple of nights, they were offering conflicting opinions about who was in control.

The last time I'd run into the "guy in the woods", he'd told me Joseph was rearing to take the girls. He'd alluded to Joseph being the one in control of things. But just last night, Joseph lead me to believe the opposite. He told me that he'd only taken my friends because he was told to. He'd indicated that the other guy made him do what he'd been doing, a mastermind behind it all.

The voices of my friends were still fresh in my mind, loudly whispering to me in hushed voices as I sat in my car the last time I'd gone to Dudley Road.

Nothing ever changed when I went back there, whether with a friend, a group of friends, or by myself. All I'd been able to do was walk around, looking for answers I'd never find.

So why did I feel compelled to go there again, right then? To jump out of bed, dry myself off, get dressed and drive there?

Why did I feel like it was the only thing I could do?

And so I went. I made no plan. I made no list of things to do, to look for. I just got up, toweled myself off with what I'm sure wasn't a clean towel, and headed out after getting dressed.

It was just after 9:30 by the time I'd crossed over to Dudley Road, quickly passing the main building, the security building, and the driveway on my right. I'd opted to just keep driving that time, to get to the turnaround spot and park there. Then I'd put together my plan. Then I'd figure out what to do and how to save Jen.

No strange noises greeted me as I got out of the car. Nothing happened with the car itself. No loud music began playing on its own. I didn't hear the voices of my friends calling out to me from the woods, or perhaps even in my head. No screams from deep in the woods. No cries for help.

For just a moment, I stood in the silence. The only sounds anywhere were those of nature, and the occasional neighing from a horse at one farm on the other side of the street. It almost, even for just a minute or two, felt blissful.

Standing just to the left of my car, I paused longer, thinking partially aloud and partially to myself about what to do.

"All of our focus has been over here and the buildings," I said out loud. "Everything we've done and looked at has been on this side of the street."

The field across the way seemed so barren as I'd turned to look. From the distance I was, I couldn't see anything remarkable over there. Just waist high grass and the occasional horse's head bobbing up and down, eating. I could only see the animals through the grass from their shoulders up.

Despite my complete and absolute fear of getting inundated by ticks — a fear that still lives to this day — I crossed the street and trudged my way into the waist high grass.

Regret washed over me, practically instantly. I could just feel them crawling up my ankles, skipping my socks and finding a nice chunk of skin to dig into. That immediate feeling of bugs crawling all over me hit me. But I trudged forward.

I'd gone in about twenty feet before I stopped and got my bearings.

Behind me, across the street, was my car. Alone in the turnaround spot.

In front of me, fields are far as the eye could see.

To my left, an old barn house on its last legs.

Slightly in front of me and off to the left was where the horses were. From that distance, I could see the fence preventing them from running off into the woods, reclaiming their freedom.

To my right, more fields. Empty of anything I could make out, though in the far distance, I could see the backs of some houses we'd seen when we drove out of Dudley Road the safe way.

Just to the right of the horse pens, kind of off center in front of me, I saw the top of what looked like an outhouse. From its roof, a shiny chimney rose about four, maybe five feet up into the air. From what I could tell, nothing was coming out of the chimney.

"That's odd," I said to myself. "Why would an outhouse have a chimney?"

After taking a few steps forward, I paused and then thought, "why would there even be an outhouse out here in the middle of this field?" It felt too modern to fit in with the dilapidated farm to my left.

Curiosity took over, so I proceeded toward the outhouse. I trudged through the grass, hoping to not be covered in insects by the time it cleared up. Hoping that whatever the outhouse was would mean something, or at least give me some sort of clue toward what was happening.

As I got closer, I realized I was slightly wrong about the building. Although small, it wasn't an outhouse. Once I'd gotten within ten feet of it, the grass around me had all been matted down, some of it appeared to be mowed by a primitive lawn mower, allowing me to see the building more clearly.

In front of me stood a building around eight feet wide and six feet deep. It looked brand new. Yellow shingles covered it on all sides. The chimney I'd seen from a distance was stainless steel and no signs of rust showed anywhere on it.

On the side of the building, facing away from the road, was a door. The entire door was frosted glass. It was nearly welcoming. The doorknob and lock both looked new, as well. Shiny brushed nickel with no signs of having been out in the weather.

The wall of the building facing the horse pen had a small window in it, around a foot and a half square. The type of small window you'd see in your grandma's bathroom next to the toilet.

The next few minutes were spent looking around in every direction, walking in a small circle, trying to look like I was lost in case anyone noticed me.

Not a single soul in any direction. Not a single sound other than horses, cicadas, and the occasional cricket. For a quick moment, it was so quiet that I could even hear the horse ten feet away from me go to the bathroom.

Against my better judgement, I did the only thing I could think of next. I reached out, grabbed the doorknob, and turned.

The sound of the latch releasing as I turned it to the right startled me. I figured there was no way the door would be unlocked. But it was.

"Do I go in?" I asked myself as I yanked the door open quickly, but quietly.

I stood in the doorway, holding the inside handle, ready to step in and pull it closed behind me. Minutes passed, although time seemed to stand still. My brain was trying to force the rest of my body to do it, to walk inside and see what it was all about.

It felt like an eternity before I stepped inside. Both feet hitting the tiled floor inside, one after another. A shiver flew up my spine as I got my bearings.

Once I'd realized I was exposed from behind, I shut the door, turning the thumb lock to secure myself inside.

In front of me was the only thing in the room, an old metal staircase leading underground. While the building looked brand new, the staircase did not. It looked old and insecure, like a fire escape hanging off an old building.

Despite having plenty of common sense, I walked to the top of the staircase and leaned down, trying to see what else I could see.

From the top, it looked like any other staircase that wrapped around a building, leading either up or down. One of those stairwells where you'd walk around the outside perimeter of the building, but could look down and see the very bottom below you.

Except I couldn't see the bottom. All I could see was a few floors down and then darkness. A couple of floors below me, the light seemed to move around the room, like a single lightbulb hung from the ceiling and someone had pushed it — something out of a cheesy horror movie from the '50s.

"Hello?" I yelled as loudly as I could muster before clearing my throat. "Hello? Is anyone down there?" I yelled again, much louder and clearer.

Seconds passed while I waited for an answer, then minutes. A virtual lifetime while I was terrified.

Was I more scared of the silence or a would be response?

Another few minutes passed. Complete silence. There was no one down there. Or at least no one who wanted to answer me.

My left foot clanged against the base of the railing hard enough to vibrate the entire staircase. It echoed over and over again as the sound made its way down the metal to the bottom. I couldn't see. Although I had intentionally kicked it to test its strength, I think part of me knew I was also testing again to see if anyone was down there.

Another few minutes passed before I took my first steps down.

The shuttering sound of my sneaker thudding on the bare metal echoed, getting louder the farther down I went.

Clang. Clang. Clang. It reverberated.

I'd gotten down to the landing on the floor below me and looked both back up to the surface and down below, to see if I could see anything in what had been darkness from the top.

It was still pitch black down there, but now it was only four floors below me, instead of five.

"I'm coming down," I yelled loudly, making sure my presence was known.

Clang. Clang Clang. My echoed presence continued downward.

The next landing was where the light seemed to move around the room. To my satisfaction, I was right about its cause. From the ceiling hung a single lightbulb with a pull chain. It was, somehow, spinning around in a two-foot arch. Like someone had really grabbed it and whipped it in a circle.

Dizziness hit me pretty quickly as my shadow seemed to fly around the room as I stood under where the lightbulb would have rested, were it not moving about in circles.

"I'm getting closer," I yelled.

Clang. Clang. Clang. Another floor down. Still utter darkness, but now just two floors below me. As I looked up to see how far down I'd gone, I found the small light from the surface was fading. What was once a beacon of hope that I could hold on to, knowing safety was just a few feet away, had now become a tiny glimmer of light. It felt miles away.

Below me, the darkness seemed to get slightly brighter. I couldn't yet tell if I was nearing the bottom, or even how much further down the stairs went.

But I pressed on, calling out before I left that landing, "Still coming down!"

No response, still. No sound at all. The faint sounds I'd previously heard from the surface had completely faded. All I could hear was the sound of my own footsteps as I descended. The sound of my panting filled every landing as I stood still, willing myself to go further down. For a moment, I could hear my blood flowing through my veins. I could even hear my heart beating for a quick second.

Clang. Clang. Clang. I descended again; the echos getting shorter, but louder.

Wanting not to delay things any further, I didn't stop on the next landing. It could have been because it was pitch black. Above and below me yielding the same thing; total blackness.

I forced myself to keep going, telling myself I wouldn't stop until I got to the bottom.

It was three more floors before I ran out of stairs.

Nothing around me, anywhere. I couldn't feel any of the walls, or even find any railing at the bottom of the stairs. The stairs just stopped suddenly. There was nowhere left to go.

I felt around, trying to find anything. A switch, a bulb, a door, anything.

When I finally found the doorknob a few feet away from the bottom step, I'd hoped more than anything else in my life until that point that it would open.

As it slid open, I had to step back to allow it to finish sliding. It was a massive door and must have weighed a ton. I felt like I was pushing an old bank vault door to the side.

Nothing could have prepared me for what I saw once my eyes adjusted.

Thirty-Seven

IT FELT LIKE I'D stood there in that open doorway for months — my body, mostly in shock, refusing to move from the spot where I stood. My legs not listening to my brain, not moving, not even flinching. I stood in awe for so long that I felt myself gasp to catch my breath. I'd stood still for so long that I didn't even realize I'd stopped breathing.

Before me stood the largest single room I'd ever seen. A single bare lightbulb hung from a plug every few feet down the wall on my right. They went so far I couldn't even see the end. Light after light in an endless line, barely lighting up the room in front of me.

To my left, tiny lights ran down the other wall. They were so far away; they were barely visible. So small that they could have been fireflies not far from my face.

It had to have been the length of ten football fields long and maybe five football fields wide.

I saw no structural supports overhead, except for a few large wooden beams that looked ancient. I'd hear them creak every so often, and I'd panic. Every time that noise filled the giant room, I remembered how far underground I was and panicked even more.

The ceiling was easily thirty feet high. Aside from the few beams I saw, there were also some of the largest ceiling fans I'd ever seen, spinning at a rate so slow that I had to wonder if they were making a difference to the temperature in the room.

Toward the center of the room was pure darkness. Not a single drop of light made it from the outer walls toward the center. I couldn't see anything, but I could hear the sounds of boots walking along the concrete floor. One after another, easily a handful of people moving around.

Once I'd taken in the entire room before me, I realized that whoever those people were, they could see me. The door I stood in was wide open, and the light from the staircase must have been shining into the room. Even from the farthest end of the room, surely someone had noticed the door open and the light pouring in. Surely they'd heard the giant door moving.

Slowly, as I regained my composure, I took my first step into the room. Careful to not make any noise, I put my foot down slower and more deliberately than I think I ever had before in my life. I held my breath again while I repeated the process with my left foot. I cringed every time I felt myself make more noise than I meant to, even though the loudest noise I made was exhaling after holding my breath for as long as I could.

Turning to place my back to the expansive room, I fumbled along the backside of the door, looking for a handle or latch to push it closed with. If I were able to open it from the other side, I should have been able to close it from the inside.

The light from the stairwell felt blinding. Every tiny drop of light hit me in the eyes so hard that I felt like I was staring directly into the sun.

I continued to fumble, reaching, prodding, looking, hoping. I wanted to get the door closed as quickly as I could. If no one had noticed me open it and stand there for as long as I did, I better get it closed before they noticed.

Every inch of the back of the door had my fingerprints all over it. But no way to close it.

Having moved out of the doorway over to the side, I felt confident that no one could see me. The light from the stairwell was likely just a drop in a giant bucket to them. I fumbled with the backside of the door, wondering why I could not close it.

I bent down, feeling along the bottom edge of the door, hoping there was a footplate or something I could find, but not see.

The cold steel felt so foreign to me. It felt ancient, like it'd been there since the dawn of man. I felt its rivets where the pieces of steel were joined. Smooth, but clearly defined. The steel plates felt to be around two square feet.

Nothing. No handle or foot hold of any kind along the bottom.

When I'd felt I was in the center of the massive door, I reached all the way out to my right and my left, at the same time. From behind, I'm sure I looked like Christ on the cross. I waved my arms up and down, as if I was trying to make some sort of snow angel out of steel. I flapped and flailed, trying my best to find anything.

My arms, on each side, were both a couple of feet short of the edges of the door.

Then it hit me. Reach up.

I threw my arms up above my head and felt it immediately. A handle. An arm, of sorts. Easily two feet above my head. Right in the middle of the door.

I wrapped my right hand around it, barely able to get my fist around the round pipe. I slide my hand from left to right and felt the hinge toward the left.

The sound it made when I yanked on it had me practically in tears. I knew, with no fraction of a doubt, that everyone in that room heard it, no matter how far away they were.

It clanged as it hit the bottom of its arc. A loud and desperate noise that echoed in my head. I still occasionally hear that sound at night, all these years later.

It was all I could do but to continue with the motion it was making and hope it would close and I could duck off into the darkness, where no one could see me.

Every muscle in my body ached as I pulled the lever to its lowest spot, yanking the door to my left. I trembled as I pulled. I gasped, virtually silently, as I finally got the door to move. Despite its size, it made no noise while it slid along its track. As I inched it closer and closer to being closed, I heard nothing after the original clang of pulling the lever down.

Minutes went by as I clung onto the lever as if my life depended on it.

The light from the stairwell grew more and more dim as I got the door closer and closer to being closed.

A sigh of relief escaped my lips as the door finally came to a close.

Despite my best efforts of trying to slow it down, to avoid some sort of major crash when it closed, I couldn't.

But it didn't matter. The door finished closing with the softness of a baby dozing off to sleep. Not a single sound. Not a thud of any kind. A seemingly soft-close door, like most modern kitchens have on their cabinets these days.

Standing there in the darkness, I waited. I hoped for more silence. I hoped that no one was coming my way.

For a moment, the footsteps I'd heard the entire time I was in the room so far had stopped. The only two sounds I could hear were the whirring of the giant ceiling fan closest to me, and the fair hum of a lightbulb just ten feet away from me on the wall.

My eyes adjusted to the darkness. As the minutes passed by, everything came into focus.

The footsteps I'd been hearing belonged to men. Five of them, to be exact. Walking around in the middle of the room, several hundred feet from where I stood.

As my eyes got used to the darkness, they all resumed their activity. It appeared they were walking in circles under a whirring ceiling fan. From my left to my right, then back again.

Upon closer inspection, they were carrying something from a table on the left to a shelf on the right.

From where I stood, I couldn't tell what it was, but I had a feeling I didn't want to know.

The wall behind me where the door was had no lights on it. It ran from the corner I was in all the way to the other wall, in complete darkness. The light bulb to my right was the closest, but still too far away that I didn't feel like it was illuminating me at all.

It turned out to be one of the biggest gambles of my life, but I ran from where I was toward the center of the room.

My footsteps echoed around the empty space. I knew they could hear me, but I felt confident that they couldn't see me. In hindsight, I was being stupid. If I could see them, they could see me.

Fifty paces at top speed. I counted them out in my head, silently, as I ran. It brought me close enough that I could see the men much clearer.

They were huge. All five of them. Easily over six and a half feet. I guessed they were all well over three hundred pounds, too.

As I came to a stop, it still didn't seem like they had noticed me. Even running as fast as I could for just about thirty seconds.

Once I could see them clearly, I saw they were all wearing full length aprons. From their chest to their ankles. They were reflective, as if they were rubber or latex. Three of them appeared to be mostly wet.

The table to the left turned out to be a conveyor belt, with an endless supply of cubes arriving at its end. Large cubes, about two square feet. I couldn't tell what they were made of, but it almost seemed like recycled metal. As if one of those large machines that crushed cars at a junkyard was constantly spitting out cubes of metal onto that convey belt.

I was close enough that I could hear them grunting at one another if one of them got too close. Sort of communicating in some sort of grunting language that only they understood. Otherwise, they were non verbal.

As I took another few steps closer, I stepped on something that made a snapping sound. It echoed over and over again, bouncing off of everything in the entire room.

They didn't stop moving.

I took another step closer.

No reaction.

Another step.

Nothing. Not even a flinch.

Could they not hear me?

I stomped my foot out in front of me as hard as I could, trying to make a loud thud, then waiting for some sort of response. Thinking that one of them would drop their cube and come racing in my direction.

No reaction of any kind.

I stomped both of my feet over and over again.

They kept moving in their circle, shuffling cubes from the belt to the shelf.

I took another handful of steps closer. I was just about close enough that I could reach out and touch one of them.

They didn't stop moving at all.

Finally, I yelled. I let out the loudest yell I could.

"Hey!" was all I could muster.

It reverberated throughout the entire room. My own voice bouncing off the walls, the ceiling, the fans, the lights, the men, the aprons. Everything.

They didn't bat an eye.

They didn't move.

They didn't stop.

They didn't acknowledge my presence.

They didn't do anything.

Thirty-Eight

They couldn't see me. It's been so many years since that moment, but I'll never forget the panic I felt standing there before them, yelling and waving my arms, stomping repeatedly.

For a moment, I wondered if I was even real anymore. Was I imaginary or were they? Was I really in that room? Was any of it actually happening to me?

I got close to one of them, as he kept going on about his business. My face near his, but close to a foot below it. I looked up into his eyes, trying to get a clear glimpse into them. Trying to figure something out. The smell of sulfur and body odor wafted up into my nostrils, stinging the entire way as I exhaled it out of my mouth. The taste of burnt popcorn, somehow, stuck in my mouth for a long time after that first breath in.

Nothing I did stopped them from their routine. Pick up object, walk to other side of room, put the object on shelf.

Over and over they did it while I stood within an arm's reach.

More time passed than I could have accounted for. Not a single change in their routine or behavior or body language.

Minutes felt like they turned to hours; the only thing I noticed was that the shelf was filling up. The supply of cubes never stopped flowing into the hands of the men, but the shelf they were moving the cubes to looked to be just about at capacity.

That's when I heard it.

From the other side of the room, the same thwack sound I'd heard when I closed the door I came in, albeit quieter. I couldn't tell how far away the door was, but it was so empty and quiet that you could hear a proverbial pin drop.

The sound of the lever rising from the bottom of its arc to the top, and then the scraping of the metal door along the concrete floor.

A bit of light came through. From where I stood, it was tiny. Only an inch tall and barely a hair thin.

The scraping continued, and the opening got bigger and bigger.

The thud when the door opened all the way echoed throughout the room, but the men didn't stop working. Whoever opened the door seemed to have been expected.

At first I thought about hiding. Running back to the darkness of the wall by the door, I'd come in. I glanced around to my left and right, then looked behind me. The darkness was so overwhelming that I didn't even know which direction I'd come in from. Had the door that just opened been the one I'd come in through? I'd completely lost my bearings at that point.

I was so focused on the door opening; I hadn't noticed that four of the men had stopped moving. They weren't joining up together, like workers on a smoke break would. They weren't acknowledging each other — or me. They just stopped in their tracks, standing perfectly still. Like a kid's toy robot that suddenly ran out of batteries. Completely motionless except for their eyes blinking. I focused on one of them who was closest to me and watched his chest rise and fall a handful of times before I was convinced they were living beings.

The last of the five men kept walking, with a cube in his hands, passing the others and heading toward the shelf. When he got there, he filled the last open spot. Then he stopped, instantly. Motionless, like his compatriots.

"I'm late," I heard a booming voice call out from the other end of the room.

When I drew my attention over to the door, I could see the tiny silhouette of a man standing in it.

It grew larger as he got closer, until the light from the doorway no longer illuminated him.

"Fuck," I thought. "He's talking to them." And I suddenly was very worried if he could see me, while I knew they couldn't.

"Mmm." One of them was responding to the new man in the room. I couldn't tell who it was, but it seemed like the one who'd just filled the last spot on the shelf.

The click clack of the new man's boots reverberated off the concrete surfaces in the room, getting louder as he approached the motionless group.

When he got to where the men were standing, he spoke again. "I'm so sorry," he said. "Have you been finished long?"

"No," the one of them farthest from the shelf replied. "We just finished."

I don't know why, but I had expected hearing them go differently. In my head, they were cavemen who would communicate solely in grunts or clicks. I didn't expect them to formulate coherent thoughts.

Also, at that moment, I realized they hadn't spoken to each other in at least however long it was that I was standing there watching them. They hadn't communicated with one another at all other than the grunting when someone encroached someone else's personal space.

"Excellent work," the new man said. Now that he was in the light, I could make out his features better. There was nothing remarkable about him. He appeared to be just some regular guy who joined the crowd of giants who were working in this giant empty room, moving cubes of something from a conveyor belt to a shelf. Nothing out of the norm there at all.

Still unsure if he could see me or not, I stomped my feet a few times. As I stomped, I winced a little, fearing the worst.

"You may all finish your day and go home early. We have no more work for you," the new man said.

"Thank you, sir," the man closest to the shelf replied.

The five men began walking off toward the open door at the far end of the room, stopping only to hang up their long aprons on hooks that were conveniently placed on a concrete column they passed.

None of them acknowledged the others. They didn't wish each other well, or say "see you tomorrow" or the like. They just sauntered off the few hundred yards, and were gone out the door.

The new man walked in my direction, the few feet from the shelf, stopping and turning to his right to inspect the conveyor belt. Everything seemed in order, based on his body language.

He turned back and headed to the shelf, still not seeing or engaging with me.

Carefully, he looked over the contents of the shelf, touching a few of the cubes, lifting one off the shelf and spinning it around one hundred and eighty degrees, as if they had placed that cube on the shelf backwards. From where I was standing and watching them move dozens of the cubes, I couldn't tell if there was a front or a back. They just looked like cubes.

"Vincent," he yelled. "This batch is ready to go. Come now."

"Yes, Theodore, I am coming," the voice replied, echoing through the door, preceding a man who came running into the room.

Vincent and Theodore. They seemed very formal.

Vincent arrived at the shelf around a minute after Theodore had called for him. He quickly grabbed a handle I hadn't noticed on the far side of the shelf, stepped down on some sort of lever, and the entire shelf popped up on casters.

As he began wheeling it away, Theodore walked toward the door. I knew that if I didn't make it to the door before they closed it, I could be trapped in the room.

So I sprinted. I ran as fast as possible, huffing and puffing the entire way there. It reminded me how un-athletic I was.

The light began blinding me as I got closer, but I persisted. I squinted and tried to shield my eyes as I arrived at the door. I looked back and saw that Theodore and Vincent were easily two hundred yards back, barely visible in the darkness.

Once I'd crossed through the door, the light became too much, too quickly. I'd been in the dark room for so long that the light made me nauseous. I felt my head spinning and reached for the wall to brace myself as I felt the vomit coming up my throat.

I leaned down and over, stepping back far enough to not puke on my shoes. As my hand slid down the wall to further brace myself, I grazed over a light switch.

My eyes were closed, anticipating the vomit making its way up the rest of my throat, so I didn't notice that the switch had turned off the lights in the room I was just in. I only knew it had happened because I heard Theodore yell. "We're still in here, you dipshits." He was loud, but relatively calm.

The click clack of his boots grew louder and more rapid as he seemed to increase his speed toward the door. It seemed like he was afraid of the dark and wanted to get out of the room.

My hearing faded out temporarily as my senses protected themselves while the vomit escaped my mouth and nose, burning along the way. The taste of burnt popcorn still lingering throughout the entire process.

I tried hard to stop myself, but couldn't. The nausea was too overwhelming and I couldn't fight it back. I felt myself sliding along the wall toward the ground, my hand trying its best to keep me upright.

The thud of my body hitting the floor hurt more than I can put into words. It felt like I was made of concrete and I'd just been dropped off the roof of a building. I hit hard and then couldn't move.

The sound of Theodore's boots grew closer, quicker, as I flickered my eyes open. The light was still too much for me, but I knew I didn't have a choice. I had to get out in front of them wherever they were going and whatever they were doing.

All I knew was that I didn't want to be there to find out.

Pushing myself up to my knees at first, then to my feet, I tried to look down the hallway ahead of me. I saw, through the blurriness of my vision clearing up, a long, stark white hallway. Nothing but lightbulbs swinging from the ceiling, still moving from where one of the men who'd previously left down that hallway had bumped into it, causing it to cast light and shadows on the walls on either side of the hallway.

As I found my balance, Theodore exited the room behind me. I knew he didn't see me in the darkness. I was, for whatever reason, invisible to him and the other men in the room, even when not under the cover of darkness.

"Assholes," he shouted down the hallway at no one, as he flicked the light switch back on. He was just a couple of feet away from me. Looming over me, looking down the hallway, still unable to see me in plain sight. But they were gone.

Wherever they'd gone off to — their homes? — they were no longer in earshot or in my direct line of sight.

Theodore turned back and went through the door, presumably waiting for Vincent and the shelf of cubes.

My head began clearing up. Enough so that I felt comfortable walking down the hallway to see where it lead. As I took my first few steps, I noticed they weren't echoing. And, as I thought about it more, my run from the conveyor belt to the door made no noise, either. I ran silently, despite not trying to do so.

I stumbled at first, but once I got my feet under me, I was able to get down the hallway fairly quickly. It seemed long from the end I was at, but in reality, it wasn't. I'd guess around a hundred feet, give or take ten.

At the far end was an elevator. Its doors were white, like the rest of the hallway. It blended in so well that I hadn't even noticed it from the other end.

To the left of the call switch was a small square device. Its original color of gray started to wear through the layer of white paint covering the buttons that looked to have been pressed the most frequent.

The only button to call the elevator was up. I saw no other way out of the hallway — or the underground structure — so I pressed it and waited.

An approaching elevator is an unmistakable sound, one that seemed louder than usual, given how quiet it was down there. From that distance, I could barely hear Vincent and Theodore at the other end of the hallway.

I stood with my back to it, watching to see what happened when the men exited the door at the other end of the hallway.

It chimed as it reached my floor, and I heard the doors open behind me.

"Hello Mike," a familiar voice said.

Thirty-Nine

I KNEW AS SOON as I heard it. My spine immediately tightened, bringing my whole body to a pencil-like, immobile, position. No matter how still I stayed, it was too late. He knew I was there. And, likely, he was there to take me.

"Your time is up," he said, as I slowly forced myself to turn around. "The time is now."

My eyes went blurry, my mind raced. There had to be some other way out of that hallway. There had to be somewhere I could run, somewhere I could escape.

"It's useless," he continued. "Turn around."

My feet rebelled against my brain. My entire body locked up, half turned around, half facing the way I had come. Every fiber of my being told me to run. Every ounce of my body told me to just flee. But I couldn't. Something held me there. Perhaps it was fear. Perhaps it was panic. Most likely it was concern for my friends. For myself.

When the rest of my body caught up with my feet, I was once again looking at the elevator, looking directly into the newly open doors. Directly into overall man's face. But what I hadn't heard the first time, what I hadn't known, was that Joseph was standing next to him. He looked angry. Angrier than I'd ever seen him before.

"Get in, Mike," Joseph commanded.

"I can't," I muttered, cowering like a dog afraid of a thunderstorm.

"You must," Overalls said.

My left foot took the first step, ignoring the commands of my brain to not step forward. Off they went, on their own, tugging the rest of my body behind them. As if I was possessed, out of control of my own muscles and bones.

The elevator chimed suddenly, scaring the shit out of me. Neither overalls nor Joseph blinked an eye as I stepped inside. Joseph's arm was outstretched, holding the doors open, waiting for me to finish clearing the entry.

"I tried to warn you," Joseph said, looking to his right at Overalls, looking for approval. "I told you that you were running out of time."

"I don't know what you psychos want from me," I mustered. "Just tell me and I'll do it! I want my friends back!"

"You should know by now," Overalls said.

"I don't!" I screamed, crossing the threshold of the elevator.

"This elevator brings us back to the surface," Joseph said. "There is no negotiating at this point. I will take Jen. Today. When we leave here."

"Why are you doing this?" I pleaded.

"We've told you. A number of times," Overalls said.

Despite the initial confusion, Overalls was in charge.

My feet were barely both planted in the elevator when the door closed. I did not turn to face the doors like I'd normally have done in an elevator. I locked eyes with each one of them, alternating. I started with Overalls, who looked straight ahead, not meeting my eye line. Joseph did nothing but stare at me.

Overalls reached past my left and pressed the only button on the elevator's panel and the elevator quickly sprang to life, shooting us up to the surface.

Neither man spoke as we rose. They stood stoically. Almost without any emotion at all. I continued to dart my eyes back and forth between them, hoping I'd be able to decipher a thought, or glimpse something that could help me.

Not a single clue. No movement of any kind, other than their blinking. Neither spoke until the elevator slowed to a stop at the top.

"You're running out of friends. Out of options," Overalls said.

"Sir, can I just take them both now?" Joseph asked.

"No," he calmly replied.

"Please," I begged. "Please don't take Jen."

"You knew the rules," Overalls said. "Joseph, go."

The doors to the elevator opened, and Joseph lept out, pushing past me.

"Yes William. I'm on my way. Tick Tock, Mike. Tick Tock."

He was gone before I realized what had happened. The only piece of information I gained from going down that stairwell and into the weird room was that Overalls had a name.

"William?" I said, still looking at him. "Who are you, William?"

"Who I am is unimportant," he replied. "What I want, nay, need, is what's important."

"I've asked you to tell me what it is," I said.

He pushed past me, preventing the doors from closing. As I turned to see where he was going, he stopped. A few feet outside the door of the elevator, by the entrance to the vestibule containing nothing but the elevator. His head tilted slightly to the left, and motioned with his left hand for me to come with him.

While contemplating if I wanted to go, he opened the outer door, letting a rush of fresh air in. It washed over me and felt better than any breeze I'd ever felt before in my life.

"Come," he said, motioning again.

When I got through the outer door, he was ten feet away. Standing in the sun, in the middle of a vast open field, with his hands clasped behind his back, looking up at the sky. It felt, from behind, like he could be smiling. Like he had some great revelation, suddenly, standing out there.

"Mike," he said as I approached on his right, "I understand there's nothing you wouldn't do for your friends."

"That's right," I said.

"This is all very simple," he began. "You see, the item you took from us is very important. It means a lot to us, to me. And we really need you to bring it back."

"Tell me," I interrupted.

"Shush. I'm not done," he said. "Until I became a part of this, I never believed. I never thought any of this was real, that any of this could happen."

"Any of what?" I asked.

"This," he gestured widely with both arms extended. "Here. Dudley Road. I never believed."

"It's just a creepy road," I interjected.

"It's not," he responded. "It's not just a road. It's not just a building. It's more than you can see or understand. It's a special place."

"What is it?" I asked.

"It's a place of pain. A place of difference. A place where your world and our world collide."

"What worlds? What are you talking about?" I asked, confused.

"Do you believe in the supernatural, Mike?" he asked, turning to look directly at me.

"I have no reason to," I said, after thinking a moment.

"You should. You do now," he said. "Where do you think your friends are? Where Joseph took them to?"

"I... I don't know."

"They're in another world."

"Where is that?" I asked.

"The supernatural. Some refer to it as the other side."

"The other side? They're dead?"

"Pish posh," he said with a snap. "We did not kill them. We don't want to kill them. We just need it back."

"I'm willing to give you whatever I took. I gave you what I had," I said, looking him straight in the eye.

"I want your soul," he said, moving closer to my face.

My skin turned white. I felt my body reactively gulp loudly, like a cartoon who knew he was in trouble. I felt my knees buckle and my body retract into itself. I was withering up. I was terrified. I was out of time and out of options.

Neither of us moved or spoke for so long. The animals that had been chirping and fluttering and neighing all stopped. It was the most incredible silence I'd ever heard.

He inched closer to my face, bending down to be on the same plane as me. He was practically touching my nose with his.

"I'm kidding," he said with a slight chuckle. "I'm joking."

"What the fuck is wrong with you?" I yelled, resisting the urge to repeatedly hit his massive face with my hands.

"I know this is all serious," he said, "but I tried to lighten the mood. The reality is, we don't want your soul. Or the souls of your friends. We just want what you took. We want to see it safely returned to us, exactly where you took it from that night."

"Wait," I said. It had suddenly come to me. "Wait a minute!"

"Yes?"

"The heart. It's the heart. It's the only thing I'd taken from the grounds."

"Very well done, Mike," he said, rousing a slow clap which somehow felt judgmental and evil simultaneously.

"So you admit it? It was the heart?"

"The heart was made by Agnes Floris. Have you heard of her?"

"No. Who is she?"

"You've heard the stories about this road? These grounds?"

"I've heard ghost stories. Fabrications of the truth. None of what I heard could be real."

"I'm not sure the specifics of what you've heard. But there is one true story of Dudley Road. Of St. Theresa's. Of these grounds."

My eyes were glued to his, dying of anticipation of finally figuring out what they wanted and what part of the legend I'd heard was true.

He took a step back, turning to face the sun. He was, as I suspected before, smiling up at it. Letting it waft over him. Letting the sun bath into his pores.

"Agnes was a nun back when St. Theresa's was an actual convent and not just a retreat. The building out back, which you found in your snooping, used to be the sleeping quarters for the women. The priest who oversaw the convent slept in the main building near the back. Sister Agnes made the heart you stole from the grounds. It was the last thing she did before the night she went missing."

"Missing?" I asked.

"Part of the story of this place is that a deranged man escaped from a nearby prison. You've heard this part, yes?"

"I have," I said. "The story says that he escaped from a prison, found his way through the woods, and stumbled onto the convent. He found some nuns outside and took one of them."

"That's right," William said. "It was dusk, and the women were leaving the main building to enter their barracks for the evening when he emerged from the woods, still in his orange jumpsuit, screaming at them. He grabbed Agnes and threatened the other four women who were with her. 'Don't you dare fucking scream,' he said. 'I'm not going back there. Not never.' The women ran inside as he took Agnes around the waist and ran off into the darkness. Her screams startled Father Michaels inside the main building. He ran outside, but it was too late. Agnes was gone into the darkness."

"Did they call the police?"

"One woman who had run inside did. Immediately. The police were on scene quickly, with search dogs and flashlights. A few days later, when they still hadn't found her, they put the word out to the town. They asked for volunteers to help find her. To help find him and bring him to justice."

"Did they find her?" I asked.

"For five nights, at the calmest point of the evening, Father Michaels and the women of the convent could hear her screams from the woods. They recognized Agnes' voice yelling for help, calling out their names, begging."

"Oh my," I said, for lack of anything better. Although I knew the story, hearing it from him seemed to make it worse. It felt like he took it personally.

"One the sixth day, they found her. One volunteer who had been searching down the road some found her in a small house off the main road. She was beaten, bloodied, and bruised, chained to the fireplace. 'He'll be back soon,' she said as soon as she saw the volunteer in the doorway. 'Help me'. She begged for help repeatedly as the volunteer called out for others to join him, to try to help break her free from the chains. The blood on the floor seemed inhuman. It was so much that the person who lost it couldn't possibly live long."

"What happened to her?" I asked. The rage and anger started welling up inside me. I could feel it in the pit of my stomach.

"Patience, Mike. Patience," he said. "It took eight men and two women with a crowbar to break the chain free from the mantel. The police and volunteers were so focused on getting her free that they didn't notice the owners of the house, dead, piled one on top of the other, in the far corner of the room. Most of the blood on the floor seemed to have been theirs. Their throats were both slit, ear to ear. When one woman finally noticed, she screamed. Agnes pointed, alerting the others to the bodies, but couldn't speak. 'He'll be back,' she said, almost whispering. 'Let's get her out of here' the officer in charge told the others, as they lifted her onto a stretcher to carry her out. She, thankfully, had no wounds. She was not cut or shot, only beaten about her head and torso."

"They carried her out of there, back down to the main road, some of them hoping to run into the escaped prisoner — now a known murderer — along the way."

"Did they ever find him?" I asked.

"Days later," William said. "Days later, after Agnes was back at the convent, checked out by the doctor, safe in her bed. He'd come back. He wanted her again. That time, the police were waiting outside the main building, lurking in the shadows, and caught him. They arrested him and brought him back to prison."

"Wait," I said. "The house you saw us in a couple of days ago…"

"That's the one," he said. "That's where they found poor, sweet Agnes."

"What happened to it?" I asked.

"Once they removed the bodies of the owners and informed their family what happened there, no one wanted the house. No one took ownership, and it just fell into disrepair, eventually falling into what it is you see today."

"And what happened to Agnes?"

"The sad story, unfortunately, only gets sadder. A few months after she'd returned to the convent, Agnes grew sick. Father Michaels feared it was from the beating she'd taken at the hands of the murderer. He summoned the doctor to come check on her, only to discover that, although she hadn't reported it, he'd raped her. Agnes was not sick, but pregnant. With the murderer's child. "

"Once she knew she was pregnant, she revealed the extent of the torture she'd suffered at his hands. The days of repeated rape. The horror of watching him kill the owners of the house. She recounted it all."

"Oh my god," I added.

"The day after she found out about the child, she disappeared again. She'd run off in the middle of the night, not even leaving a note or telling her best friend where she was going. It wasn't until morning that they realized she was gone. When the other nuns awoke, they assumed she'd gotten up early and gone for a walk, as she often did.

She had. But only for a short walk. She'd walked out of the barracks, around the side of the building, toward the road. She stopped, only for a moment, and placed the heart you've taken by the door. Then, just a short walk away, she hung herself from the oak tree across from the entrance."

"Holy shit," I spat out. "Holy shit, this is all real? No. No way. You're fucking with me."

"No, Mike. I am not. This is, sadly, all too real. So, you see, the heart is important to us here. All of us. It reminds us of Agnes. Of her pains. Of what she went through. It reminds us of how short and fragile life is or can be. It reminds us of the pain we all felt."

I was still reeling from his telling of the story. I was still trying to understand how this had all happened but there was so little record of it, just rumors and myths. It took a few minutes for me to realize.

"But I put it back," I said. "I put it back a few nights ago!"

"You did not," he exclaimed. "Do not lie!"

"I did. I swear. I put it right back outside the door, where I took it. I put it down and ran back to the woods, only to find out Dan had disappeared."

"I recall seeing you that night, through the window of that very door," he said. "I saw you approach the door with the heart and then run away. But when I opened the door moments later, after you'd retreated to the woods, the heart was not there."

"But I put it down!" I yelled.

"I thought you were pulling a fast one on me," he said. "I looked around for a moment, but it was not there."

"But I put it back! I gave it back to you! Give me my friends back."

"Despite what you say," he said, "we have no heart. And, thus, your friends shall remain with us!"

"But I did what you asked," I pleaded. "I brought it back and left it by your door. I saw the door close a minute after I stopped looking for Dan. I knew you'd come out and taken it. I thought you brought it back inside!"

"Unfortunately, no," he said.

"Someone else must have taken it."

"What?" I'd confused him.

"After I put it down, someone else must have been here and run out and taken it, while I was distracted looking for Dan in the woods."

"That seems unlikely," he said.

"Unlikely, yes. But impossible?"

Over and over, I replayed the night Dan went missing in my mind. I factored in what William had told me. I tried to see it from all points of view. Nothing made sense other than another person coming and taking it. Nothing explained how I put it down, walked away. William opened the door not even a minute later, and it wasn't there.

Was it even possible? It would have been so fast. Wouldn't I have heard or seen someone else out in the woods that night? Maybe I was too completely distracted looking for Dan to notice.

"I know what I need to do," I said.

"And that is?"

"I need to find whoever took it and bring it back."

"Tick Tock, Mike. The time is running out. By now, Jen is with the rest of them. Soon, Wendy. Then you. Once you join them, there is no turning back. There is no return." His formal tone had given me the chills.

"I know," I said, trying to sound confident.

"Twenty-four hours," he said. "Then Wendy."

Forty

I RACED TO WENDY'S as fast as I could, surely breaking some laws along the way. Tires screeching as I pulled into her driveway, barely waiting for the car to come to a full stop before jumping out.

My hand hurt from knocking on the door so hard.

Silence from inside.

Again, I knocked. Louder.

Barely audible shuffling came from inside. I somehow knew it was Wendy.

"Hi," she said, opening the door. "What's up?"

"Is Jen with you?" I asked immediately.

"No. I thought she was with you. What's happening?"

She moved herself out of the way of the door and I stepped inside, rushing past her to the couch.

"I think she's gone now, too," I said.

"Gone? You mean with them? Taken?"

"Yes," I said, without making eye contact.

"What the fuck is happening, Mike?"

"I just left there. I found some giant underground structure with all sorts of weird shit happening. I still don't fully understand what I saw down there. But before I could leave unnoticed, William picked me up. He forced me to go with him."

"Where did you go?"

"It's not where I went that's important," I said. "It's what he told me."

She stared in silence as I forced myself to find the right words. I fumbled over everything that popped into my head to say. No way that I could explain things would make much sense, but I knew I had to try.

"You're freaking me out," she said. "Are you going to tell me?"

"I don't know how," I started. "He said I needed to return the heart. That dumb stick thing we took."

"You put it back, didn't you?"

"I swear we did. The night Dan went missing. I put it by the door we took it from. I know I did. I know for sure. But Overalls says I didn't return it, that they don't have it."

"Where did it go if they don't have it and you put it back?" Wendy asked.

"I don't know. I know I put it back. I put it down and ran back to the woods, hoping no one would see me. That's when Dan disappeared. I'm completely certain I left it by the door."

"Do you remember seeing it when you left? Do you remember seeing anyone else there that night?"

"No. Wait. No. I remember running away from the door, trying to find Dan. It was so dark, except for the light above the door."

"Did you tell him that someone else must have taken it?"

"I tried to, but it didn't seem like he cared. He just insisted I had to put it back, or they'd take Jen next."

"Where do they go?" Wendy asked, now sitting across from me, but looking down at the floor.

"I don't know. I'm not sure I want to."

"Do you think..." she paused. "Do you think they're dead?"

"I don't know." I said. "I hope not."

It was all I could think to say. I had no idea where they were or if they were all right. I didn't know why any of it was happening. There had to be some sort of explanation, more so than what they'd told me. There had to be something more than my returning the heart. There had to be more that both they and I were missing.

"Can I rely on you to stay put?" I asked her.

"I called out of work. I'm not going anywhere," she said. "I have no plans to leave this couch unless I'm going to my bed."

"Good. Stay safe. I'm going to go back to the woods and see if anything comes back to me."

Forty-One

As I pulled out of Wendy's driveway, I remember seeing her peer through the window at the front of her house, right by the end of the driveway. The look of worry and terror stuck semi-permanently to her face. A look that seemed to beg for it all to be over, and soon.

My car was on autopilot. I'd driven from Wendy's to the woods, the convent, the nunnery or whatever it was and vice verse so many times that I didn't even have to think about it. My hands just moved. It left my mind free to come up with some sort of solution, or at least an explanation, or where the heart had gone after I'd put it down.

The sun was still high overhead, so I knew I had plenty of time to get there and just sit, thinking. Trying to force myself to remember anything out of the ordinary. Where was this dumb stick thing? Who took it? Why do Joseph and William want it so badly? Who were they?

Once I'd parked under the big oak tree across the street, I shut the car off and turned to my left, peering through the chain-link fence, toward the direction where I knew the door was. That same, single, dimly lit door. The thought briefly crossed my mind: is this the tree she hung herself from?

I reclined my seat back and closed my eyes, hoping something would come to me. That something would bring me back to that night when Dan went missing. Maybe I'd remember seeing something or hearing something. Maybe I could somehow relive that night again, in my head and possibly pull some subconscious memory to light.

Before I knew it, I was waking to hear clanking on my window. My eyes were still groggy and struggling to focus. It was night. And not twilight. Dark. Very dark. It must have been the middle of the night.

I shook my head a few times to shake out the cobwebs. That's when I saw him. A police officer standing on the right side of my car, off the road. Tapping on my passenger window with the butt end of his flashlight.

The ignition chimed as I turned the key over to turn on the electronics to put the window down.

"You can't sleep here," he said as soon as the window was open enough. "Are you okay, son?"

"I know. I'm sorry," I said. "I got tired and pulled over so I wasn't driving drowsy." The lie had just come naturally. There'd been so much of it, it was easy to just roll one off my tongue.

"Are you okay, son?" He repeated. He couldn't have been over twenty-five.

"I'm fine now, thank you. I just needed a brief break."

He turned the flashlight on and looked around inside the car, both front and back.

"Anything illegal in there?" He asked, almost jovially.

"No, sir. Nothing."

"Are you in any trouble?"

You're goddamn right I am, I thought. Not that he could do anything to help me. I shook my head in an affirming way.

"Okay then," he said. "Get on home. It's late."

The clock on the dashboard read 12:21. It was late.

"Yes sir," I said. "Of course," and turned the ignition the rest of the way, while reaching back to grab my seatbelt.

He said something else as I pulled away, but I couldn't quite tell what it was, or maybe I just don't remember all these years later. I just remember looking back and seeing him walking back toward his cruiser.

I'd been asleep for six hours. Six full hours wasted. Completely wasted. And I had nothing to show for it. I had had no dreams about the heart, or any memories pop into my head.

There was only one person, aside from me, who hadn't been taken. Just Wendy, alone at her house, probably terrified out of her mind.

As I drove home, I continued trying to think of what could have happened. Where did the heart go? Did someone come along after I'd left it and take it? Was someone following me — besides Joseph and William — would could be trying to mess with me? Did I have any enemies who would do that to me?

When I pulled into the driveway at home, I'd prepared another lie to tell my mother about where I'd been. But she was, thankfully, asleep, so I didn't need to explain. Just a note written on the counter, as usual:

See you in the morning. Lock up and turn the lights off.

Part Three

Forty-Two

A LOUD BANGING WOKE me up that morning. It sounded like clasps of thunder, echoing through the quiet night. One louder than the one before it. Almost completely deafening, shocking me with every clasp.

As I opened my eyes, I realized I wasn't at home. I wasn't in my bed. I hadn't been asleep at home. I was in my car, parked under the oak tree across the street from the convent.

"What the fuck?" I said quietly to myself.

How was I back there? Had I even left?

The banging got louder and faster, as if a giant robot was running toward me, clanging its enormous feet on the pavement. It shook the car, and, by proxy, me inside of it. I knew if I tried to close my eyes, it wouldn't go away. But I was so scared. It horrified me to know what was happening.

A sudden jolt hit me when the backend of the car seemed to lift off the ground. At first, just a little, but then higher and higher, until I was looking down the hood at the ground in front of me. The rear-view mirror showed nothing except the night sky. The side view mirrors showed just trees. But something — or someone — was definitely back there, lifting the car off the ground.

Before I could control myself, I was screaming. Nonsense words, making no sense, were flowing out of my mouth like the lyrics to my favorite song.

"Fuck you! Fuck you!" I screamed. "Put me the fuck down!"

The windows were all closed, but I knew that whoever was back there could hear me.

The car slammed down onto the pavement. Then up in the air it went again, immediately. Like a kid playing with the lid of their toy box, the car went up and down ten times in rapid succession.

Then, suddenly, it stopped. The sound of immediate silence cut straight through my gut, paralyzing me.

I closed my eyes tightly. Hoping that by the time I opened them, I'd be back home, in bed. That this was all just a bad dream and none of it was real.

My eyelids hurt from squeezing them shut so tightly. My head began to throb from the pressure I'd put on myself. My arms trembling by my side, stuck parallel to the armrest.

The silence seemed to last for minutes. The pure quiet, again, of not a single sound. No nature. No passing cars. No other humans. Not even the faint hum of a television or radio playing in the distance. Total and complete silence.

It felt like a lifetime had gone by before I could open my eyes. And even still, I had to muster up the courage to do it. I had to internalize what was happening and convince myself it was safe to open them.

But it wasn't.

As soon as I did, I saw what was going on.

There, in front of the car, stood Joseph. About ten feet or so from the bumper. For a fleeting moment, I thought of turning the car on and flooring it, trying to run him over, to escape by any means necessary.

A blip of motion caught my eye in the rear-view mirror. As I focused on the reflection, I saw it was William. About equidistant from the back of my car, as Joseph was from the front.

I was — excuse the cliche — surrounded.

I looked forward and backward, waiting for one of them to make a move. For something to happen. I calculated whether I had enough space between the car and Joseph to speed off and flee the scene.

But there wasn't room, nor was there time.

William stepped closer to the car and began banging on the trunk with both fists. Slamming them down, over and over again, surely leaving a set of huge dents back there.

As I focused on him, wondering why he did that, I lost sight of Joseph at the front of the car. He vanished into thin air.

William stopped banging and walked to the front of the car. He stood right where Joseph had previously stood, staring right into my eyes. Completely locked on me.

He opened his mouth to say something, but I couldn't hear him. Or perhaps I couldn't understand what he was saying.

As I sat there, motionless, trying to figure out what was happening, something I couldn't have expected happened.

Joseph came out of the woods and stood next to William. Arm to arm. Shoulder to shoulder. Aside from their weight, they were the same size and lined up in front of me like some sort of a grotesque fence around a yard.

William turned his head to Joseph and briefly said something that I couldn't hear. Just as Joseph nodded, the two linked hands and began to grow.

I shook my head because I couldn't believe it. They were virtually doubled in size before I understood what I was seeing.

Now, the two of them, easily ten feet tall, stood over the car and leaned in.

"We are all powerful," William said. "You must comply."

"You will not survive," Joseph added. "You must comply."

"Holy fuck!" I yelled as I turned the ignition and threw the car into drive, while simultaneously hitting the gas. I steered around the two giants, barely missing the swing of William's enormous hand, blowing right through the stop sign at the end of the road.

The engine cried as I flew around corners and made turns, trying to get as far away from them as I could, still not fully understanding what had just happened.

My heart was racing. My eyes filled with a combination of sweat and tears. My lungs gasping for air, as if I'd just run a mile in gym class.

I pulled off to the right of the road I was on. Just five minutes up the road from the convent. From Dudley Road.

Without even thinking about it, I'd shut the car off and jumped out. I, for some reason, thought I needed to put space between myself and the car, so I ran. I ran without looking at where I was going or what was in front of me. My eyes were stinging from the sweat, doing their best to see in the dark.

It felt like I'd run miles. It felt like I'd run for an hour, as fast as I could, as long as I could, as hard as I could. I felt like I was on the brink of death.

The ground welcomed me as I fell. My body hit hard and quickly hurt in a way I couldn't remember ever feeling before.

My hands brought themselves up to my eyes, with no intervention from my brain. They rubbed and rubbed, trying to clear my vision.

When I could finally see, I realized I was in a cemetery. I didn't recognize exactly where I was, but I recognized the location as just a couple of miles up the road from Dudley Road.

It felt calm. It felt peaceful. As if I was protected in that space. As I sat, arms on my knees, back against a tree, I felt safe. I felt as though, no matter their ill intent, William and Joseph couldn't hurt me where I was. I'd left them, in their giant state, behind, on the road outside the convent. Surely they couldn't have followed me there. They couldn't have gotten there as quickly as I had. And they definitely couldn't touch me in there.

Why did I feel that way? What was it about that cemetery? What was it about where I was at that moment that made me feel so untouchable?

Then I heard it — a faint whisper from nowhere.

"You're not safe anywhere," it said. "Not safe at all. And neither are your friends."

I jumped to my feet and looked around. There was no one.

As I ran through the cemetery to get back to my car, I tripped on a tree root and fell hard on my face. It felt like I'd broken my nose on the ground.

When I came to, I managed to focus my vision on the only thing in front of me. There, staring me in the face, was a tombstone.

A tombstone with my name on it.

A tombstone with my date of death just three days from that night.

It felt like a hallucination. Surely it wasn't real. Surely it was whatever power the two of them had playing a trick on me.

There was no way it was real.

The only thing I knew for certain was that it felt like I had three days left to figure it out, or they would kill me. And probably all of my friends.

Forty-Three

I WOKE UP DRENCHED in sweat, confused about how I'd gotten home. I fumbled for the clock on my nightstand, but the room was too dark and, it was out of reach.

My eyes hurt as I rubbed them, as if I'd rubbed them too hard, too vigorously, or too quickly. It felt like I had punched myself in the face.

After I couldn't find the clock on my nightstand, I decided to stand up and stretch. Perhaps find a towel on the floor I could use to dry off. As I swung my legs around to the side of the bed, there was no drop-off. Where my legs would usually fall to hit the floor, feet landing solidly on my carpet, there wasn't room to fall. Was I on the floor? Had I somehow fallen asleep on the floor instead of my bed?

My hands jutted out in front of me, as if on their own, reaching, trying to find the soft gray carpet of my bedroom floor.

But there was nothing soft, nothing gray, nothing comforting to be found. What my hands felt — though my eyes couldn't see — felt hard and dusty. I knew right then that I wasn't home. I didn't know where I was, but I knew I wasn't home.

"Hello?" I called out. My voice echoed. Then the echo echoed.

"Hello?" I called louder. A louder echo. Then another louder echo. My voice bouncing off what sounded like bare concrete walls.

Dust flew up into my eyes, causing somewhat of a sting. It must have been my yelling that caused a disturbance on the floor where I was sitting.

"Hello?" I yelled a third time.

Nothing.

No echo returned the sound of my voice that time. No echo of the echo. Just quiet.

I reached out in front of me, trying to feel for anything around me. Anything to illuminate the room. To help me find my place, find my way out of the place that I'd woken up.

But I found nothing — air in every direction.

Frantically, I tried to stand up. Since I knew I was on a floor, I pushed myself up to my knees, still unable to see even my hands in front of my face, though I knew they were there.

It was a darkness I'd never experienced before, even in a dark room with window shades drawn. There's always a sliver of light somewhere. There's always some tiny glimmer from something that your eyes adjust to, that you can use to find your way.

There was none of that. No sense of direction. No sense of up or down. Left or right. I simply felt confused.

From my knees, I reached out as far as I could reach. Nothing.

"Hello?" I shouted so loud that my throat burned instantly.

"Hello?" my echo returned.

"Hello?" its echo called back.

The room sounded virtually endless. My calls out into the darkness floated off in some direction I couldn't discern, only to bounce back at me. To hit me in the face with the sound of nothing but myself.

From my knees, I pushed up to my feet, struggling to find my balance in the pitch blackness.

I hit my head so hard on the ceiling it echoed.

The "thwunk" of my echo hit me a moment later.

My back was arched, hunching me over, preventing me from standing up straight. The room must have been just five feet from floor to ceiling.

And still darker than I'd ever seen before.

I touched my face, then my neck, then my shoulders to make sure I still existed. That I could still feel touch — that I could still feel something.

My own skin felt warm. Not like I had a fever of some kind. Not like I'd slept funny and maybe under too many blankets. More like I'd been sitting next to a camp fire too closely. As if I'd been playing with matches and maybe accidentally touched one to my skin. But instead of it just being on my finger or my hand, it was everywhere.

Since I couldn't stand up anyway, I sat myself back on the ground, roughly where I was when I'd woken up. Although I swore I'd felt a pillow and blanket when I woke, neither was within reach of where I was sitting. Nothing around me other than darkness. No sounds other than my own breathing, and, occasionally, the sound of my heart thumping in my chest.

"Hello?" I tried again.

The sound seemed to die right in front of me. There was no echo. No traveling of my voice. As if I'd spoken directly into a pillow.

"Hello." A voice called back. I could feel the breath on my face. I could sense someone so close to me that it made me physically ill and my body involuntarily jumped backward, slamming into a wall — or some other solid surface — behind me.

No echo from that thud. No sound at all.

Until I heard footsteps. Coming closer to me.

Step.

Step.

I tried to scurry further back, but there was nowhere to go. I reached to my left and right to see if there was an escape along the wall, but there was none.

A third step landed right by my outstretched leg. I felt it brush against my jeans.

"Who are you?" I demanded.

I sensed whoever it was crouching down, closer to me, virtually on top of me.

"I am he," the voice said in a crackly semi-whisper.

"Enough with this bullshit," I yelled as loud as I could. "Who are you? Why am I here?"

"You know why you're here," the voice said back.

"We've been over this," I said. "I don't. I don't know why I'm here or how to make this end."

"Do you like not seeing?" The voice asked in a slightly louder whisper. "Do you enjoy it?"

"The dark doesn't scare me," I said, trying to sound as unafraid and macho as I could.

"Mike," the voice said loudly, "the room you're in is not dark."

I fumbled for anything I could reach to strike that person, to try to make some escape in some way.

All I found was a hand, his hand. Right by my left side, resting on the ground. From it, I could tell the person in front of me was much larger than I was. The fear in my stomach intensified instantly.

"Turn the lights on, you coward," I demanded. "Let me see your face."

"That's the irony," another voice said, coming from my right. I tried to gauge how far away, but I couldn't. "You can't see," it continued. "We've taken your sight from you."

"What?" I yelled. "That's not possible. Turn on the fucking lights!"

The hand I'd discovered on my left a moment ago was suddenly resting firmly on my shoulder, holding me down on the floor and back against the wall.

From a short distance away, I heard the sound of someone snap their fingers. The moment it happened, light came rushing into the room. I instantly threw my hands up in front of my face to block it.

The sudden onslaught of light, coupled with the small room I was sitting in, was more or less too much. I just about passed out from the shock.

"You see," the voice from afar said, "we take, we give, we have the power."

As best I could, I shielded my eyes from the bright lights along the hall in front of me, seemingly the entire width of the room I was in. I'd wanted to be able to adjust fast enough to see the faces that went with the two voices.

These two men before me — one holding me down, just inches from my face, the other just ten feet away — were not Joseph or William. They were not men I'd seen before.

While I was trying to make out their faces and adjust to the light, the man holding me down snapped his fingers and everything immediately went dark.

"As I said," the voice from across the room called out, "we are in control."

I was speechless, cowering, scared for my life.

"You'll return the heart," the man in front of me said. "it's important to us all."

"I told the others! I don't know where it is!"

"You had better find out, then, Mike," the other man said. "You had better find out soon, as well."

Something came over me — to this day I don't know what — but I swung out in front of me. Though I couldn't see, I knew the proximity of the man holding me to my fist, and I did my best to hit him. I swung as hard and straight as I could. But I didn't land. I didn't connect with him at all. I swung and hit the air.

As I tried to regain my composure, assuming they'd be laughing at me, I realized his hand was gone from my shoulder. No one was restraining me against the wall anymore.

"Hello?" I whispered, half expecting someone to hit me and half expecting someone to scream.

My echo called back. Its echo reverberating my desperate cry.

"Goodbye," one of the voices said, seemingly far away.

"Wait, help me!" I called out, only to hear the sound of my echos reverberating through an empty room. No sounds of doors closing as they left. No elevators or stair treads. No sound of any kind. Just complete silence from where they'd been just moments before. They left, somehow, but made no sound while doing so.

I leaned back against the wall, with the knowledge they'd made me blind, wondering how I was going to get out of it.

If they'd done it to me, if they'd terrorized me as much as they had, I'd wondered what they'd already done to my friends. I had no idea if any of them were alive or dead, missing or at their houses with their families, trapped somewhere or lost in the woods. I felt an immediate panic wash over me. A sense of responsibility, not just as the oldest member of our group, but as the one who'd brought us all into the mess in the first place. I felt as though I'd let them all down. As though I had some simple way to end this all and just didn't know it yet.

All I knew, sitting there in pitch black silence, was that I had to find them. I had to save them. I had to figure it all out and get everyone home safely.

The thought of my friends in peril made me nauseous. The vomit made its way up my throat before I could bring my hands to my mouth to stop it. Before I knew it, I was throwing up all over the floor around me, some on myself.

The only thing close to as terrible as throwing up alone in the dark, without the gift of sight, is the sound of it echoing back to you a moment later. Every sloshing sound. Every moment of heaving. Every ounce of everything in your stomach hitting the floor around you, your jeans, your sneakers, your hands. Echoing back at you from the blackness.

Then, a split second later, reliving it all again from your echo's echo.

Forty-Four

I SAT THERE IN the darkness, counting seconds as they passed. I hoped my vision would come back when I'd gotten past a certain point or gotten to a specific number. That, somehow, time was the only barrier between me and being able to see again. Although, somewhere inside, I knew time was the enemy.

As I crossed five hundred, I started to give up hope. I went from counting silently to myself to counting aloud. First, quietly, then louder and louder.

Tens of minutes had passed.

"One thousand, eight hundred sixty-five. One thousand, eight hundred sixty-six. One thousand, eight hundred sixty-nine."

And there it was.

Just over thirty-one minutes, but my vision came back. I could see again.

At first, my eyes throbbed. They burned with the infectious bright lights from in front of me. I blinked as fast as I could, attempting to force my body to regulate and regain control.

It hurt beyond words.

Once I was able to, I stood up, remembering to duck so I didn't hit my head on the short ceiling of the room.

I'd gotten a peek around the room before, when my vision came back temporarily, but I could finally take stock of what was around me.

Before me, a long narrow hallway. On each side were a series of doors. I counted ten on each side of the hall, a handful of feet apart from one other, and staggered so no two doors were across from one another. You could draw a zigzag between them all.

The hallway was maybe fifty feet long and dark, other than the light from one window near the ceiling. A small, round window that looked like a porthole from an old ship. I wasn't out on the water somewhere, was I? On some abandoned boat in a marina?

As I stepped out from where I'd been sitting, I could finally stretch my back and stand upright. I felt — and heard — the bones in my back and my knees crack with relief. I was thankful to see, but just as thankful to stand fully upright.

At the end of the hallway stood a single door facing me. While all the others crossed from my left to right and vice verse, the one solitary door facing me was far at the end of the hallway. My mind thought it was surely the way out of wherever I was.

My first few steps were uneasy. My equilibrium was slightly off, but not that sensation of trying to walk on a boat. The porthole window threw me for a loop, but once I'd started walking, I was convinced I wasn't on water.

As I approached the first door on my left, I took the few steps over to it and jiggled its handle. A modern doorknob, but slightly rusty. Some of the paint flaked off in my hand as I first tugged and then pulled at it. Making sure I wasn't missing something, I pushed and pulled a few times. It seemed to be locked.

The next door on my right seemed light years away. I drug my feet one in front of the other across the hallway to find that it, too, was immovable. Either locked or stuck, or both.

I continued down the hallway, trying door after door, hopelessly getting closer to the sole door facing where I'd been sitting just a short while ago.

Not a single door budged. All twenty that I tried were solid in their frames, immovable by both my will and my feeble attempt at sheer force.

As I left go of the last door handle and turned to my left, eyeing the only door in the hallway I'd yet to try, I heard a faint scratching sound.

It was silent, incredibly faint, and had my sense of hearing not been heightened from having lost my vision for a period, I probably wouldn't have heard it at all.

Tiny scratches. Like a mouse standing on its hind legs, trying to get up a wall or table leg to get those few crumbs you'd missed when you cleaned the dinner table. Just ever so faint, but definitely tiny.

Before grabbing the last door handle, I ventured back toward the other end of the hallway, pausing along the way, trying to identify where the scratching was coming from, listening intently.

As I passed door number seven on my left, the scratching got louder and faster.

A loud thud suddenly quieted the rest of the hallway. THUMP from behind one of the doors.

The scratching stopped immediately. Whatever made that sound was afraid enough to stop.

THUMP another sound came, seemingly from behind a different door.

I braced myself, not knowing what was next or what was happening.

THUMP from yet another door, the sounds getting closer to me, seeming louder as they approached.

THUMP from another door, then immediately from the door diagonally across from it.

THUMP THUMP THUMP in rapid succession. Now, suddenly, the thumping was at the door closest to me.

I jumped back a few steps as another THUMP happened. This time, two thumps came from the same door.

I stood as still as a statue. I made no sound. I intentionally held my breath as long as I could. Whatever was on the other side of that door seemed angry. It seemed large and it seemed like it wanted to get through the door to me.

Through the dimly lit room, now with dust particles flying about, making it more difficult to see, I thought I saw the handle of the door start to move. Just a tiny bit from left to right. As if someone on the other side didn't know it was locked and was trying their luck.

A louder THUMP came from the door closest to me. Followed by another at the door in front of me.

They went back and forth in rapid succession, with increased frequency. What started as a few seconds apart now sounded like a rapid fire machine gun. Back and forth on either side of me, faster and louder.

The door in front of me jerked back and forth violently within the frame.

Someone, or something, wanted out of that doorway and into the room with me.

Still being as quiet as I could, I turned and ran toward the last door I hadn't tried. Hoping it'd allow me out of the room. Hoping that it, for whatever reason, would free me. And also hoping that whatever was on the other side of the door didn't connect back to where the thumping was coming from.

As I approached it, before I could reach out and grab the knob, all the doors behind me began to shake violently, like the first one had. In succession. I could hear the doorknobs twisting and turning. I could sense the anger from the other side of each door. Angry they couldn't get out. Angry they couldn't get to me. Angry they were restrained. I could feel it all.

I closed my eyes and grabbed the final doorknob. It turned, slowly.

As hard as I could, I pushed the big wooden door. It took all of my effort to get it moving from its stationary position.

Dust kicked up all around me, causing me to cough and lose my breath for a moment.

The other side of the door was dark, but quiet. I didn't sense anything scary on the other side, so I pushed myself through it, falling to the ground, facing up back toward the door.

The door closed itself behind me.

The dust settled.

My eyes adjusted to the brightly lit room.

As I came to and turned around, I knew immediately where I was.

I, somehow, was back home in my bedroom. The door that led to the hallway I was just in was, somehow, my bedroom closet.

To be sure — to be safe — I opened it again to see if it led back to where I'd just been.

All I found were my clothes hanging nonchalantly on their hangers.

And as I pushed my way to the back of the closet, to be extra sure there were no trap doors or hidden boogeymen, I saw it. Out of the corner of my eye, hidden behind an old sleeping bag, just barely visible.

The sticks shaped into a heart.

That stick shaped heart that I knew we'd returned to Dudley Road. That I'd personally placed down on the ground, right where I'd taken it from.

That, somehow, ended up back in my bedroom. In my closet. Hidden.

Now that I knew where it was, I knew I had to get it back to them. I knew it had to be returned and that, in return, they'd bring my friends back. They offered me a trade and I could finally accept their terms.

I picked it up, looked it over, made sure it was still intact, and raced out of my bedroom, down the stairs, and out into the driveway.

I immediately noticed Wendy's car parked behind mine, as it had been so many times before.

But there was no one near or in her car that I could see.

I walked up to it to get a closer look. No one.

The hood was cool to the touch. No one had driven it recently.

But if the car was in my driveway, where was Wendy?

Forty-Five

I PUT THE HEART-SHAPED sticks down on the hood and walked around the car, checking all the door handles to see if it was unlocked. To my surprise, the only door that was unlocked was the rear passenger door. The rest were locked.

When I pulled it open, a foul stench hit my nose. To avoid puking in her car, I quickly jumped back and leaned over the row of bushes that lined the sides of my driveway, immediately dry heaving for a solid minute.

The car door, still ajar, seemed to stare at me in my stance of almost-puking. Mocking me. Laughing at me.

"Just let it air out a minute", I thought to myself. "Don't go back over there." And, although I was a good ten feet away, I could still smell it. I could see it escaping into the air. The same way you can see the heat coming off an outdoor grill. Those cartoonish heat waves floating up into nothingness. The stench from the car did the same.

From a safe distance, and once I stopped dry heaving, I straightened myself up and took a step closer to the car. By now, it'd been a few minutes since I first opened the door and the smell waves I'd previously seen seemed to have dissipated.

Slowly, I took another step closer. One by one, until I was standing right by the open door. I placed one hand on the open door and the other one on the roof of the car and slowly leaned in.

The stench was still there, although not as bad as it was at first.

Just the usual things I'd expect in the back of Wendy's car were present. A backpack — clearly still there from the school year — and her purse. Small and blue, with a long strap that'd often criss-cross her body. Nothing out of the norm there.

As best I could, I threw my body across the center console between the two front seats and unlocked the driver's door. I couldn't help but notice that the keys were still in the ignition.

By the time I'd gotten around to the driver's seat, something felt uneasy inside me. Not a sense of fear. Not uneasiness. Not pain or horror. Guilt. What I was feeling, at that moment, was guilt. The guilt of knowing — assuming, at that point, I guess — that Wendy was now gone. With the others. Dead? Maybe. Alive? Hopefully. But somewhere else.

The door creaked loudly as I pulled it open, common to older cars, even back then — a loud pop as it reached its widest open position.

Bending down, I looked in, hoping to see something out of the normal. A sign of struggle. Anything to give me a clue what had happened.

Then, I saw it. Plain as day, right in the cupholder. A piece of paper.

Although folded, at first, I knew it was something. I felt it calling to me. I felt, in my stomach, that the piece of paper was for me.

I quickly grabbed it and stepped back out of the car to catch a breath of fresh air before opening it.

It was folded in quarters, and as soon as I opened the paper fully, I saw it.

The names of my friends. One by one, listed out, separated by half an inch.

First, Brian's name had a single, solid line drawn through it. Mostly straight, with a black pen. From the very edge of the B to a little past the n.

Kevin's name was next to Brian's. His name had a number of lines drawn through it. Not a scribble, but deliberate lines, one on top of one another.

Dan's name completed the top row of three. His name was feverishly scribbled out, his entire name blacked out, as if being crossed out by someone furious.

Below the guys' names and between Brian and Kevin's names was Jen's. Her name scribbled out just as much, if not more, than Dan's.

And, to its right, Wendy's. Scribbled over, crossed out, giant Xs written all over it, and rubbed so hard with a pen that there was a small hole through the paper.

It was obvious that the person doing the name crossing was growing more angry with each name crossed off the list. Angrier — at me — by the day.

My name was at the very bottom edge of the paper, as if added as an afterthought. In very small, deliberate, spaced-out lette rs. M i k e.

I could sense this feeling of time running out.

But, aha, now I knew! I knew I had their stick heart again. Even though I had no idea how it'd gotten from where I'd left it to in my closet, or how it repaired itself from being shattered like it was the last time I saw it. I knew all I had do was return it to them again. Bring them back their stupid heart, still sitting on the hood of Wendy's car in front of me, and I'd get my friends back. Wouldn't I?

Forty-Six

There was enough room between Wendy's car and the garage in front of my car to maneuver my car out of the spot I was parked in. Although I had to do an eight point turn, I was able to get my car out without having to move Wendy's.

The heart sticks riding shotgun next to me as I made a right out of the driveway. For some reason, I felt compelled to buckle it in. Which, in hindsight, was as crazy as this whole thing probably sounds to you.

The drive seemed to take forever and be instantaneous all at once. I couldn't tell you anything about it, even moments after I got there.

I don't know what songs played on the radio, or what the news or weather were. I couldn't tell you how many cars I'd seen on the way, or how many lefts or rights I'd made.

I had just arrived as the sun was setting. The night sky settled in, awaiting the crisp oranges and yellows on the horizon to disappear and for night fully take over.

The car skidded to a halt, directly under the giant oak tree I'd parked under more times than I'd care to count, and after freeing the stick-heart from the seatbelt, I leapt out of the car, quietly closing the door behind myself.

I don't know why, but that night, I felt the need to be more sneaky than usual. As if someone was going to finally see me and call the police.

No cars were coming from either direction, though the lights in the house on the corner were on, so I waited a few minutes before crossing the street to make sure no one was looking out the window.

The night air felt chilling, although it wasn't cold. The weight of it all felt crushing.

When I finally felt it was safe, I sort of ran/hopped across the street, trying to take as few steps as possible with large, stupid, comedic leaps.

As usual, the security gate was open, so I was able to walk right in.

Keeping to the right, as usual, I made my way along the perimeter of the woods, staying in the shadows of the trees as the horizon grew dimmer and dimmer, the night sky's darkness coming fully into control.

Periodically, as I crept, I looked down at the heart. I half expected it to glow, float, or do something mystical or magical.

I almost laughed out loud at myself. What a stupid thing to expect. Even with everything that'd been going on, with everything about that place, the history. Even with all that, I was stupid to expect this pile of ordinary sticks to do something extraordinary. Especially since nothing had happened, the last time I'd returned it.

The night had fully taken over by the time I got to where the door was. Just minutes before, I'd been getting out of my car with the sun just crossing the horizon. And now, there I stood, in the woods, just out of sight of anyone who might look, waiting. I still don't know what I was waiting for. A sign. A noise. A welcome home banner to unfurl above the door. Perhaps the single light above the door to turn itself off.

I waited.

Minutes passed.

I continued to wait.

Nothing happened.

No movement. No sound. There was no motion of any kind.

The moment I lifted my foot to take a step toward the opening separating the tree line from the building, I heard it.

"Hello?"

I put my foot back down and froze, unsure if I should respond.

A moment passed, and the voice repeated, "hello?"

My eyes involuntarily blinked repeatedly, as if I was trying to clear my eye crusties out and re-focus on something in front of me. My head darted left and right, looking for any sign of life around me. I turned my back to the door for a moment, and let my eyes adjust to the dark forest in front of me. With just barely a hint of light from the light above the door shining over my shoulders, I wondered if I'd see anyone or anything out there. Wondering if I'd see the source of the voice I'd just heard, clear as day.

"Hello?" I heard again, most definitely behind me. Calling out from nothing.

I spun around immediately, making no sound of my own.

There was no one.

Nothing disturbed, nothing moved, nothing out of place at all.

"I told you it was nothing," a second voice said.

I'm not sure if it was because of the longer sentence or the words spoken or what it was, but I immediately recognized it. It was Brian's voice.

"I swear I heard a branch snap," the first voice said.

Tears fell from both of my eyes like someone had just turned on the faucet.

It was Dan.

I could hear their entire conversation. The fear in their voices. The uncertainty. I could sense them near me, but couldn't see them anywhere.

The light above the door went off, and I knew it was time to act.

"Guys, I'm coming for you," I said as I leapt from the woods into a full sprint, crossing the span in front of me in just a few seconds.

In one fell motion, I put the heart down by the right of the door — just where I'd picked it up, just where I'd returned it just a few days ago — and backpedaled toward the tree line, making sure the heart was never out of my sight.

When I was safely in the woods again, I heard the faintest of whispers from right beside me. So quiet, yet so loud, sending shivers down my spine in a way I've never since felt.

"Mike? Is that you?" Dan asked.

I could feel him standing next to me. I could sense his body mass. I'd stood next to Dan thousands of times in my life and that moment, right then, felt identical to that.

"It's me," I whispered back.

"Where are you?" I heard Wendy's voice ask.

"Where am I? Where the fuck are you guys? Are Brian and Kevin and Jen there?" I asked, hoping for some answers.

"It's dark," Wendy said. "Everyone is here. Brian and Kevin have been sick for a few days. They can hardly stay awake anymore."

"You have to help us," Jen said.

"I don't know where you are," I said. "But I know you're not here. I'm at the convent. I just put the stupid heart thing back for the second time. I think that's why they've taken you all and put you there. I tried returning it once already, but it somehow found its way back to me. I'm trying, guys, I'm doing my best!"

"I don't know where we are," Dan said, "but it's not right. Something isn't right here."

"Can you see me?" I asked.

"No," Dan replied. "But I felt you earlier. I thought I heard a noise in the darkness and then I just felt you standing there."

"What the fuck!" I exclaimed, a little louder than I'd intended to. "This has to end now, doesn't it? Is anyone hurt?"

"We're not hurt. But every day that goes by, I feel worse and worse," Dan said. "The longer we're here, the harder it is to be awake, like we're running out of energy. It feels like it's been weeks," he said.

That feeling of guilt washed over me again. I felt it settle in the pit of my stomach, hard.

"Should I stay here and wait?" I asked.

"For what?" Jen and Wendy asked, almost simultaneously.

"For them to find the heart? To know they've got it this time?"

"What do you think will happen once they have it?" I heard Dan ask, seemingly further away than he was before.

"I don't know. Fuck. I don't know. But something has to happen, right?"

I was looking for assurance. As if any of them, wherever they were, had the answers.

"Can you see anything?" I asked them.

"It's just woods," Dan said. "Trees and darkness as far we can see. As far as I've been able to walk. Before Jen and Wendy got here, the guys and I had been wandering around the woods, trying to figure out where we were."

"What's different about it?" I asked.

"What do you mean?" Dan replied.

"Is it just woods? Are you actually in the woods?"

"Oh my God," he said sharply. "We are. We're in the woods where you are."

"How do you know?" I asked.

"The sun never comes up here, it's dark all the time. It's like it's always the middle of the night," he began. "So we've been trying to sleep when we can. Just one of us staying awake at a time, to make sure we can wake everyone else up. We are trying to keep ourselves on a regular schedule so we know day from night. But something happened the other night that I just remembered. I'd thought it was a dream, but now I'm certain it wasn't."

"What was it?" I heard Jen ask him.

"A scream."

"A scream?" I asked.

"The scream. That same one we heard out in the woods that one night we were out there. The woman screaming for help."

"You're sure?" I asked.

"Positive," he said. "I'd bet my life on it."

They were there. Somewhere out in the woods. I'd quickly wondered if I'd be able to find them if I went looking.

"It can't be real," I said. "Wherever you are, it's not reality."

"What do you mean?" Wendy asked.

"Dan said it's never day time, right? How could that be real?"

"Oh shit," Dan said. "You're right. Even if it was winter, we'd have some daylight. It wouldn't be this dark all the time."

And that's when it hit me. My friends were being held prisoner in some sort of alternate reality. An alternate reality based on the one that William and Joseph must have created, based on the only thing they knew: the woods around the convent.

"I heard your voice a week ago, Dan," I said. "Was that you?"

"I've been talking out loud here a lot, dude," he said. "What did I say?"

"You said something about me having to do what they tell me to," I said.

"What? No. I don't even know what you're talking about," he said.

"Jean jacket guy."

"Fuck. The weirdo from my backyard?" He asked.

"And all the other weird shit that's been happening? He has a friend, too. A much meaner friend. The friend seems to be in charge of whatever's happening."

"Is this all some fucking joke?" Jen demanded. "Are you guys playing one of your pranks on us?"

"I wish we were," Dan said. "We're not."

As soon as he stopped talking, their voices were gone.

Silence filled the woods again, aside from the casual insect noises and the sound of the trees swaying in the light breeze.

Nothing could have stopped me from noticing the light above the door flicker off and then back on.

I, again, froze. Nothing could have pried my eyes away from that door. Not even God himself could have come down and yanked me away from that spot in the woods, staring directly into the window on the door, waiting to see what would happen.

Minutes passed.

Nothing happened.

More time passed. It seemed like hours.

And then, right as I was about to give up and leave, the door swung open.

Forty-Seven

"WISH ME LUCK," I said aloud, hoping my friends could hear me in their alternate world.

The light flickered ever so slightly — just a tiny, momentary flicker. And I knew in my heart that they did. I knew that they'd heard me.

I mustered up every bit of courage, every ounce of bravery, every morsel of my being and forced myself to step out into the light.

The door, now just forty or so feet in front of me, still stood open. No movement came from inside it. No lights came on other than the one outside, above the door.

I stood motionless. I stood paralyzed with more fear than I'd ever felt before in my lifetime.

I waited.

Although terrified beyond words, I'd hoped that something would happen. I was ready for the entire ordeal to be over.

Seconds felt like hours. Minutes felt like days. But I stood my ground and waited.

Eons of time passed. Proverbial lifetimes.

Somehow, somewhere deep inside of me, I found the courage to speak. To call out.

"Hello?" I yelled, hearing my words bounce off the tall brick wall in front of me and deaden in the forest behind me.

"Hello?" I called again.

The door flew the rest of the way open, changing from its position of half open to fully open, resting against the brick wall on the left side of the door frame.

The light flickered, then went off.

My eyes quickly tried adjusting, focusing on the now pitch black doorway, hoping for someone to emerge, rather than something to emerge.

Just as I began focusing, the light came back on.

In the doorway stood the silhouette of a person. A man, from what I could tell from the shape, height and build. A man who looked to be standing motionless.

"Hello." The silhouette called out to me, stepping forward in the door frame, but not quite yet outside.

"Hello?" I called back.

"I see you've returned the heart," the voice said. "Finally."

"I returned it once already," I said. "I know I did. But it returned to me. It came back to me on its own."

Silence.

"Hello?" I called out again.

The figure took another step forward, standing fully out of the door, directly below the light, which came back on as he stepped below it.

I was too far away to tell who it was. The voice wasn't familiar, and the clothes weren't the normal clothes that either Joseph or William had been wearing.

Fighting against every urge I had, I took five steps forward. I got closer, hoping I could see who it was.

He bent over to his left and reached down to pick up the heart. He seemed to clutch it to his chest, holding onto it as if he never wanted to let it go again.

My body took over, ignoring the impulse control from my brain, and took another five steps forward.

Now just fifteen feet or so in front of me, the man turned back my way and stepped out one more step.

It was then that I realized the man who was in front of me was me.

Somehow, I was standing face-to-face with myself. Wearing the same clothes I had on, the same Red Sox hat I'd not taken off since the season ended. It was a carbon copy of me. Identical.

"What the fuck?" I yelled. "How is this possible?"

"Anything is possible," the clone replied.

"But why? How?"

"When you mess with things you don't understand, sometimes unexplainable things happen," he said.

"I gave you the stupid heart back. Bring back my friends!" I demanded.

"Not just yet," he said.

Although it was me, it was my face and clothes and hat, the voice was not mine.

"This is a trick, isn't it?" I asked. "You're not real."

"Or maybe you're not real," it replied quickly, sarcastically.

I shut my eyes tight, hoping that when I'd open them again, things would be back to normal. That something would make more sense than it was.

"It won't work," he said.

"Shut up!" I yelled, fighting back tears. "Shut up, shut up, shut up!"

With my eyes clutched tight, I felt him approaching.

By the time I opened them and regained focus, he was nose-to-nose with me. An identical copy of me, within a fraction of an inch of me.

"What is happening?" I yelled.

"It's almost over," he said.

I noticed a flicker of light in his eyes. A tiny fleck of blue peeking through the brown. A bit of a hiccup in whatever was making me see myself.

"You're not me," I said. "This isn't real," I repeated.

"It's not," he said. With a wave of his arm in a big, flamboyant flourish, he changed from a clone of me to Joseph. A face I will never forget.

"You see," he said. "Anything can be anything with the right know how," as he laughed.

"Where are my friends?" I demanded again. "Bring them back!"

"In due time," he said. "In due time."

He leaned his head ever to slightly on the left and nodded.

Before I could turn to see what he was nodding at, I felt the sharpest pain on the back of my head that I'd ever felt.

I remember falling to the ground and seeing literal and figurative stars.

As I tried to roll over to see who Joseph had nodded to, I felt another thump on my head.

I blacked out immediately.

Forty-Eight

I CAME TO WITH the worst throbbing I'd ever experienced. My head hurt so badly that my vision was blurry. My head seemed to scream at me, as if I'd done something wrong to deserve this pain.

My mind was racing. Where was I? What happened? Am I going crazy?

I shook my head to free my vision from the blurriness, but it just made the throbbing worse.

Although I couldn't see very well, I could tell I was in the dark. Judging by how quiet it was, I thought I was outside, maybe in the woods.

"It's not real," I said to myself. "It's. Not. Real."

At first, I just repeated it in my head. Over and over again, while I waited for something to happen. Something I knew was inevitably coming my way, eventually.

The more I said it to myself, the more I realized I was starting to say it out loud.

Before I knew it, I was yelling my makeshift mantra. Yelling so loudly my throat burned, echoing the pain I still felt in my head. The throbbing and the burning, combining to put me in the worst pain I'd ever felt.

Despite how much it hurt, I shook my head again, trying to shake free the blurriness and confusion of where I was and what had happened.

Was it still the same day? How long was I unconscious for? I couldn't tell. I couldn't even feel the difference in time between when I'd blacked out and that moment.

Oh, God. The pain. It felt like a cinderblock swung by Thor had hit me. I reached back and felt the bump on the back of my head, quickly growing from a bump to a welt, to a mountain. It seemed to grow as I touched it. The longer I held my hand up against it, the larger it felt.

"It's not real," now repeatedly escaping my lips involuntarily. Words just poured out, as if my brain was trying to convince itself that it was true. It felt like the whole matter was completely out of my hands. My body had just taken over and was well on its way to whatever it needed to do to reinforce what it thought. That it wasn't real.

My vision came back, slowly, and I could make out the shape of a tree trunk in front of me. At first, just a long brown rectangle, but then the bark came into focus. The longer I held onto the desire to figure out where I was, the less blurry my vision came, and the less my head throbbed. Eventually, I could tilt my head up to look at the branches overhead. Those branches confirming what I had suspected, that I was in the woods. But where?

"Hello?" I called out, again involuntarily. "Hello?"

But no one responded.

Another few minutes later, I could finally shake my head without immense pressure and pain at the back of my skull.

Then, as I shook, I realized I was only moving my head. I couldn't feel my arms or legs. I couldn't move any parts of my body other than my head.

"It's not real," I said aloud, but only quiet enough that I could hear it myself.

"It's not real."

"It's not real."

"It's not real."

I kept saying it, trying to will my limbs to cooperate. Trying to convince my body that we still had control. Trying to convince my entire existence that what was happening wasn't real, and that I could move if I wanted to. That I could, against everything, get to my feet and go for help.

"This has gone on long enough," I muttered to myself. "I need help."

When I tried tossing the weight of my body to my left, I didn't move.

The same when I tried moving to the right.

My limbs were still numb, dead.

When my vision returned to normal, I looked down and discovered that I was tied to a tree. My back pressing up against the cold, hard bark. My head bouncing off of it with every attempt to adjust my body. With every attempt to move, even an inch, it felt like I made matters worse. It felt like I had somehow tied myself tighter to the tree.

"How is that even possible?" I said condescendingly to myself. "Don't be a moron."

The trees around me were suddenly in complete focus. In every direction, there were trees. They covered the night sky, but the moon peeked through with just a sliver of light. A bit of moonlight, as if instructed by God himself, directly hitting the one thing a short distance in front of me that I could tell was not a tree.

The dilapidated house we'd found in the woods weeks ago. The broken and crumbling brick of the corner closest to the trail was unmistakable from where I sat.

"This isn't real," I said again, aloud.

"Ah, but it is," a voice called back. "It very much is."

No one was in my line of sight, either left or right. I turned my head as far as I could in all directions, but I didn't see anyone.

"It's very real," another voice called out from the same direction as the first.

"No, it's not," I yelled. "It's not!"

"It is," the first voice said. It was close enough that I could feel hot breath on my face. Just inches away. Almost pressing up against my skin.

But there was no one there. Not a person in sight. Not a body. Not a soul. Nothing.

"It can't be," I said. "It's not!" I yelled twice.

Thump.

I felt the force of something hit me on the back of the head, right about where the initial whack had knocked me out.

"Do you feel it?" The second voice asked.

I tried to place the voices as they spoke. I think, on some level, I tried to convince myself it was William and Joseph, although I wasn't sure it was. I felt, at that moment, that if I knew it was them, I wouldn't be afraid. The evil you know, and whatever the rest of that old saying is. If it were them, it wasn't something that might be worse. As horrible as my experiences with them had been, I knew what to expect of them. I knew what they were capable of. I knew what they had intended to do to me.

I shook my head, hoping to stave off blacking out again. Hoping that I could stay conscious and continue deciphering what was happening.

It worked.

"I gave you your stupid heart back," I said. "I saw you pick it up, Joseph. I know you have it now. Where are my friends?"

"They're here," the first voice said. "They're here with you. Don't you see them?"

"No! You're lying!" I yelled. My friends were nowhere in sight. Just to be sure, I whipped my head in all directions, hoping I'd see a sign of them. A glimmer of light or life or something.

At the last possible second and out of the farthest peripheral point in my vision, I saw a tiny bit of motion — a teensy blur of colored movement, from within my vision to outside of it.

I tried my best but I couldn't move my head further to the right to see what it was.

I struggled for a minute before I heard a third voice.

"Mike?" It was female.

"Hello?" I yelled out. "Who is it?"

The flash of colored movement raced past me from the right to the left, dodging in and out of shadows, intentionally staying out of the streams of moonlight making it through the branches of the trees down to the ground. Like some sort of supernatural force aware of its surroundings.

"Mike, it's me," the voice said. "It's Wendy."

"Wendy?!" I yelled. "Wendy? Where are you? Where are we?"

"Wendy," the second male voice said, "we told you not to help him."

"Fuck you," Wendy said.

"No need for that language," the first voice said. "You were warned."

"I don't understand," I said. "I gave it back, like you've been saying for weeks. You have it now. Why are Wendy and I still here?"

"It's not just us," Wendy said. "Everyone. Everyone is here."

As if triggered by Wendy's words, blasts of movement spurned from all directions, running out in front of me, careful to not be in the light. Careful to not let anyone see them.

"What's happening?" I asked no one and everyone at the same time.

"They don't care," I heard Dan's voice say.

"They don't," Jen added.

"The heart means nothing to them," Kevin said.

"It's just a means to an end," Dan added.

"Silence. All of you," the first voice commanded, shaking the tree they tied me to and the rest of my surroundings.

I instinctively flinched.

"They're not here," Wendy said.

"What?" I asked.

"They're not here," she repeated.

"Where is here?" I asked.

"We don't know," Dan said.

"But this is where we've been," Brian responded.

"Are you all okay?" I asked, still unable to see any of them, other than the blurs of color zipping by me as they moved about in the woods.

"We are," Dan said.

"We're fine," Kevin said. "Annoyed as shit, but fine."

"So you're not hurt?" I asked.

"No," Jen said.

"We're fine," Brian said

"This must be part of it. This was part of their joke, their plan. Their game," I thought to myself.

"It's not," the first voice said. "I am Joseph and I am real. You have seen me. You have felt my wrath. You have shown me your fear."

He knew what I had just thought to myself. He had read my mind. He knew what I was thinking.

"You're not real," I thought again.

"Wrong again," the second voice, who I was then certain was William, said.

"Don't listen to them," Dan said. "When they realize you're not afraid of them, they'll give up."

But I was afraid of them. I was terrified. I had no idea where I was or what was happening still. I wished I could just go back to Johnny Rockets. I wished the worst of my problems was someone complaining that their fries were cold or their drink was empty too long. I wished I was back in school and my only problem was that I forgot my homework at home.

My head throbbed with another sturdy whack on the back.

On some tiny level, it felt good to feel pain on the other side. It evened me out some and felt, just a teensy tiny bit, better.

"I have nothing else you want," I said. "I've given you the thing you were after."

"You did," Joseph said. "Twice, actually. But we gave it back," he added. "We gave it back because we're not done with you yet."

"What? How?" I commanded.

"Ignore them," Dan said. "Don't listen."

I had little control over what I was doing. I had no choice but to listen to them and hear what they had to say.

"Mike," Wendy said, "listen to me. Listen only to me."

"Mike, it's okay," Dan said. "It's okay. We're here with you."

"Mike," Wendy said again. "Listen only to me. I am your only ally."

"Nonsense," Joseph said. "Your friends are here for you. But if you don't be careful, we're going to kill them all. Including you."

"Listen to him," Brian said.

"He's serious," Kevin added.

"They're not here," Wendy said. "It's just you and me. Focus on my voice and no other voice."

"Wendy," Joseph said, "I have warned you twice and I will not repeat myself a third time."

A clasp of thunder struck so loudly that I felt the tree vibrate behind me for a few seconds. My arms and legs were still numb, but my body itself feeling the Earth move beneath and behind me.

A sense of fear I'd not yet felt before washed over me, from head to toe. For a moment of terror, I felt it. The fear ran through my body. I felt my arms and legs. I felt the warmth of my hands clasped together behind my back, pressed up against the tree. I felt the bark. I was able to grab it, if only for a split second.

"Yes," Joseph said. "Good."

"You mustn't listen to them," Wendy said again. "They're not in control now."

"Wendy. Quiet."

For a moment, I stopped responding. I stopped trying to understand. I stopped trying to explain anything and I just let myself sit there, alone and quiet.

I had seen no other person. The warm breath on my face was all I felt. I had only felt myself, the tree, and a gut full of fear.

"There's no one," I said out loud. "It's just me," I told myself.

"We're here. You've felt the pain," Joseph said.

"It's just you," Wendy said. "You're in the woods. You're by yourself. What you're seeing right now and what you're hearing and feeling are not real."

"It's not real," I said out loud.

"It's not real," Wendy echoed back.

Another, louder, clasp of thunder shook the ground below me again. The tree shook behind my back. I felt it move with my hands, but I did not budge. I didn't flinch. I didn't acknowledge what had happened. I didn't show fear.

"That's it, Mike," Wendy said. "Alone in the woods."

"Where are you?" I asked Wendy.

"Don't listen to her," Dan said. "She's working with them!"

I knew, right then, that it was the opposite. Dan, Kevin, Brian, and Jen had all been there so long. They'd been turned. They were working with William and Joseph. They were not my friends anymore. They were part of the evil.

But Wendy? Wendy had just gotten to the other realm, the other world, whatever the fuck it was. Wendy hadn't been there long enough to be turned against me. Wendy was, in fact, my only ally.

"They can't hurt you," Wendy said. "They can't hurt any of us."

"They can't hurt me," I repeated. "This isn't real and they cannot hurt me."

Thunder clasped again, not even not phasing me.

Lightning hit the top of a tree not far from me and I saw it shoot from the tip to the ground, shattering the trunk and every branch along the way, sending splinters in every direction.

I didn't move. I didn't budge. I didn't acknowledge any of it.

"Our friends aren't here," Wendy said.

"Yes they are, shut up girl!" Joseph commanded.

"They're not here. Their voices are in your head."

"They're not real," I whispered to myself. "Not real."

"They're all here!" Joseph yelled. "They're here and they work for me now!"

"They're not, don't listen to them, Mike," Wendy reassured me. "I'm the only one here. I'm in some sort of holding area. I'm in limbo, I think. You have to…"

I heard the beginning of a clasp of thunder and then every bit of sound I heard was white noise, like a television tuned to a channel that didn't exist. It grew louder and louder until it was so deafening that I couldn't stand it anymore.

My ears trembled from the sound. My eardrums vibrating from the sound. My hands could not rise and block out the sound.

It was the loudest and most confusing sound I'd ever heard and felt. It was completely disorienting.

In my gut, I knew that it was just a distraction tactic. Wherever Wendy was and whatever she was about to tell me was so important to William and Joseph that they had to stop her.

Perhaps they didn't have control over where she was. Maybe they weren't strong enough to silence her. Maybe she'd gotten free of whatever restraints they had her in and the others were just stuck in some other place.

But, whatever it was, they prevented me from hearing the next words out of her mouth by making it so loud with noise that I couldn't hear anything.

Forty-Nine

I struggled for a few minutes, hoping I'd be able to make out what Wendy was trying to say, to tell me. I tried to force my brain to ignore the white noise, the static, the distraction, and focus on the sound of her voice, which I could barely hear through the sound. It was faint, but I could hear her.

Somehow, I could sense her struggling to make sure I could hear her. Her voice, though faint, strained from yelling to make herself heard.

It felt like such a waste, like such a futile effort to hear what she was saying, to get any sort of help, hint, or clue about what was happening.

There I sat, in the middle of the dark forest, still struggling to get free from the tree I was tied to, still baffled by what was happening to me, around me.

I noticed motion from the corner of my eye, moving from my far left to just out of my peripheral vision, just in the quick blink of an eye.

"This is getting out of hand," I heard a voice say. It took me a second, but I recognized it as William.

"It is," Joseph said. "But you know the rules."

I don't think I was supposed to hear what they were saying, but I somehow could.

More movement from my left, this time coming more into view.

It was Joseph.

"You've seen what your future holds now, Mike," he said. "Your friends are gone, and if you keep this up, you're going to join them."

His tone had a stronger sense of disdain, of more anger than I'd heard from him before. I could feel it this time. His words pushed through my chest, hitting me so hard it felt like I'd been punched.

"I gave you what you wanted. Keep up your end of the bargain, please!" I begged. "Give me back my friends!"

"Bargain?" He scoffed. "There is no bargain. You haven't kept your end of the agreement. Why would I let your friends go now?"

"I did!" I screamed. "I gave you your stupid heart back! You said it was so important and now you don't care that I've given it back? That seems hardly fair!"

"Fair? Fairness is not stealing something that doesn't belong to you in the first place, is it?" He snapped back.

"Don't listen to him," I heard Wendy's voice, ever so faintly. "He's the bad guy."

"No shit," I thought to myself. "Of course he's the bad guy."

"Silence!" he commanded. "Silence", he yelled again.

The white noise intensified to where Wendy's voice was completely muffled. I couldn't hear her at all anymore. Just Joseph, who was now standing directly in front of me. His hips were at my eye level, menacingly looming in front of me.

He stood, turned around, and took a few steps away from me. He paused there, as if he was deep in thought.

"Do you want to die?" he said after a few seconds, the white noise stopping the moment he started speaking. "Do you want this to be the end of your life on Earth? The end of your existence, as you know it? Never to see your friends, or your family again?"

I forced myself to not respond immediately, to ponder what he was asking. To really think about why he asked that.

"Is that what happened to my friends?" I asked, virtually inaudibly. "Are they dead?"

He turned back and moved so quickly toward me, crouching down to meet my eye level, that I couldn't even comprehend how he'd done it.

"What do you think?" he asked. "Do you think they're dead? Do you hear the voices of dead people often, Mike?"

My head was spinning, my thoughts not making sense. He was right. If they were dead, how was I hearing their voices? How was I hearing their voices if they were dead, if they were gone?

"I don't know what's real, anymore," I said, quietly, still. "I don't know up from down, right from wrong, left from right. Everything is so abnormal. It doesn't make sense."

Joseph stood up but still leered down at me, looking down his nose as if he was a disappointed professor leaning over a student's desk while he returned a test with a big red F at the top.

"Joseph," I heard William start to speak.

Joseph's left hand extended out immediately, in a gesture to silence William before he could get his thought out.

"Everything and nothing is real. Reality is only what I let it be. Reality is only what I show you, and it will continue that way until I'm done with you. Until you return the heart," he said.

I was so instantly confused. He was talking as if he'd not already had it back. That thing I'd placed right back where I'd taken it from, twice. That thing that I no longer had. That thing I'd seen him just recently come out of the doorway to pick up. He knew he had it back. I knew he had it back. So why was he still fucking with me?

I didn't answer him. I sat still, making eye contact, not really knowing what to say.

The silence filled the space around me for some of the longest seconds of my life. They turned into minutes. The minutes felt like they were turning into hours. That's when I noticed more movement.

It was William. He seemed to float in without moving his legs, to where he stood right in front of me, next to Joseph.

"Has he returned it?" William asked.

"No," Joseph said. "He's still stonewalling."

"Mike," William said, crouching down, getting close to my face. "We've been more than lenient with you. We just want our heart back. It's sacred to us. It gives us peace, it gives us comfort. It's very important to me, to Joseph, to our people, to our religion. We just need it back."

Maybe I can reason with William, I thought to myself. "William, I understand," I said, trying to maintain eye contact with him. "You both keep insisting I need to return it, but I have. I brought it back already. I put it outside the door. Just a short while ago, Joseph picked it up, while masquerading as me, and held it in his hands. I don't have your heart anymore."

He stood up immediately, without saying a word, and turned to Joseph.

"What does he mean?" he asked Joseph.

"He's lying," Joseph said, instantly.

"He seems pretty sure of himself," William said, leaning closer, as if to shield their conversation from me.

"He's lying," Joseph merely repeated.

William turned, briefly, and looked at me, making as little eye contact as possible, despite my efforts to capture his gaze.

"So you don't have it?" he asked Joseph.

"No," he said.

But I knew he was lying. He knew he was lying. We both knew it, but only one of us understood why he was lying. He intentionally didn't make eye contact with me as he and William talked.

Fifty

"THEN WE HAVE NO other choice," William said. "Send him."

Before I could even try to understand what William was saying, Joseph had quickly quickly taken four or five strides toward me, and put his right thumb on my forehead. He chanted something quietly, practically to himself, in a language I couldn't recognize, and my eyes forced themselves closed.

When I opened my eyes, Joseph and William were gone. The room I was in was dark, but not pitch black. My eyes started adjusting as I moved my head around, trying to see anything and figure out what was happening.

"Mike," I heard a voice. It was Wendy.

"Wen?" I called out. "Where are you? Where am I?"

"You're here now," she said. "This place that they sent us, that they sent you to. I don't know what it is or where it is, but we're all here."

"Everyone is?" I asked.

"Everyone," she said. "But I need to warn you."

"What?"

"The others aren't in control anymore."

"What do you mean?" I asked.

"Dan, Kevin, Brian, and Jen. None of them can control what they say or do. It's like they're puppets, not in control over themselves anymore. When I first got here, Dan could talk to me. We could have conversations. The others have seemed different since I got here. But something changed with Dan the other day. It's like he snapped."

"How?"

"I don't know. It's like the longer they're here, the less in control they are."

"What do you mean?" I asked. "Give me an example."

"It's like," she started. "It's like they are all against us. Dan keeps telling me that, because I'm the only one left who can talk to you, I need to tell you to return the heart. Like our friends are on their side."

"What the fuck?"

"Like they're brainwashed," she said.

"Are you hurt?" I asked. "Are they?"

"They hurt no one, unless you count having their brains scrambled in some bizarre way."

"No physical pain?"

"None that I've seen," she said.

"Are we in the woods? Is it nighttime?"

"I don't know," she said. "I don't know where we are, and I don't know if it's day or night. There's no sun here. The sun never comes up, and it never gets brighter than it is right now. I've never seen the moon, either."

She was talking crazy. What she was saying made little sense. How was that even possible? I didn't think it was.

"Mike?" I heard another voice. It was Dan. I could see movement off in the distance, growing bigger, as if it was moving toward me. "Mike, is that you?"

"Remember what I told you," Wendy's voice said. "Remember."

"Dan? Dan? It's me." I called out, as the shadowy figure got close enough for me to make out Dan's face.

"Mike, holy shit," he said. "It's really you."

I reached behind myself to free my hands from the ropes, but found I was no longer tied up. And there was no tree behind me. Wherever I was, it wasn't the woods anymore.

He bent down and hugged me.

"I'm so glad you're here," he said. "You can finally end this now."

"I don't know how," I said, quickly.

"What do you mean? Not more of this bullshit," he said. "They're tired of you playing dumb. Just give it back to them."

The way he said "give it back" sounded so eerily like Joseph, like his voice and his demeanor. It could have been a recording of Joseph's voice. It could have been him. It seemed like Wendy may have been right, that they weren't in control of themselves anymore.

"I gave it back," I said. "I don't know what else I can do. I put it back. Joseph took it. He has it. I just told them that, and they still sent me here."

I finally adjusted my eyes to the darkness. I could see Dan's face, make out his features. But something felt off. I could sense that he wasn't himself. Something about his eyes, they were dim. Not black. Not dark, but dim. As if the color has been pulled out of them and his iris was only a tiny shade brighter than his pupil.

"This is my fault," I said to myself. "You did this. You did this all."

The guilt felt heavier on me than it ever had before.

The person in front of me wasn't Dan. It may have been his body, but it wasn't Dan.

Fifty-One

Had Dan been under their control the whole time? I'd heard his voice so many times since he vanished that I'd started wondering if anything I'd heard had been true. If anything he had said was of his own decision or if they were controlling him entirely.

What about my other friends? Were any of them still in control other than Wendy?

So many quick visions started flashing before my eyes. Like a whole lifetime of possibilities quickly showing themselves to me, based on everything that had happened and everything that I knew.

Nothing seemed real anymore. Even the things I thought I knew, for sure, weren't real.

"It's a simple matter," I heard Joseph say. "Just give it back."

I looked around, trying to see if I could find where he was. Trying to prepare myself for whatever he would throw at me next.

"Don't listen," I heard Wendy's voice say. "He's in control of everything."

I closed my eyes as tightly as I could, to the point of blacking out. For some reason, I thought that if I couldn't see what was happening, I could erase it all. To wish it away. To hope it'd just all stop.

"That won't work," I heard Joseph say. "It's too late now."

"Too late for what?" I called back, without opening my eyes.

"It's too late to go back. This is your life now."

"No, it's not!" I yelled.

"You'll never see your mother again. You'll never see your family. You'll never see your real friends."

"Yes, I will!"

I kept my eyes shut tight.

"This is the end, Mike."

The way he said my name sent shivers throughout my entire body. With a hint of sarcasm and hatred. I'd felt the sarcasm from him before, even anger. But I'd never felt hate in his words until that moment. For whatever reason, Joseph hated me. He was convinced I still had their heart and wouldn't give it back, despite us both knowing he already had it.

"Mike," a different voice spoke. William. "Mike, this can all end."

"What?" Joseph asked, cutting William off. "It's over. We agreed."

"Joseph, this is what it will take to get it back."

They were bickering. They weren't on the same page. Not anymore.

"William, we discussed this. We agreed. That was his last chance."

"I gave it back," I said, still not looking.

"You did not!" Joseph yelled. His voice echoing like thunder through a canyon. Booming loudly, directly through my body, causing me to quiver and inadvertently open my eyes.

The voices were Joseph and William, but the people in front of me having the argument were Dan and Kevin. Their bodies, their movements, their mannerisms. It was them, but it was not their voices.

"I did, you know I did." I said, timidly, virtually quietly.

"Mike," William said. "When did you put it back?"

"I don't know, I've lost all sense of time," I said. "But I did. I put it back and Joseph took it."

"From where?" William asked.

"It doesn't mat-," Joseph said.

"It does," William interrupted.

"I left it by the door. The door where I took it," I said.

"Was the light on?" William asked.

"What does it matter?" Joseph asked, moving Dan's body closer to Kevin's.

"It matters to me," William said, now turning Kevin's body toward me. "It does matter."

"I," I said, pausing to think for a moment, "I think it was yesterday."

Kevin's body immediately turned back to Dan's and moved in so close their noses were almost touching.

"Is he telling the truth?" William asked. "Did he bring it back?"

"I've told you ten times," Joseph said, getting louder. "He did not."

"I did," I said. "I put it back by the door and waited. After a while, a man appeared. It was me."

"You?" William asked, still looking at Dan's body, Joseph now taking a step backward.

"It was me," I said. "And the next thing I knew, I was tied to the tree."

"Joseph?" William asked, stepping forward. "Joseph, what did you do?"

"I did nothing, William," he said. "What do you mean?" His face turned to a look of shock, of disbelief.

Confusion wasn't an appropriate word to describe what I was feeling.

"I know that I did not do that. I was not there," William said.

"Neither was I," Joseph said. "I don't know what he's talking about."

"Tell me," William said. "Tell us."

He turned to me, taking a step between Dan and me, seemingly trying to shield me.

"I," Joseph said. "I... well... I."

"Tell me!" William's voice boomed through everything. He echoed twice as loud as Joseph's did the last time he'd yelled.

"I took the heart," he finally confessed. As soon as he said it, he turned away. I could barely make out his body from behind Kevin's, William still blocking me.

"You did what?" William demanded. His voice was louder than before. Kevin's body seemed to grow a foot instantly. Now towering over Dan's.

"I had to," Joseph said. "I had to."

"Why? Joseph? Why? We've lived for so long in peace. Why did you have to take it and not tell me it had been returned?"

"It was the only way to get you to see," Joseph said. "The only way for you to see it is time to move on."

"Move on to where?" William asked.

"Both of us," Joseph said. "It's time for both of us to move on."

"What are you talking about?" William asked, shrinking back down to Kevin's normal size.

"Yeah," I chimed in. "What the fuck are you talking about?"

Neither of them acknowledged I'd said anything.

"We've protected him for so long," Joseph said. "It's time to let someone else take over."

"We serve our master," William said. "He is our master and we serve him."

My head was spinning. I did not know what they were talking about.

"And we have served him well," Joseph said. "He gave us the gift of everlasting life, but I think I've served my purpose. I think we've served our purpose."

"Joseph, how can you say that? We were born to serve him. We were born and given so many gifts to serve him, to protect him."

"William, you have been like a brother to me for more years than I can even remember. We have been through so many trials and tribulations, but I think it's time we move on. It's time we go home."

"We go home when he calls us home," William said. "It is not our time. Not yet."

"I took the heart..." Joseph said. "I took the heart because I wanted him to see that we can fail. That we've outlived our usefulness."

"He sees all," William said. "He knows all. You cannot trick him."

"I had to try," Joseph said. "I want to go home."

It finally hit me. All their talk of serving him and going home. It finally hit me.

Their master. The one they were talking about — for the first time in front of me — must have been God. It didn't make sense otherwise. The convent. The abilities they had. The taking over of bodies. The hiding of my friends. All of it. Unless they had some supernatural powers from some other origin, it had to be God.

"If we fail," Joseph said. "He'll bring us home."

"He shalln't," William said. "And how could you lie to me? How could you deceive me in this place? In our home?"

"I had to," Joseph said. "He has been promising to bring us home for ages, for lifetimes. And he has not. He says we have more to do, but I believe we are through."

"Joseph, this is not the way," William said.

I shrunk back a bit, inching away from them. Not that I thought I had anywhere to go or an escape of any kind. But I wanted to let them have their time to sort things out.

"We were cruel to this boy," William said. "Unnecessarily cruel to him! To his friends!"

"We had to," Joseph replied. "We had to keep the heart away from here. We had to prevent him from seeing what we'd done."

"What we'd done? Why?" William asked, barely audible.

"Without it, he wouldn't know."

My head was spinning. My eyes were wider than they'd ever been. My brain trying to decipher what was happening, what I was hearing.

"It is our tie to him," William said. "Without it, we are on our own. How could you not tell me we had it back?"

"I had to show you," Joseph said. "I had to show you it was our time to go home. That without the heart, without him being able to see us and track us and keep tabs on us, that he'd have no choice but to call us home."

"He will call us when it is our time," William said. "Like all the others before us, and all the others that will come after us."

"Our time to go home is now," Jospeh reiterated. "It is now."

"Where is the heart?" William asked.

"It's safe. It's away from here. It's where no one will find it."

"Joseph, where is it? We need to bring it home," William said.

"We can't," Joseph said, falling to Dan's knees, sobbing. "We can't. I can't keep going on like this."

"Joseph, we have to bring it home. We have to bring it back here. We've taken this too far. We've done too much to these children."

"Will he forgive us?" Joseph asked. "When he sees all we've done, will he forgive us?"

"He forgives all," William said. "We have not broken his rules. We have simply strayed from his teachings."

"I've tried, for so long, to do good. To help these people. To guide them."

"I know, Joseph. I know."

"I just want to go home. I want to go back and be with him."

Joseph was now fully in hysterics. Dan's body throbbed up and down as Joseph wept. His tears were visible, even from the distance I was from him.

"If we return the heart to its rightful place, all will be forgiven," William said, then turned to me. "Mike, I'm sorry you got caught in the middle of this. I'm sorry we brought you through this with us. I'm sorry we've done this all. I have thought, for all this time, that you had, in fact, taken the heart and not returned it. I thought you still had it. Joseph lied to me. He lied to us, and I am so sorry for what we've done to you and your friends."

"I will retrieve it," Joseph said. Dan's body collapsed to the floor. I'd assumed that it was Joseph leaving Dan's body as a vessel, returning Dan to his own body. But Dan didn't move.

"Is he…" I started to ask.

"He'll be fine," William said. "You all will be fine."

He took the few steps that separated us and knelt down in front of me, leaning close.

"I am so sorry," he said, reaching out. "This will be over soon."

A flash of light blinded me for a quick second. When my eyes adjusted back to normal, Kevin was gone. William sat in his place, in the same position, knelt down before me.

His arm reached out toward me, his palm extending out toward my forehead.

The last thing I remember was his hand touching my forehead. After that, everything went black. Again.

Fifty-Two

"MIKE," MY MOTHER CALLED. "Mike, are you up?"

I was barely awake, the sound of her voice jostling me the rest of the way.

The alarm clock by my bed read 10:29 am. The little dot indicating the alarm was on wasn't illuminated. I'd slept in. I was at home.

"Mike?" she called again. "Dan's on the phone."

I'd never sprung up in bed so fast before.

"I got it," I yelled down, like I had a thousand times before.

"He.. hello?" I said.

"Hey, did you just wake up?" Dan asked.

"Dan? Is that you?" I said. "Is it really you?"

"Of course it's me. Who else would it be?" he said.

"Where are you?" I asked, still so confused.

"I'm at home. Come get me and Brian. Let's get Kevin and go to the mall. The girls are working."

"What?" I asked, for lack of anything more coherent coming out of my mouth.

"Me. Brian. Kevin," he said in a caveman voice. "Girls. Work. We go. Car. You."

I couldn't help but laugh.

"Give me half an hour, I'll be there," I said. "Is everyone... is everyone okay?"

"Everyone's fine. Are you okay? You're being fucking weird," he said.

"You're sure everyone's fine?" I asked again, looking down at my body to make sure I was okay as well.

"Everyone's fine, except you, you weirdo."

I hung up and jumped out of bed. So many thoughts and questions running through my head.

Fifty-Three

I PULLED INTO THE driveway at the Dan's house and bound my way up the stairs, straight into the kitchen.

Kathy, as she was so many times in the past, was there, making lunch for Dan and Rachel.

"Hi, Mike," she said. "You hungry?"

"No, thank you," I said, giving her a hug on the way by, barely slowing down. "Hey Rach!"

Dan's door, as usual, was closed. I didn't wait to knock, I just burst through.

There he was. In the flesh. On his bed. Like always. Music playing through his stereo, magazine in his hands.

"Hey," he said as I came in. "Shut the door."

Slowly, I closed it behind me. Still unsure. Still uneasy about things.

Was this really Dan? It looked like him. It sounded like him. It sure acted like him. But was it him?

"Do you remember the CD I borrowed a couple of weeks ago?" I asked him, seeing if he knew the answer.

"Candlebox?" he asked. "That's excellent, isn't it?"

"Yeah, that's the one," I confirmed. "Do you remember which track it was that I heard on WAAF that night?"

WAAF used to do a nightly battle of new songs most week nights. I had heard Candlebox's "You" come on in one battle, but didn't get the band's name. The next day, I called him and sung two or three words from the chorus and he knew what I was talking about. He knew the song. He already had the CD. If it was the real Dan, he'd know.

"It was 'You'", he said. "You called me and asked about it."

I leapt across the room and hugged him.

"You okay?" he asked. "You seem off today."

"I'm fine," I said. "I'm perfectly fine."

Fifty-Four

IT TOOK ME A few weeks to actually talk about the events of that summer, even with my friends. Even with the friends who were affected by everything.

The memories were still vivid in my mind. Everything that had happened had been pressed into me in a way that wouldn't let me forget it.

When I sat them all down to discuss things, to ask what they had experienced, they all sat silently staring at me.

They sat while I spewed on about the heart, the darkness, their voices, the screaming in the woods, everything. They stared at me with rarely blinking eyes. They looked at me like I was crazy.

"What happened?" Wendy asked after a few minutes of silence once I'd finished talking.

"You were there," I said. "Don't you remember?"

"Mike, what are you talking about?" Jen asked.

"That's a fucked up story, Mike," Brian added.

"I don't know what you're talking about," Dan said. "None of that happened."

"None of it?" I asked, questioning my own sanity.

"We went there. You took the dumb stick thing, that was it," Kevin said. "None of that other wacky shit you said happened."

There was no explanation. None of it made sense.

How was I the only one who knew what happened? Not a single one of the five of them remembered anything.

"Tricked ya," I said, not knowing what else to say. "It was all part of a story I'm working on."

Dan and Kevin laughed. Brian scoffed. Wendy and Jen just looked at each other, confirming I was as weird as they had thought I was.

Epilogue

Although we've grown apart after all these years, Dan and I still keep in touch on Facebook. Ironically enough, he and Jen reconnected on Facebook years ago. They're now married and have two kids. They still live locally.

Brian and I are Facebook friends, but don't interact much. I like his band's postings; he likes my author page's postings. It's a mutual, but not beneficial, friendship.

Wendy and I were connected for a while, but aren't anymore. I don't know why. I sent her a message a while back, but never got a response. In preparation for finalizing the book, I tracked her down and emailed her. She responded and gave me her blessing to use her name.

Although Kevin was on Facebook in the early days, he's not anymore. He was never big on computers. I bet he still has a non-smart phone. In preparation for finalizing the book, I tracked him down and got in touch. He gave me his blessing to use his name.

I brought up the summer of 1997 to Dan once, asking him how much he remembered. If he remembered Dudley Road at all. I hinted at the things that I still vividly remember but didn't mention any of the specifics of what had happened to me, what had happened to us.

He didn't remember any of it.

"Do you still have the heart you took?" he asked me during one of our infrequent chats.

He remembered that bit of our time at Dudley Road. He knew I'd taken the heart.

"I do," I said, telling a small fib. "It's in the closet in my old bedroom at my mom's house." That's where I'd kept it for the short period it was in my possession before returning it for the first time, and then again after it had returned itself to me, hidden away.

One day, on a drive up to my mother's house — she still lives in the same house that I grew up in — I decided to take the back roads. I don't remember why. Perhaps 495 was full of traffic or I was trying to kill time or something. But, along the way, I started recognizing things. Roads. Trees. Signs. Houses. I sort of knew where I was.

And that's when I drove by the safe end of Dudley Road. The horse farms I'd driven past a dozen or more times all those years ago are still there, still flourishing.

My body took over from my brain, and I made the left down the road. I turned, unintentionally, onto Dudley Road.

The nice houses and the horse farms all passing on both sides as I instinctively drove toward the turnaround spot, where the road turned from pavement to dirt, the spot I'd spent countless hours parked at, wandering through the woods.

My daughter Samantha and my wife Megan were with me. Both along for the ride, but not understanding what we were doing or where we were going. Samantha, just two and a half at the time, didn't know what was going on. Megan asked me why we were going down the road we were on.

"Remember that creepy story I told you when we first met?" I asked.

"About the guy who escaped from jail?"

"That's the one."

"Yeah, what about it?" she asked.

"That's this road," I said. "I just need to do something."

As we approached the front of the convent, I slowed down. I took out my phone and snapped a few pictures.

It was exactly as I remembered it, albeit the grass was a little overgrown.

"I'll be right back," I said, as I put the car in park in the same spot, by the big oak tree that I'd parked under back then.

"Where are you going?" Megan asked.

"Just stay here. I'll be back in a minute. Lock the doors," I said, jumping out of the car.

Then I did something I'd never done before. I buzzed the box at the security gate.

"Yes?" a voice came from inside.

"It's been a very long time," I said. "But are William and Joseph here?"

"William? Joseph?" The voice squawked back.

"Yes," I said.

"Oh, no," the voice said. "They left years ago. Why do you ask?"

"I'm an old friend," I said, unable to think of anything that would make sense to this stranger.

"Mike?" he asked.

"How... how did you know my name?" I asked.

"They said you might come back some day. William left something for you," he said. "Come to the door."

The gate made a loud buzzing sound and popped open just a few inches.

I looked back at my wife and daughter and waved, then gave them the universal signal for "I'll just be a minute", by raising my index finger.

The gate swung open with just a small push, and I stepped inside. My body instinctively knowing where to go and which door the voice on the box was talking about.

It took me a few minutes of standing just away from it before I mustered up the courage to approach, a million thoughts racing through my head. Though I've done my best to recount everything, to recollect it all as I was working through writing this, I still felt there were so many questions left unanswered. So many things that never fully made sense. So much of it fuzzy, yet so clear.

The moment I finally stepped forward, the door swung open and the man, whose voice I recognized from the speaker as soon as he spoke, greeted me.

"Hello Mike," he said. "I'm Jacob."

A small envelope was in his hand as he reached out to me.

"William left this for you. He instructed me to not open it and to give it to 'Mike' if one ever came asking for him or Joseph."

"Thank you," I said, looking down at the envelope. It had no markings on the outside, but was sealed with a wax stamp in the shape of a heart.

"Be well," the man said, closing the door behind him.

As it closed, I noticed it there, on the ground, in the spot where I'd both taken it and returned it twice — the heart.

I smiled to myself as I made my way back to the car.

Megan was looking at her phone when I gently tapped on the window to get her to unlock the doors.

I flipped the envelope over, inspecting it before deciding to open it there and not wait until we got to my mom's.

Its edges crinkled under my fingers as I popped the wax seal off.

In it was a single, small piece of paper. The side I'd taken out was blank.

On the other side were simply the words:

I let you remember.
William

I felt a smile come across my face as I buckled up and put the car in drive.